Withdrawn

YOU SHOULD HAVE SEEN THIS COMING

YOU SHOULD HAVE SEEN THIS COMING

SHANI MICHELLE

Swoon READS

New York

A FEIWEL AND FRIENDS BOOK

An imprint of Feiwel and Friends and Macmillan Publishing Group, LLC
120 Broadway, New York, NY 10271 • fiercereads.com

Our books may be purchased in bulk for promotional, educational,
or business use. Please contact your local bookseller or the Macmillan Corporate
and Premium Sales Department at (800) 221-7945 ext. 5442 or by email at
MacmillanSpecialMarkets@macmillan.com.

Library of Congress Cataloging-in-Publication Data

Names: Michelle, Shani, author.
Title: You should have seen this coming / Shani Michelle.
Description: First edition. | New York : Swoon Reads, 2022. | Audience:
Ages 13-18. | Audience: Grades 10-12. | Summary: Hayden has visions of
the past, using her ability to extract justice and cash from her classmates,
and Cassie has visions of the future, helplessly watching her boyfriend fall
in love with someone else and seeing her own kidnapping—so when Cassie
disappears, can Hayden save her in time?
Identifiers: LCCN 2021027785 | ISBN 9781250294777 (hardcover)
Subjects: CYAC: Extrasensory perception—Fiction. | Kidnapping—Fiction. |
High schools—Fiction. | Schools—Fiction. | LCGFT: Novels. | Thrillers
(Fiction) | Paranormal fiction.
Classification: LCC PZ7.1.M5156 Yo 2022 | DDC [Fic]—dc23
LC record available at https://lccn.loc.gov/2021027785

First edition, 2022
Book design by Michelle Gengaro-Kokmen
Feiwel and Friends logo designed by Filomena Tuosto
Printed in The United States by Lakeside Book Company
Harrisonburg, Virginia

ISBN 978-1-250-29477-7 (hardcover)
1 3 5 7 9 10 8 6 4 2

For Ben Levkov,
I didn't need to be psychic to know you were "the one."
I'm so lucky to have you as my partner.
I love you.

1

Cassie

"Almost got it," Hayden Jefferies says. She's crouched in front of the teacher's desk, wiggling a straightened-out paper clip into the lock.

"We're good," Brody—my Brody—tells her, watching the hall from the window in the classroom door. "No sign of Donnelly."

Hayden has some serious concentration going on. Nose scrunched, eyes lasered on the keyhole, hands steady. Her copper-brown hair falls in front of her face, but she doesn't seem to notice or care.

"Yes," she says as the lock gives a click and the drawer pops open. "That is how you do it!"

Brody rushes over to her.

"One, two, three," she says, referring to the three phones sitting in the drawer. Mr. Donnelly must have confiscated them earlier in the day. He's pretty much the phone police of Lightsend High. If he sees one, even gets a hint that someone has one out, he takes it and keeps it until the end of last period. No exceptions.

"You did it." Brody picks up two of the phones in one hand and takes

*Hayden's palm in the other. He gives it a light squeeze. "Thank you.
This may be the key. We're going to find her."*

*Hayden gives a shrug and sucks in her bottom lip. She has one of
those oh-it-was-no-big-deal-anything-for-you expressions.*

I don't want to see any more.

Their eyes are locked on each other.

I need to look away. Only I can't.

The gaze they're sharing is intense. Too intense.

*Brody lets go of her hand and wipes a strand of hair off her face, his
hand grazing her cheek. He lets it linger there.*

They're going to kiss. I know they're going to kiss.

*There's a sound at the door, and both of them snap out of their love
trance and turn to look.*

I don't see who it is.

My vision is over.

I'm back in my room, back on my bed, back to streaming *Gilmore
Girls*. I hit pause. Why can't my life be like Rory's? That's what
I want. A mother-daughter wisecracking team, great boyfriends,
where my biggest concern is whether to go to Yale or Harvard or
that my mom doesn't like that her parents are super rich.

I stand up and shake out my arms.

"Breathe," I remind myself.

Before I know what I'm doing, I'm holding the framed photo
of Brody and me, tracing the outline of him with my finger. We're
at the town fair a few years ago. I'm carrying a colossal pink cotton
candy. Brody had the guy make it triple the normal size because he
knows how much I love the stuff. I'm laughing, my head thrown

back, over something Brody said, and he's looking at me, eyes filled with love.

He could always do that, make me laugh, smile, forget the otherworldly things I have to deal with. At least he used to.

Now when I think about Brody, all I see is him and Hayden. The constant visions of them that have been popping up since the start of summer and have been going strong ever since. The first one didn't even feel like a vision. I was sure it was real, that I was living it. The second one almost got me. It still featured the two of them, only a different scenario. But now, having just finished vision number 888 of Brody and Hayden, I'm practically a pro. I know what I'm seeing is just a glimpse of what's to come.

My phone buzzes. I know who it is, but I look anyway.

It's Brody. A text.

Brody
Can we please talk?

My body clenches. I can feel my heart beating faster than usual. I'm tempted to answer. I want to answer. I still love him, but I ignore the message. He's going to fall for someone else. I've seen it. I need to prepare for the inevitable.

Ice cream. That's what Audra would say. Piles and piles of ice cream.

My best friend thinks junk food can solve everything.

I head to the kitchen but stop short when I see my dad there.

"Oh, Cassie," he says, putting down the *Wall Street Journal*. "I didn't know you were home."

"I am," I say.

"You doing okay?" he asks.

I nod.

"Good. Good." He glances at me and then into his glass of brandy. My dad never looks at me too long. I'm not sure if it's because I resemble my mom or because he thinks I killed her.

"School good?"

"Yep."

He's still studying his drink. "Brody treating you right?"

"He is." I don't explain that it's over between us. I don't want to get into it, and I know my dad doesn't want to hear it. Especially not if I were to mention the word *vision*. I could use every four-letter word I can think of, and I don't think he'd care, but try to talk about seeing the future and you'd think I told him I put poison in the school Jell-O. I learned long ago to keep my mouth shut around him about my visions.

"Invite him over for dinner one night this week," he says. "Always like his company."

Translation: He likes having a buffer so he can pretend he's spending time with me without actually having to deal with me.

"Okay."

He folds up his paper and picks up his drink. "I should go finish up some work and then call it a night. Don't you stay up too late, it's a school night." It's only eight p.m., but he wants to escape. "I'll let you have some privacy. I know how you teen girls are."

I force a smile.

I wish his words were true. Then he'd know that I just want him to be there for me.

2

HaYDen

No one does a good saunter anymore. I shake out my arms and loosen my body before I meander into the girls' locker room Tuesday morning, doing my best to channel an old-timey sheriff in a Western film. Time to show the elite who's boss.

Brooke Tamison and Fiona Gavini are standing off to the side. Both look up as I approach.

"Well, well, well, what do we have here?" I ask, stopping right in front of them.

Brooke's whole body goes rigid. "We're in the middle of something, Hayden. Get out," she commands. Her dark green eyes narrow into slits and her nostrils flare. She's perfected the look of someone in charge, I'll give her that.

A for effort, but she's not fooling anyone. She's scared of me. The little tremble in her voice is a dead giveaway. I can't really blame her. In my two months and change at Lightsend High, I've developed quite the reputation.

"Just what I need," Fiona mumbles, throwing her head back, hitting the locker behind her.

I cringe. She couldn't have meant to hit it that hard. I almost ask her if she's okay, but then I remind myself that she's the enemy. One of the school's we-think-we're-above-the-law-and-better-than-anyone crowd. The ones I can't stand. The ones I'm taking down.

She lets out a sigh. One of defeat? Surprise? Disgust? It's hard to tell.

"You know . . ." I shake my head. "If you're gonna have a clandestine meeting, you really should come up with someplace more original. You're making it too easy. It's like you want to be caught."

I take a seat on the wooden bench in front of them.

"Don't know what you're talking about or what you 'think' you know," Brooke says, using her fingers to make quotation marks, "but this is between Fiona and me."

She puts her hands on her hips and glares down at me, but regardless of our positions, we both know who's in power.

I make sure to give her my sweetest smile. "Now it's between the three of us, isn't it?"

She knows she's in trouble. They both do. I am the school's self-appointed Robin Hood. Taking from the rich, spoiled, and corrupt, and giving to the poor—i.e., me. It's the only after-school activity I find remotely entertaining.

"How do you keep doing this?" Fiona asks.

Now it's my turn to play clueless. "Doing what?"

She sighs again.

We both know what she's talking about. She wants to know how I keep finding out all this dirt on everyone. If I told her, she wouldn't believe me, so I don't bother to explain.

Not that this instance needed any noteworthy skills. Not with

Brooke. She's a special kind of egomaniac. The kind that doesn't believe anyone will dare cross her. The kind where you just have to wait, listen, and watch, and you'll have something on her in no time.

"You're just as bad as all the people you hate," Fiona tells me.

She's saying this to *me*?

I don't dignify it with an answer.

Not when the people she's talking about told so many brutal lies about Leighton Chutney that she's now being homeschooled. Or hit a dog with their car and just left it there. Or put laxatives in Kristoff McLeigh's protein shake before his big football game with all the scouts watching.

Not even the same playing field.

I get justice. Or at least, a little revenge. So what if I pocket something on the side?

"Stop talking," Brooke hisses at Fiona, before turning her attention to me. "You don't have anything on us." The glare she flashes could make blood turn cold.

"No?" I ask, plucking the thumb drive Fiona's been holding from her hand. She really should have stashed it in her bag.

"Two cheaters for the price of one. Well, price of two. You can both pay up," I say, lying back on the bench. I want to take in and savor every second of this. Sure, there are people at Lightsend who've done worse than Brooke, but this is personal. Brooke's the one who went *Mean Girls* on me when I started school here. The compliments on my clothes that everyone knew were really insults. The whispers. Trash talk. Blocking my car in for hours. Spilling coffee on me. And little Miss Fabulous Fiona was always along for the ride. "Or if you prefer," I continue, "I can let Mr. Thadwell know that one of the school's top students got there by cheating, and another had a side business that helped her do it."

"That drive proves nothing," Brooke scoffs.

"Come now," I say, matching her condescending tone. "Do you really think this is all that I have on you?"

Truthfully, yeah, it is. But she doesn't need to know that. I'll find something else. I always do.

I toss the drive up in the air and then catch it in my palm.

Right as it smacks my skin, my whole body shudders.

Now? *Really??*

There's nothing I can do but watch.

A lavender bedroom. Cluttered desk. Books, papers, nail polish, makeup, laptop, some kind of trophy. I'm not quite sure where I am or what I'm seeing.

A hand pulls a drive out of the computer and shoves it into the pocket of her jeans.

"I have no choice."

Of course. It's Fiona's voice. It's her eyes I'm seeing through. I'm in her room. She's on the phone, talking through her headphones.

"If I don't give it to her, she'll show the picture to everyone."

I can't hear the other side of the conversation.

"Easy for you to say, but you know my parents. They'll flip. 'What were you doing taking a picture like that anyway? Did you send it to that boyfriend of yours? I knew letting you get this serious was a bad idea.' They'll ground me till graduation. They'll never let me see you again."

It must be Nico she's on with.

She wipes her eyes with the back of her arm. "I'm such a clod. I made you erase it, and then I didn't do it myself. I should have known Brooke would pull something like this. She's been struggling in English. Kaplan ripped her last two essays apart, and you know she'll do anything to be number one."

Fiona tightens her hands into fists. "It's karma. I didn't say anything when they all turned on Leighton, and if I don't do what she says, I'm next. I don't know how I'm going to keep this up. Ms. Kaplan will figure it out. Only so many theses I can come up with. How am I supposed to write two of everything she assigns?"

There's a pause.

"I am not just letting her share the photo."

She stands up and grips the back of her chair.

"Yeah, I know there's nothing to be ashamed of," she says, her voice rising. "But you try telling that to my mom and her snobby friends, to the admissions boards, to the judges in my next pageant. They won't see it that way."

As quickly as the vision started, it ends.

Brooke is already halfway out the door.

"Not so fast," I call after her. "We're not done. Not even close."

Fiona is just watching me.

I stand up and smooth my sweater. If I pretend like nothing happened, maybe she won't ask why I just spaced out for who knows how long.

"Fine," Brooke says, moving closer until she's shoulder-to-shoulder with Fiona. "Get it over with. What do you want from us?"

"I want you both—"

Crap.

Payback is supposed to be a feel-good moment, not a my-stomach-is-telling-me-I'm-evil one. I can't get Fiona's voice on the phone out of my head. *Shake it off, Hayden.* It's not like a few hundred dollars will matter to her. It's spare change. She drops more than that on a take-out lunch for her and her friends. I've seen her flaunt the to-go bags at least a dozen times.

"I need . . ." I hold back a wince. A lock of hair is twisted around my finger so tight that the tip is white. I loosen it, letting the strand fall back in place.

"I need . . ." *Annoying conscience.* "I need you to erase the picture you have of Fiona."

Fiona may not be my biggest fan, or even one of the "nice" ones at Lightsend High, but she doesn't deserve what Brooke is doing to her—or for me to make her pay for it.

Fiona's eyes go super wide, but she doesn't say anything. It's Brooke who speaks up.

"Don't know what you mean."

I shake my head. "Are we really going to do this again? We all know you do. So how about we jump ahead? You will erase the photo. If it shows up anywhere, so will information about you. It's all pretty simple. Oh . . ." I put out my hand. "And you can give me five hundred for my time and effort."

"What?! We're not paying you five hundred," Brooke says.

"Correct," I answer. "*She's* not. You are."

Brooke crosses her arms and flips her light blond hair over her shoulder. "This is ridiculous."

"And trying to shame your 'friend' and getting her to do your work isn't? Nice priorities you have there." I put out my hand. "Pay up."

"You think I carry that around on me?"

"Yeah, I do."

"Ever hear of Venmo?" she says. Like I'd be amateurish enough to leave a trail.

"Just give me the cash."

Brooke rummages through her purse, mumbling about how I charged Ollie a lot less. She pulls out a hundred-dollar bill, two fifties, and three crumpled twenties and shoves them at me. "Here, this is all I have."

"You can pay me the rest tomorrow."

Her top lip curls. "You think I have time to go to the bank tonight?"

"Fine," I relent. I can be reasonable. "Thursday morning, before lunch. At your locker. You know what happens if you don't pay."

Brooke gives me a ginormous eye roll and turns on her heel, her hair whipping me in the face as she goes.

"Real nice," I say, backing up.

Fiona is still standing there. She hasn't moved. "What about me?"

"What about you? No one's keeping you here."

Her brow furrows. "You don't want any money?"

I sit back down on the bench. Yes, I want money, but not like this. "Not from you. Wouldn't be very Robin Hood–ish now, would it?" I say the last part more to myself.

"Huh?" she asks.

"Nothing. It doesn't matter."

Fiona looks down. She's been rubbing the same small scuff

mark on the floor with her shoe—a shoe that probably costs more than my car—for the last few minutes. "Thank you," she says. "I don't know how you knew or why you helped me. I know I haven't been . . ." She closes her eyes. "It's just all so hard. I didn't want to make waves. I knew Brooke was . . . I should've . . ."

I stop her. "It's fine. I get it." Why risk being an outcast? Being on the outside is hard when you're not used to it. I've become a pro over the years. Five schools in less than five years can do that.

Fiona nods, opens her mouth to say something, but hesitates.

"What?"

"You're not going to show anyone the photo, are you?" she asks at warp speed.

"I don't have it."

She lets out a heavy breath. "And you won't say anything about it, either?"

I hold up my fingers in the Girl Scout pledge. "Promise." I'm tempted to give her the whole your-body-is-nothing-to-be-ashamed-of-and-screw-Brooke-for-trying-to-make-you-feel-like-this speech, but she's not going to want to hear it from me. Instead, I say, "You know, if she were to release it, it's a crime. She could get in serious trouble."

She snorts. "Brooke? That girl gets away with everything."

Most people in town do. The rich ones anyway.

"Not anymore," I tell her.

Fiona gives me a skeptical smile. "Well, either way, thank you. I owe you one."

That I will take. At this school, you never know when an IOU will come in handy.

Maybe helping others really does pay.

3

HaYDen

"Come on, Greta, don't do this to me. Don't make me stay at this school any longer than I have to. I want to go home." I tug at the driver's-side door of my car, but it's not budging. I give one more pull, using all my strength. It doesn't do any good.

"Fine. You win." I open the back door and climb over the seat to get to the front. A couple of girls from drama club are watching. I smile and give them the middle finger. They leave, but not without glancing back in my direction a few times.

It takes three tries, but Greta finally starts. "That's my girl." I pat the steering wheel. "I know you're hungry. We're going to get you some fuel." She's been surviving on fumes, but I finally have the cash to fill her up.

Greta is a fighter. Been on the road for decades. Mom and I bought her eight years ago from a woman—my car's namesake—whose kids forced her to give up driving.

Greta the person, despite the fact that she could barely walk and had horrible reflexes, did not want to let her vehicle go. Knocked the keys right out of her son's hand when he tried to give them to my mom. Greta yelled and cried, which in turn made my mom yell and cry.

She's like that.

It was a scene. I had to make my mother take a walk down the block while Greta's kids assured her they'd drive her places and that she could take Lyft and Uber if they weren't around.

Eventually, Greta relented, saying Uber wouldn't be the same, but that my mom and I should take her car and be good to her. That she had meaning. I told her we would, and to this day I still try to keep that promise. Even if there are times I can't afford to take care of her like I want.

There are only a few cars at Grayson's Gas Station when I pull in, and I'm able to get a pump right away. Normally I pay right there, but my credit cards and I have dealt with enough rejection this week. The hundred Brooke gave me will do perfectly. Even gives me a legit way to break it.

The bell over the door rings when I go inside, but the guy at the counter doesn't turn to look. His back is to me as he fiddles with the coffee machine. A coffee would be nice, but I'm not wasting the ninety-nine cents.

I slide the hundred-dollar bill toward the guy. "Ten on number two." I want to do more, but I also want to make sure the cabin has enough heat.

"Sure," he says, turning around.

And, oh my god.

It's Ray Brody. I should have recognized that mess of dirty-blond curls.

Time to find a new gas station.

His dimpled smile turns into a scowl when he realizes it's me.

I have to admit that makes me a little happy. If I have to suffer, at least he does, too. "Just when I thought my day couldn't get any better," he says, letting out a sigh. "The Grim Reaper comes to pay me a visit. Here to extort me?"

"Maybe," I answer. "Day's still young."

He rests his elbows on the counter and leans toward me. "Give it your best shot. Let's see what you can find."

He's so close I can see myself in his pupils. They're wide, almost eclipsing the hazel color surrounding them.

"I'll leave that to your admirers," I say, backing up and giving a side-eye and wave to the two girls standing a few feet away at the magazine rack. They're not subtle about why they're there. They're practically drooling. Not that it's unexpected. More members of what I like to call "the Brody Bunch." Ray Brody, who most people just call Brody, has had a harem of girls around him ever since he and Cassie Lee ended things earlier this year. Seems to be someone new almost every day.

He notices the girls and winks.

I roll my eyes. "Cassie replacement numbers 772 and 773?" I ask.

He stiffens at the mention of his ex. It's like he's about to say something but then just takes my hundred and puts the change on the counter.

I look from him, to the money, back to him. Chances of me having an episode are small, but still . . .

"What?" he asks. "You need me to put it in your hand?"

Why does it have to be him at the counter? And since when do golden boys like Brody have jobs? At a gas station, no less? If anything, I'd expect him to have an internship at some bougie place where acceptance requires a bribe from a rich relative, and the actual work involves lounging around networking with other privileged people.

He's waiting for an answer.

I know what I have to do, and I know how it's going to sound. Still, it beats the alternative. "Actually," I say, "can you put it in my bag?" I open it and hold it toward him. "You know, flu season, germs, money is super dirty."

Brody shakes his head but does what I ask. "Another one for the book of Grim."

I don't react. People like him feed on that, and I already played into it once. A couple of weeks ago, eight people moved to the other side of the room when I sat near them during study hall. Word had gotten around that I have the inside track on people. Brody walked in during the mass exodus from my area. He said, "Whoa. Looks like we have a Grim Reaper in the room." I may have answered, "And it looks like we have a pompous asshole, too."

I shouldn't have engaged, because he plopped down in the seat right next to me. "You know, you have the scoop on everyone else. I think we should learn about you," he said, and picked up my bag from the floor.

I grabbed it back before he could unzip it. "Touch it again, you'll *wish* I was the Grim Reaper."

If I thought that would intimidate him or scare him away, I was dead wrong. He just laughed as if I amused him. "I like it, living up to the name."

"Guess it's better than living up to the stereotype of every frat-boy douche in all those old movies."

"You mean the rich, hot guys?" He relaxed back in the seat, his hands behind his head in a power pose. "Yeah, I'll take it. That tracks."

The teacher came in, and I decided to ignore the ass next to me and concentrate on my Spanish vocab, but Brody wasn't done with me.

"What?" I asked after I caught him staring at me and jotting things in a notebook.

"Irritable and angry," he said, writing down the words as he spoke. He shut the cover. "Keeping tabs. Only fair, right?"

How someone like Cassie—now don't get me wrong, I don't like the girl, but of all the people here I detest her the least—was able to date him is beyond me. She's one of those classic nice people. My first day of school, she asked me to join her table at lunch and offered to show me around or whatever. Obviously, I said no, but in three schools she was the first person to genuinely make an effort. And yet, somehow *she* wound up with Brody for years. That says something. I mean, the guy is infuriating.

"Anything else?" he asks now. "Or do you just want to stand here admiring me, too?"

I give him my best disgusted look, raise my bag in salute, and head to my car.

He's watching me. I can feel it.

I reach for the pump, stopping before I take it. I give a small prayer that I won't have another episode.

Not in front of him.

I clutch the handle and wait.

Nothing.

I let out a sigh of relief. Usually I don't have two visions close together, but it's happened.

"We're okay," I tell Greta, patting the dent on the driver's-side door. Most of the scrapes and dings on the car are courtesy of human Greta, but this one is all mine. Almost killed me.

After the tank's full—or at least as full as it's going to get on ten dollars—I try to open the door, but Greta is still in a mood. Why did I shut it all the way? "Come on, I fed you," I plead with my car. She doesn't care. It's back through the rear door.

I don't have to check if Brody is watching. I know he is. He's always watching me.

I make it to the front and turn the car on. Works first try this time. Things are looking up. I pull out of the gas station, roll down the window, and crank the radio as I go.

The weather has been really warm for fall, and I'm here for it. The wind feels good, the music feels good, the money in my bag feels good.

By the time I get home, the stress of the day, of Brooke and Fiona and Brody, are gone. I'm actually happy.

"Baby!" my mom says, taking my hands and twirling me around the room the second I walk inside. "You're home."

I love when she's like this.

"I am," I say, taking a seat on the stool near the counter that separates our kitchen and living room. I jiggle my bag. "And guess what? We have enough for this month's electricity bill now."

"Oh, sweetie!" She kisses the top of my head. "Thank you for pitching in. Those kids are lucky to have my brilliant daughter tutor them."

"Yep," I lie.

"And don't you worry," she says, pulling a box of pasta out of the cupboard. "I think I sold another article. We're going to be okay. More than okay."

"I know," I tell her, and I really want to believe it.

4

HaYDen

Thursday comes, and the bell rings to signal lunch. Finally. It's money time!

I already have the rest of what Brooke owes me spent. Most of it will go to pay down the credit cards, but I'm putting aside a twenty for a splurge day at the grocery store. I am so sick of pasta and peanut butter sandwiches.

"Careful. I wouldn't do what you're about to do."

I look over. It's Cassie, standing by her locker with her best friend, Audra Rafferty.

"Yeah, I'm talking to you," Cassie says.

"You don't know what I'm about to do."

She cocks her head. "You sure about that?"

I don't have time for this. I told Brooke I'd meet her just before lunch. This girl is not going to keep me from collecting what's mine.

"Whatever," I say. "I'll be fine."

"Don't say I didn't warn you."

A part of me does want to know what she's heard. Cassie and Audra are the kind of people who fly above high school hierarchy.

The bratty rich kids welcome them, but so does everyone else. They're able to float from group to group, so there is a good chance they're in on all the gossip and whatever people are saying about me. Cassie would probably jump at the chance to help me if I let her, too. The only one in this school who ever would. Even after all my snubs, she still tries to check on me every now and then to see if I'm "settling in" or need anything. Like I'm her after-school project or something. I never take her up on it. I'm not a charity case, and I don't do friendship. I don't need her help now, either.

"About time," Brooke says when I show up at her locker.

I'm perfectly punctual. Not that it should matter. I'm the one with the upper hand here.

She's standing very rigid. Her whole demeanor seems off. I guess I really scared her.

"So," Brooke says, angling the right side of her body toward me. "How do we do this?"

Seriously? "You give it to me, and we're done."

"Give you what exactly?" she asks.

I don't need a vision or a warning from Cassie for my Spidey sense to erupt. Brooke is up to something.

When I don't answer her, she does it for me.

"If I give you more cash," she says, "you won't spread lies about me? Is that right? Like you've been doing about everyone else."

No. No. No.

She's setting me up. Calling my bluff. Probably taping the whole thing, making herself out to be the innocent victim.

"Don't know what you're talking about," I say. "I just wanted to borrow your physics notes."

Brooke's hands ball into fists. "Liar. Own it. You're trying to spread stories about me, ruin my reputation. I'm not going to stand for it."

And I'm not going to stand here while she calls me out. I walk past her and turn the corner. There are two men standing there. A tall, skinny white guy and an average-height, stocky black man. Both have the words SHERIFF'S OFFICE printed on their uniforms.

She called the police?

The two see me and head my direction.

Crap.

No way I'm sticking around for this. I cannot have something else on my record. I turn to go.

The tall one calls out, "Hayden Jefferies? We want to talk to you."

That's my cue. I book it out of there. I run down the hall past Brooke.

"Aww, someone's in trouble," she calls after me.

Of course I'm the one paying for my crimes, while she gets off scot-free. Fiona was right. Brooke gets away with everything.

I hear footsteps running behind me. It's just one set. The other officer must be going in another direction. The guy's not far behind me, but I have a tiny bit of leeway. If I am going to lose him, I need to do it now.

I slip inside the nearest classroom, making sure to shut the door behind me. The room is full of students, but beggars can't always be choosers.

"Can I help you?" the teacher asks.

I don't recognize her. Hopefully she doesn't recognize me—or know of my reputation.

"Yes," I say, trying to buy myself some time. I press myself against the wall, away from the window on the door, hoping I won't be seen by passersby—namely anyone from the sheriff's office. "I'm supposed to make a plea on behalf of the school paper. We're . . . umm . . . short of people and desperately need writers. Any of you interested?"

I look around the class. No one looks too familiar. They're not juniors—I'd be able to tell if they were my year. Probably freshmen or sophomores.

A girl in the back squints at me. "I'm on the paper, and we're doing fine."

"I didn't mean the *paper* paper," I cover. "I meant the lit mag."

"The school doesn't have a lit mag," she says.

"No kidding. That's why I'm here." I'm a decent liar, but this is not going well.

The teacher stands up. "Maybe I should call the office."

"No need," I say, peeking out the door. "I'm about to leave."

There doesn't seem to be anyone milling around the hall, so I make another break for it. I don't have much choice. I need to get to the girls' locker room, go through the gym, out the back exit, and then I'm home free.

Every step I take, I'm sure I'm going to get caught. I don't have that far to go, but I can almost picture one of the officers jumping out, or Brooke, or some teacher asking me why I'm wandering without a hall pass.

Somehow I make it to the locker room. To my relief it's empty. Only who knows for how long? I need to get through the gym and to the exit. I open the door ever so slowly. It lets out a whine. I freeze. It doesn't seem to have drawn anyone's attention. I survey the gym. No Coach Bates. No Coach Hill. There's no class in there, either. They could be doing something outside, though, which means they may return any minute.

Time to run again. I open the door a little wider. This time the squeak it makes is super loud.

"Hello? Is someone there? Hello?"

Where is that coming from?

"Hello?" the voice says again. There's a pounding emanating from inside the storage closet in the locker room. "Hello?"

"Shh!" I warn.

"Please," the voice continues, "get me out of here."

Why now? I need to go.

"Hello?"

I go over to the door and try the knob. It's locked. My whole body tenses. Of course this is happening at this very moment.

"Get him in there," a voice says. "Hurry up."

A bunch of people are pushing Nick Kellog into the closet and locking the door. I can't make out who they are, I'm just seeing backs, but they're all in gym uniforms. A few hoot and cheer as Nick bangs on the door, hoping to be released.

This whole thing shouldn't come as a surprise. Besides me, Nick is probably Lightsend's biggest outcast, and the school has more than its fair share of assholes who I'm sure take great pleasure in torturing him. Still, the timing of this latest stunt couldn't be any worse.

"You still there?" he asks.

"Yeah, I'm here." Even though I should be halfway across the gym by now. "Hold on. I'll get you out."

Somehow whoever put him in there had a key. As for where they put it . . . ? I don't have time for a scavenger hunt. I grab one of my credit cards—at least it's good for something—and jimmy open the lock.

"Thanks," Nick says once he's free. He doesn't stick around for small talk. He goes straight for the door.

So much for being careful and discreet.

I follow him, both of us running through the gym and toward the exit.

We make it outside. Only, that's as far as I get.

A hand lands on my shoulder. "Not so fast."

5

Cassie

"I still don't get why you warned her," Audra says, sliding into the passenger seat of my car. We're making the most of our open lunch period and picking up food from Brennan's Bistro. It has crab cakes to kill over. "She's the enemy."

"She's not the enemy." I'll admit part of me—the less rational, collected, analytical part—wants to blame Hayden for the Brody situation, but the rest of me knows it's not her fault. "She didn't do anything. At least not yet."

Audra tilts her head at me, her lips pursed. Even without the stare-down, I know she thinks I'm being ridiculous. I can't help it, though. I find myself constantly reaching out to Hayden, and it's not one of those know-thy-enemy things.

"She's struggling. She needs the money," I add, not sure if I'm trying to convince Audra or myself.

"How do you know?"

I lower my sunglasses. Now it's my turn to give *her* a look. Audra knows exactly how I know. Other than Brody, she's the only person I've told my secret to. I tried with my dad years ago, but he didn't want to hear it.

"Okay, fine," she says, "but still . . . you are way too nice."

I wouldn't exactly call it nice. I just saw Hayden walking into an ambush from Brooke and thought maybe I could give her a fighting chance. A small one, anyway. The girl needs a break. Not all my visions about her have Brody in them. I've seen how Hayden lives, how alone, how lonely she is all the time. We're not the same, I have friends, but part of me feels like I understand her. "Did you order?" I ask.

"Yeah," Audra answers. "You know I did. Quit switching the subject. You need to stop with the whole Hayden-Brody thing. Have you seen him around her? He hates her."

That's on me, too.

"You're crushing the guy's heart," Audra continues. "You gotta give him a break. He loves you."

"He seems to be moving on very nicely," I mutter.

She shakes her head. "Yeah, because you pushed him away in order to create a self-fulfilling prophecy."

We've been over this. A quadrillion times. For months now.

When I don't answer, she keeps going. "Not all your visions are right."

"I know that, but this wasn't *one* vision. It kept happening. It *keeps* happening. It's never like that. This is a warning."

"Fine." She throws up her hands. "A warning that you should keep Brody away from Hayden, then. Not that you were supposed to dump him."

"I don't want someone who doesn't want me. I want to be his first choice."

Audra lets out a guttural groan. "You are. Hayden wouldn't even be on his radar if it wasn't for you. He probably wouldn't even know her name. He doesn't want *her*, he wants *you*."

"Look, we're better as friends. You know that. It's for the best." I know Audra is only trying to be a good friend, but she doesn't understand what I've seen. My visions don't only look real, they feel it, and most of the time they come to life. And the way Brody and Hayden act around each other in them—just thinking about it makes me cringe. It's all I can picture when I see Brody now. Even when I see other girls hanging on him, it doesn't feel like those visions do. It kind of makes a relationship impossible. I pull into the parking lot of Brennan's Bistro and turn off the car. I feel tears brimming, but I fight them back. "Do you want to run in or do you want me to?"

"I'll go," she says, her voice softer, "and I'm sorry. I didn't mean to upset you. I'll drop it for today, okay?"

I nod, still looking forward. I don't want to cry. I'm sick of crying over Brody. And I'm sick of talking about Hayden. She's already taken up too much of my brain space.

By the time Audra comes back with the food, I've composed myself. "That smells amazing," I say.

"I know, right?" she says, popping a garlic truffle fry with Parmesan into her mouth and handing the bag to me so I can take one.

"Why did I tell Valerie we'd pick up her lunch?" I ask. "We could have just sat here and ate. I'm starving."

"Because you," Audra says, pointing a fry at me, "have become enamored with the musical and everyone in it since you joined the crew."

"Maybe." I've been throwing myself into the behind-the-scenes stuff for Lightsend High's production of *Grease*. I find painting the sets relaxing; my mind seems to turn off while I do it. No visions, no thoughts of my ex, just the brushstrokes on the flats as I bring the backdrops to life. "But I promise, I'm not staying after school to work on the play today."

"The physics test," Audra says, gripping the top of the take-out bag. "Don't remind me."

We've been trying to find a time to study all week, but between my set stuff and her dance classes and babysitting her sister, we haven't been able to make it work.

"You'll ace it," I assure her.

"I hope so," she says. "Either way, after that test, we are going out."

I turn on the car. "I don't know."

"Well, I do. You need to get out, have some fun, not think about you-know-what."

I nod. I know she's right. I need to exile Hayden and Brody from my mind.

Now if only I could get my visions to cooperate.

6

HAYDEN

"If you'll excuse me," I say, trying to turn away from the officer, "I have to get to lunch."

"Nice try," he tells me. It's the shorter black guy, and according to the badge on his shirt, he's not just part of the sheriff's office—he is the actual sheriff.

"I didn't do anything." I know I should probably be pleading the Fifth and keeping my mouth shut, but I don't want to be brought to the station and have to have my mother come pick me up. "I'm sure Brooke said all sorts of things about me, but you can't listen to her. She's the one you should be dragging out of here in cuffs."

"No one's dragging anyone away in cuffs." He motions to a bench a few feet away. We go and take a seat. "Listen, Hayden, the accusations against you are serious."

"I told you, you can't listen to Brooke."

"It's not just Brooke. She gave us written testimony from several students. And a teacher."

I did *not* blackmail my teacher. My mom had been sending me a million bizarre texts. I needed to make sure she was okay, and Mr. Donnelly saw me texting her back. He demanded my phone, and I was upset. When I held it out to him, I may have told him not to use it to send any of his private pics to Vera from Tinder—that they were really inappropriate. His face went pale, then green, and then a little red, but he didn't take my phone as he slunk back to his desk.

If that bothers him, he should try getting a trig test back and having to see what he was up to while correcting my paper.

"Some say you're threatening to spread lies for cash, others say you hacked them to find personal information," he continues.

"Lies. I didn't hack anything. I wouldn't even know how."

He twirls the gold band around his left ring finger. "Your history with your past schools seems to say otherwise, and Mr. Donnelly says you had some personal information about him."

I don't know how to answer that. I consider telling him that I catfished my teacher, but that could be easily disproven if Donnelly actually met Vera. Instead I try to divert the conversation.

"You know you're wasting your time on me, right? It's Brooke and her friends who have things to hide. Things much worse than this."

"What kind of things? Do you have proof?"

I don't. Only what I saw, and I can't exactly tell him that. I don't need proof when I approach the Brookes of the world. They're so afraid that I'll spill their crimes, they just go along with what I say. I didn't even have anything concrete on Ollie Easton, just a gut feeling that he was hiding something. When I told him I knew what he did, his look confirmed I was right. He paid up without even asking what I knew.

That tactic isn't going to work here.

I shake my head.

I'm done for. The word of the kids who own the town versus the word of the freak whose mom rents the tiny, run-down cabin in the woods is not really a contest. Hell, *I'd* probably believe them over me.

Telling him the truth about what I can do is out of the question, too. He won't believe me. *Hey, Sheriff, sometimes when I touch an object, I see things that happened in the past.* He'll ask me if I want to plead insanity at my trial.

It's not like I can show him I'm for real. Visions don't work on cue, and even if they did, they're not all winners. Like the one where I touched Mr. Thadwell's keys. I saw him racing to the television to catch *Jeopardy!*, with his wife saying she was getting worried, because he never misses it. Not exactly a get-out-of-jail-free card.

I don't have any more hands to play. "So what now? What does this mean?" I ask.

He purses his lips. "The Tamisons have asked to file charges."

I rest my elbows on my knees and put my head in my hands. Brooke really does think she's above the law. She doesn't care if I expose her, because she made sure I'm not credible. And she knows Fiona won't turn on her. Not with the threat of exposing the picture.

"But," the sheriff continues, "Principal Thadwell wants this all worked out internally."

I lift my head. Thank god for rich, high-rated schools not wanting to tarnish their reputations. "So detention?" I ask. Might be wishful thinking, but come on, just like I don't have any hard evidence on the people I blackmail, other than a bunch of people accusing me of things, they really don't have any proof that I committed a crime, either.

"It's to be determined," he says. "There will be a meeting tomorrow morning."

I nod.

"Make sure your mother's there."

I bolt upright in my seat. "My mom? No, that's not going to work. I can handle it myself."

"Hayden," he says. "She has to be there."

I get up and start pacing. "What if I just agree to a suspension, promise to be a model student, and do community service? Does that work?"

"Your mother needs to know what's going on. This is a nonstarter. Principal Thadwell will call her and tell her to come down if you don't. Do you want it to come from him or you?"

"Me," I say, my voice almost a whisper.

I close my eyes.

My mom at school? I might as well pack my bags tonight. There's no way this is going to end well.

7

HaYDen

The whole ride home from school, I play calming music. *Everything is great*, I tell myself over and over.

I pull over before I turn onto the small dirt road that leads to the cabin. I'm near the parking lot for the walking trails around the falls. It's a good mile or so from where I live, and for the most part, out of range from my mother. I rest my head on the steering wheel. *I can do this. This is no big deal.* I let myself sit for a few more minutes, trying to clear my mind, trying to get rid of the anxiety and fear I'm feeling. I'm not sure it's working, but I'll find out soon enough.

I put Greta in drive and make my way home. *Everything is great*, I start telling myself again.

I park the car and slowly walk to the cabin, still silently chanting. I open the door and see my mom sitting on the couch. She's embroidering. There's a little smile on her face. So far, so good.

"Hi, Mom."

Everything is great. Everything is great.

"Hi, baby. How are you?"

Serene. Happy. Great.

"Hanging in there. But I do need to tell you something. I got in some trouble at school, and they want us both to come in tomorrow morning."

I'm so relaxed.

"What kind of trouble?" She moves the needle through the fabric, but she still seems calm.

I tell her the story in my most soothing voice.

"Oh, Hayden. What did I tell you? This was our chance to start over again."

I feel myself getting agitated. *Cute puppies playing in the snow. Babies laughing. Lying on a warm, sandy beach.* I'm not going to react. I'm not going to point out that if she could hold down a job, any job, I wouldn't have to find creative ways to make money. I wouldn't have to be the mom in this relationship.

Mom stabs the needle in and pulls the thread out the other side, her hands shaking. She repeats the motion, each time getting more forceful.

Crap.

La, la, la, everything is good. Rainbows. Warm chocolate chip cookies. Snuggling in bed, watching the rain fall out the window.

The tension in her shoulders melts away.

"Mom, are you going to be able to do this tomorrow?"

"I'll have to."

I sit down next to her. "But there's going to be a lot of people. A lot of emotions."

"You need me. I'll be okay."

I put my hand on her arm. "We can just leave, start over."

She shakes her head. "No, I can do this. We're staying. I'm making you a home."

A worry line creases her forehead. I'm not sure if the emotion is coming from her or from me.

"It's going to be a big day." She stands up and kisses the top of my head. "I'm going to go rest."

"Sounds good. I love you, Mom."

"I love you, too."

I know she does. I just don't know if it's enough to get her through the meeting. The last time she went to one of my schools, she wound up curled in a ball in the corner crying, banging her head against a wall.

It was when she finally admitted that she wasn't just super empathetic, she was an actual empath. That she can sense how people are feeling. Not their actual thoughts, thank god, but their emotions. Only she doesn't know how to control it. The more people there are around, the more chaotic things become, with each of their emotions warring inside her, the strongest fighting for control.

And now, thanks to me, for the first time in forever she's going to have to face a crowd. A crowd of high schoolers and angry parents and teachers.

Basically, I'm throwing her to the wolves.

8

HaYDen

"How are you doing?" I ask my mom when we pull into the parking lot at school the next morning.

She's gripping her knee and staring straight ahead.

"Maybe we should wait until after the bell sounds," I say, putting the car in park. "It will be fewer people in your immediate vicinity."

Mom bites her lip. "No, you can't be late. It won't look good."

"What if I go in and say you're finishing an emergency phone call and that you'll be here in a minute?" I don't love the idea of her walking in alone, but I think it beats dealing with the rush of people in the hall before classes start.

"Maybe that's a good idea," she says.

"Mom, you don't have to do this. You can call in. Or I can wing it. We can find a way around this."

"No. Hayden, I am the mother, and I am calling the shots. We are doing this. Go inside, get to that meeting, and I will be there in a few minutes. I'm going to fight for you."

I nod. I hope she can feel the love I have for her.

The whole school is lining the hallway when I walk inside. It's a good thing Mom agreed to wait in the car.

I should have known that Brooke would spread the word. But it's not only the students; the faculty is here too. You'd think they'd tell everyone to get moving, but nope, they're feeding on all this just as much.

Well, I'm not going to show defeat. I hold my arms up like a wrestler walking into the ring as I make my way down the hall. "Enjoying the show?" I ask the crowd. Probably not helping my case. I should be acting like the poster child of contrition, but there's no way I'm letting Brooke and her cronies think they won.

My arms drop when I pass Cassie. She's wearing that I-told-you-so look.

The smugness of it pisses me off. "You know," I say, not caring that we have an audience or that my voice is carrying down the hallway, "if you're going to warn someone they're being set up, you should *really* warn them. Not allude to it. Spell it out. Help a girl avoid all this."

"Why should she have to warn you?" Ollie, one of my more recent blackmailees and an all-around general asshat, calls out. "Don't you know everything?"

If I knew everything, there was no way I'd be in this mess. I'm not sure why I answer him, but I do.

"Apparently, *I'm* not the one with inside knowledge around here." I turn to glare at Cassie, but she and Audra are already walking away, heading into the bathroom. Must be nice to have the freedom to go where you want.

I see the sheriff, Mr. Thadwell, his assistant, Ms. Quill, and my guidance counselor, Ms. Drake, watching me from the main office.

I flash a sad smile their way and try to milk the moment. "I didn't do anything. I'm just an innocent bystander here who got caught up in Hurricane Brooke."

"All right, all right, enough," Mr. Thadwell says. "Ms. Jefferies, come inside here please. The rest of you go to class."

"Bell didn't ring yet," someone yells.

Mr. Thadwell massages the back of his head, right over the remaining section of hair. This place is probably what made him go bald. Seconds later the bell sounds. "Now go," he says to the onlookers. "Ms. Jefferies, where's your mother?"

"She'll be right in."

We go into his office. Brooke and her parents are already there. It's like looking at a real estate ad. All three of them sitting together, legs crossed, perfectly coiffed hair, not a frizz in sight. Brooke with hers pushed back by an ivory-colored headband. She's wearing a pink skirt with a matching blazer over a lace top. There's a giant flower pinned to the lapel. She's even in tights and pumps. It's like she googled how to look sweet and innocent. Her normal look is a lot more Kardashian/Jenner. Both of the elder Tamisons are in tailored suits. I can only imagine how much they shelled out for them.

They're hogging the chairs. Other than Mr. Thadwell's spot behind his desk, there's nowhere else to sit. I suppose he doesn't usually get this many people in his office at once. "Gretchen," he calls out to the administrative assistant, Ms. Quill. "Can you get us a few chairs?"

"I'll help," the sheriff says.

He steps out, and it's the Tamisons, Mr. Thadwell, Ms. Drake, and me. The silence oozes around us. The tension shows no sign of easing up. I try to think happy thoughts just in case my mom is nearby.

"Anastasia," I hear the sheriff say a minute later.

At the sound of my mother's name, I twist around to get a look. Did he get that from my file? Or does he know her?

"Phillip." She puts her hand on his forearm to steady herself.

What is going on?

He pulls her to the side, and I can't see or hear them anymore. Has my mother been hiding something from me?

How does she know the sheriff? She never leaves the house.

Ms. Quill gets stuck bringing all the chairs in while my mother and *Phillip* talk about who knows what.

When they finally enter the room, Mr. Tamison stands and points at them. "Is this why there won't be any charges? Because she has an in with the sheriff?" He has that angry evil look I've seen on his daughter hundreds of times. "I won't tolerate this."

My mom gets right up in his face. All five feet of her. Mr. Tamison may be over a foot taller, but she is more than holding her own. "*You* won't tolerate this? You know what I won't tolerate? Some rich prick thinking he can come after my daughter."

"Excuse me?" he says, his chest jutting out.

"You heard me," she says, matching his posture.

Oh, here we go.

She looks ready to pounce.

Butterflies landing on a cat's nose. A mountain in autumn right after the leaves change. A winning five-million-dollar lottery ticket.

It's not doing any good. She's feeding off not only her own emotions but Mr. Tamison's, too, and they're strong. Even I can sense that.

"Let's cool down," the sheriff says. "Brooke, Hayden, please go wait in the hall."

"We should be able to stay," Brooke protests.

For once I agree with her. I want to be here for my mom, and I want to know what's going on. This is my future at stake. I should have a say, or at least get to plead my case.

Apparently no one cares, because we still get the boot.

I take a seat on the bench in the main office, in front of Ms. Quill's desk. The admin gives me a small smile. I think she's about to say something but stops when Brooke takes the spot next to me, sucking all of the air out of the room.

"You can't find somewhere else to go?" I ask Brooke.

"And miss this opportunity to watch you suffer?"

I put in my earbuds and wait. I'm not listening to anything, but it keeps Brooke from talking to me.

About twenty minutes later the Tamisons storm out.

"What happened?" Brooke asks.

"It's taken care of," her mother says. "Get to class."

"But—" Brooke says.

"To class," her father orders.

They don't look particularly happy, which is hopefully good news for me.

"Ms. Jefferies, you can come in now," Mr. Thadwell says.

I'm trying not to be nervous. I don't want to set my mom off even more.

Roly-poly puppies. Roly-poly puppies.

It's not working. My skin feels warm and cold and clammy all at the same time.

All eyes are on me as I step into the office, but my eyes are on my mom. She's sitting in one of the chairs, her body contorted, with hands clenched on the armrests. She's focusing on me so intently that I know it's taking everything she has to keep it together.

Come on, puppies, do your magic.

"Well," I say, hoping to speed things up. "What's the verdict?"

It's my guidance counselor, Ms. Drake, who speaks up. "You have no extracurriculars, which we fear may be giving you too much free time to find unsuitable activities."

Wait. Are they referring to my blackmail as an activity?

"We think you need some more supervision and guidance . . . ," she continues.

Oh no. *Guidance.* Am I going to have to do community service or mandatory therapy or something even worse?

"Which is why," she says, "you're going to be working in Sheriff Rafferty's office."

"Excuse me?"

"After school most days," he pipes up. "And occasional weekends. We'll make a schedule that works for us both."

I shake my head. "No. I can't afford to volunteer. I need to get a job."

"This is a job," the sheriff says.

He doesn't understand. "A *paying* one," I say.

I look to my mom. How could she agree to this? She knows I'm seconds away from landing a spot at the grocery store. I've been applying everywhere since we moved to Lightsend, and it's the first place that's shown any signs of hiring me. I'm supposed to go back in for a final interview on Monday. I won't be able to work there if I'm stuck at the sheriff's office all the time. And if I can't earn an income or get money from my classmates, we won't be able to pay our bills.

"It is a paying job," my mom says, her voice strained.

"What?" I look to Sheriff Rafferty.

He nods. "We have some money in the budget for office help."

"And you want me? Town pariah working at the sheriff's office? Girl accused of both making up stories about people for profit *and* hacking their lives?"

"This way I can keep my eye on you," he says. "Keep you out of trouble. I don't think you'll be doing that again. You don't want those consequences. Trust me."

My mom is still watching me. She gives me a little nod. She wants me to agree.

Something is definitely up, but I'm not going to complain. It's a paying job. I'll do whatever it takes.

"Okay," I tell him. "Hayden Jefferies, teen detective, it is."

He lets out a laugh. "I said office help, Hayden. You won't be working on any cases."

Details, details.

9

Cassie

Audra lines her lips with precision before filling them in with her go-to matte stick, My True Obsession. It's red, with warm undertones that look amazing against her dark brown skin. My best friend likes to sleep as late as possible in the morning, so she does her makeup in the school bathroom when she gets in and between classes. She starts the day with a fresh face but by lunch is totally glammed up. Most of the girls in our school are. With everyone snapping and posting pictures every three seconds, people want to be Insta-ready. I, personally, am just an eyeliner-and-lip-gloss girl, but I like spending the extra time with Audra.

She glances at her watch. The bell already rang, but we have a lot of leeway on Friday mornings. Our first-period study hall is with Ms. Warmack. She's so obsessed with the school musical that as long as I say we're working on the sets or in the library researching something, we have free rein over what we do with the period.

"Another one?" Audra asks, looking at me through the mirror while wiping away some excess lipstick.

I nod as I continue writing in my journal. I keep track of all my visions—even if they're ones I'd rather not relive—along with what I think they mean, and how I'm feeling. It was my psychologist Dr. Mukherjee's idea to keep track of my thoughts, and it helps. Writing, painting, drawing, and that type of thing sometimes feel like my only escapes. "Yep. Last night. My own personal soap opera starring my ex. Lucky me."

"I know you don't want to hear this again, but I—"

Her voice slips away, the bathroom slips away. My pen falls from my hand and clatters to the floor.

I'm sitting alone in Audra's car outside the store at Grayson's Gas Station.

Audra opens the driver's-side door and tosses a bag of Sour Patch Kids at me before taking a seat behind the wheel. "I deserve all the chocolate," she declares, ripping open some peanut butter M&M's. "That physics test was brutal. I swear Ms. Perez is trying out some form of torture on us." She looks over at me. "And FYI, he wasn't in there."

She has to be talking about Brody. If we just took the physics test, it's Friday, Brody's one consistent shift at the gas station, and undoubtedly the reason Audra had us stop here. She's been trying to create accidental run-ins between Brody and me since we broke up.

The me in the vision ignores the Brody comment. Instead I'm hyper-focused on scouring the contents of my backpack. "Shoot," I say, a huge scowl on my face.

"What?" Audra asks.

"I did it again. Drop me back off at school?"

"Why?" Her face scrunches up like she sucked an extra-tart lemon. "It's the weekend. We're finally free for a few days. Don't make me go

back there. We're supposed to do something fun together. You promised."

"I know, but I forgot my journal in my locker. You know I hate when I do that. I won't be able to have fun if I'm thinking about it there. Besides, I'm having 'feelings.'"

"Fine," Audra says. "Reason accepted." She knows how important that thing is to me. "But won't the school be locked by now?"

"No, they have a rehearsal tonight in the auditorium. It'll be open."

We pull up to the entrance. "Okay, hurry up," Audra instructs me, "and we can still catch everyone at the Grille."

"You go without me. I think I just want to stay in and write."

"Cassie . . ."

"I'm sorry. You understand, though, right?"

Audra looks like she wants to argue, but decides against it. "Fine," she says, "but still hurry. I'll drive you home, and then I'll go join them."

"I was thinking I'd walk. Clear my head."

She shakes her head. "It's a mile, and it's already dark. I veto this idea."

"It's also Lightsend. I'll be fine. I'll be on lit roads the whole way home."

"Uh-uh. My dad would kill me if I let you do this. How about I drive you home, and you can walk on the treadmill in your basement?"

I know she's just looking out for me, and I love her for it, but I need the air. I need the alone time.

"Audra . . . thank you, but . . ."

"It's building up again," she finishes for me.

"Yeah, it is." I feel on edge, my chest is tight, and it's like I can feel the blood moving through me. I need to regroup. "I'll be okay. I promise. I'll even pin you my location. It'll be like you're on the walk with me."

She doesn't look convinced, but I don't wait for her to protest. I squeeze her hand and get out of the car. "Thank you," I call out, and wave as I head toward the building.

Rehearsal hasn't started yet, and the school feels really empty. Like it's deserted. I know there must be a janitor or teacher somewhere, but still, it's kind of eerie. I rush to my locker and take out my journal. I hug it to my chest and promise myself I will not forget it again.

There's a creak from down the hallway.

"Hello?"

There's no answer.

Must be the wind, or the building settling. Nothing to worry about. I start back to the door, but I hear it again. Footsteps this time.

"Who's there?" I say. I turn around. Nothing.

I look around again. It's not dark, but it's not bright, either. About half the hall lights are off, creating large shadows all around me. I know it's my imagination, but I feel like they're closing in.

There's a buzz, and I jump. It's just my phone. I glance at it and see it's Audra texting me. I'm about to respond when I hear a creak again.

"I said, who's there?" I call out.

Still no response.

This isn't a mind game or shadows messing with my head. I know someone's there. They're watching me. I can feel it.

"Hello?"

What do I do? What's my best move?

Leave.

But how? What's the safest way? The main entrance? The emergency exit? Scream and hope someone is nearby to help?

Think, Cassie.

I freeze in place, trying to sense where they're hiding, to hear their breathing, to see something.

I need to go. I need to get out. I need to get to people. Now. *I race toward the emergency exit, my heartbeat quickening with each step. As my hand touches the door, someone slams me against the wall. I can't move.*

A cold, hard piece of metal rests against my neck, and everything goes black.

"No," I scream.

"Cas?" It's Audra. She's by my side, holding me upright.

I'm back in the bathroom. The fluorescent lights flood my eyes. "No, no, no."

"Are you okay?" she asks.

I'm not. I've had a vision of us after the physics test before, but it wasn't at all like the one I just saw. The old one ended with us raiding my freezer and making massive ice cream sundaes . . . not me with a knife at my throat. Something changed to make this happen. Something big. I've *never* seen a vision like this. Not one of me in jeopardy. I try to inhale, to take a deep breath, but it only makes my chest feel tighter.

It was just a vision, and visions can be changed. It was just a vision, and visions can be changed. It was just a vision, and visions can be changed.

The thought reassures me for a second. Until a different one hits.

I'm in danger.

Serious danger, and I don't know how to get out of it.

10

HaYDen

need to get my mom out of here. She's been holding it together, but being around all these people is clearly taking its toll. She is slipping down the chair, her arms twisted together and her knee bouncing nonstop.

"We're done, right?" My eyes scan over all the adults in the room. I'm not exactly sure who's in charge.

"Yes," the sheriff says. "I'll see you Monday."

Mom lets out a low groan. She's trying to stifle it, but it's not working. "Hey, I got you," I say, rushing to her side and helping her up. "Let's get you to the car."

I keep my arm around her waist once she's standing, but she shakes me off. "I'm okay."

I try to think of all my usual happy thoughts, but it's hard when I see her like this.

Mom takes my arm, and we make our way through the hall. No one's out here, but they're close. The classrooms are filled with people going through who knows what.

We make it halfway to the exit when Mom stops. She crouches down by the lockers and cradles her head in her hands.

"Mom? Are you okay? Let's go," I say, trying to pull her back to her feet. "We're almost to the car. We'll get you home."

"No." Her voice is pained and her eyes are welling with tears. "Don't you hear it?"

"Hear what?"

"The screams. The terror." Mom's rocking back and forth on her heels now.

"We need to go."

I reach for her, and she grips my arms. "You have to help."

"I'm trying," I tell her.

She shakes her head violently. "No, no, no, no, no, no. Not me. There." She points to the bathroom.

"Mom."

"Please, Hayden."

"I can't leave you here."

She tries to pull herself up, but she can't. "You have to help her."

I'm wasting more time arguing. She's not going to relent, so I give in and agree to check out the situation in the bathroom.

I push the door open and see Cassie bent over the sink, hyperventilating. Audra is standing by her side, rubbing her back.

"Everything okay?" I ask.

Cassie snaps to attention at the sound of my voice.

"You. You," she says. Her arm is outstretched, simultaneously pointing at me and clutching some book. "You're what changed. You did this. This is your fault."

I look to Audra for help but don't get any. Her focus is on her friend.

I have no clue what Cassie's talking about. I didn't do anything to her, but the wild look in her eyes tells me she certainly thinks I did.

There's something about her expression that reminds me of my mother. The nights she used to wake up screaming.

"What did I do?" I ask. I keep my voice calm, soothing.

"You changed things. You changed everything."

She's not making any sense, but I'm used to being around someone like this. I wait, hoping she'll continue talking. She doesn't. Instead tears streak down her cheeks, and as she goes to wipe them, her book slips out of her hand.

I pick it up for her, and I get a flash.

The book. It's a journal. Footsteps. A knife. A glint of light. A muffled noise. Then darkness.

I drop the book. Cassie snatches it back up.

"Cassie," I say. "Did someone hurt you? Are you all—"

"No." She cuts me off, her voice infused with sobs and sniffles.

I'm not sure which question she's answering.

"What—"

She turns away from me.

"You should go," Audra says, her voice so quiet I almost don't hear her. She gives me a small, pitying smile and then focuses her attention back on Cassie.

I don't know what else to do, so I go.

My mom is still by the lockers, but she is no longer alone. The sheriff is there.

"Hayden," he says, "I'll take your mother home. You get to class."

Before I can respond, he swoops her up and is carrying her out. She is curled up like a ball in his arms, her head buried in his chest. And the way he's looking at her? There's way too much concern in his eyes. That is not how you look at a stranger, not even one in a massive amount of pain.

What the hell is going on here?

My mom doesn't go out, she doesn't see people. She doesn't *know* anyone here. Yet, clearly, she knows Sheriff Rafferty. How, though?

Are they having an affair?

Is that possible?

No, that doesn't make sense, but neither does the way his eyes were fixated on her. Something is going on. It doesn't add up.

The sheriff pushes the door open and carries my mom out of the building, and I'm just left there watching.

11

HaYDen

My mom doesn't answer any of my texts or calls. Not one. I've been trying her all day, with the exception of Donnelly's class. By the time school is over, I'm out of battery. When I get to Greta, I plug the phone into my charger, but it's a lost cause. You have to hold it at just the right angle to make it work, and I don't have the patience. Not that it matters; if my mom hasn't answered by this point, she's not going to pick up now. I just need to get home and talk to her. I know I need to get my emotions under wraps first, but my mind is at war with itself. Half of me is terrified for my mom's well-being after all she went through at the school today, and the other half is pissed at her for keeping me in the dark about whatever it is she has going on with the sheriff.

I can't let those feelings overtake me now, though. I need her to answer me, and that won't happen if I come in like a tornado. I use the ride to calm my mind. I turn on the radio and let the music wash over me in the hopes that it will help me—and in turn, my mother—relax.

Mom's not in the living room when I get home. I knock lightly on her bedroom door, but I don't wait for an answer.

"Hey," I say, letting myself in. "How are you doing?"

She lifts her head off her pillow. "Hayden, hi. I'm okay. Tired."

I take a seat on the edge of her bed and take her hand. She looks better than I expected. "Thank you for coming today."

She squeezes my palm. "I want to be there for you."

"I know, but I also know it was hard."

She doesn't argue that. It's true.

We sit there in silence for a minute, and I can't help it. "How do you know the sheriff?" I spit out.

"I don't."

She's lying. I try not to let the annoyance overtake me. "He called you by your first name, and I saw him carry you out of there."

"He was just being nice."

"Mom . . ."

She turns away from me, her hand slipping from mine. "Hayden, I've had a long day. I just want to sleep."

I feel a twinge of guilt. She has had it rough, but then I remind myself that she just lied to me. "And I just want answers. It will only take a minute."

"It's nothing," she says. "He's the sheriff. I called for info on the town before we moved here, and he was very helpful."

"And that's it?"

"That's it."

I'm not buying it.

"He was very familiar for someone you only spoke to on the phone once."

"Hayden," she says, turning back to me. "Not everything is a puzzle to solve. He was helping out a fellow resident. That's it. Now please, let me sleep." She closes her eyes, signaling that the conversation is over.

My mom is very stubborn. The next few days I try to get more out of her, but she sticks to her he-was-helpful-on-the-phone story, no matter how much I push.

I don't have much better luck with the sheriff, either. I started work yesterday, but this is the first time we've been alone in the same room for more than thirty seconds.

He's sitting at his desk in an area nicknamed the pit while I sweep.

So far my job primarily consists of straightening up, making coffee, doing the dinner pickup, and nonemergency phone line coverage. They won't even let me touch an actual file.

I'm not about to blow this chance, though. I've been wanting to grill the sheriff since our meeting at school. I sweep closer to him. He's typing something on his computer. He doesn't look up, even when I'm practically by his side. It doesn't seem like he's going to give me an opening, so I just go for it.

"My mom says you and she go way back," I lie.

"She does, does she?"

His face shows no expression. I have no idea if he's buying this, but I already jumped in, so I'm going all the way. "Yeah. She told me the story, but I forgot. How'd you meet again?"

He closes his laptop. "Hayden, I know you like gathering information on people, but there's nothing to get here. Your mom needed help, and I helped her. That's what I do."

"Helped how?" I ask, wanting to see if their stories match.

"Carrying her out of the school," he says.

I stifle a groan. He knows that's not what I meant.

I want to continue questioning him, but Audra enters the building. She walks right past the front desk and right over to me.

Or not.

"Hey, Daddy," she says, giving him a kiss on the cheek.

"He's your dad?"

Of course he is. Sheriff Phillip Rafferty. Audra Rafferty.

In my defense, I did have a lot going on the day I met the sheriff. I was not exactly contemplating the name on his shirt. And once I knew it, it wasn't like I was focusing on his family life. Or on Audra.

Plus, the two of them look nothing alike. They both have dark brown skin, but that's pretty much where any similarity ends. He's about five-eight—average for a man. She's five-nine or five-ten—tall for a teen girl. None of their features look alike. Nothing from the shape of their faces (hers is squarish, his is oval) to their earlobes (hers free, his attached).

"Don't look so shocked," she says.

I realize I've been staring and look away. "Sorry."

The sheriff raises an eyebrow at her, and she gives me a smile. A fake one for her father's benefit. Audra doesn't like me. Never has, but after the incident with Cassie in the bathroom, I can tangibly feel the hate she's sending my way. "It's fine," she says. "No one thinks we look alike. But wait until you see the smile."

"Huh?"

"I have his smile," she says, and gives his cheek a pinch, but no grin appears. She's doing this little show for his benefit, not mine.

She wants something from him. "But otherwise," Audra says, "I look like more like my mom."

That I'd been able to suss out for myself. Delaney Lamont is the face of the Channel 6 morning news, serving Lightsend and other middle-of-nowhere New York towns. I haven't seen the show—we don't have a TV—but her image is plastered everywhere: on the sides of buses, on billboards, on posters.

I heard someone say she was Audra's mom, but even if I hadn't, I would have known. Audra is the spitting image of her mother.

"She hasn't seen my smile yet," Sheriff Rafferty says. "You need to earn that."

He gives me a stern look. Another reminder that I'm still on probation here. I've probably gotten forty-five warnings from six different people that if I overstep, I will be kicked out and forced to face the Tamisons' wrath. That I need to prove Rafferty made the right choice in giving me a chance.

Although maybe I'm not the only one who needs probation. I wonder what Delaney Lamont would think of him hanging out with my mother. But would he really cheat on someone like that for a recluse who's afraid to leave the house? My stomach turns. What if that's the appeal? Less chance of getting caught or ratted out.

Audra rolls her eyes at him and pretend-whispers to me, "Don't be fooled. He's really a big softy."

"Mm-hmm," I say. I don't know what kind of man he is, but if he's involved with my mother somehow, I plan to find out.

"Right, Dad?" she asks. "Tell her."

She is laying it on thick. Too thick. She's 100 percent after something. No way she'd be this nice to me otherwise. Not when her best friend thinks I did something horrific to her. I can't get that expression on Cassie's face out of my mind—or that vision I had when I held her journal.

It could have been nothing, I remind myself. She could have been writing in it while watching an episode of some FBI/catch-the-killer-type show—and that's what I saw. Or it could have been something much worse. It could have been a look at someone who hurt her. I have no way of knowing, and it's not like Cassie's going to open up to me. I tried talking to her at school yesterday. Twice. But all the goodwill she used to have for me is long gone. She just shook her head and walked away.

"So to what do I owe the honor of your presence?" Sheriff Rafferty asks his daughter.

"Guess who aced her physics test?" she says. She pulls a red metal bottle with a Baby Yoda sticker attached to it from her bag and goes to the water cooler to fill it up.

"That's my girl," he says.

The way he's beaming at her, I feel a small ache. I wonder what it would be like to have a dad like that.

While it's not directed at me, I do see the sheriff's smile. The resemblance to Audra is there. They both have this wide grin that causes a tiny dimple to form right below the right eye.

Maybe my dad is where I get my height (six inches taller than my mother), or my slightly crooked nose, the gap in my front teeth, thick eyebrows, golden eyes—or everything else that sets me apart from my mom. Including my visions. Not that I'll ever find out. My mom won't tell me anything about him other than we're better off on our own. I'm not sure that's true, but saying that just hurts her, so I leave it alone. Usually.

I get back to sweeping. I don't need to see any more of this family bonding.

"As much as I love the news, that's not why you stopped by. What are you really here for?" Sheriff Rafferty asks. He was able to see through Audra's act too, not that she made it hard.

"It's about Cassie."

That gets my attention. I'm curious now. A special trip to her dad's office just to talk about her friend? I turn back to them.

Audra is giving her father one of her humongous smiles. She's trying to butter him up again.

He sits back in his chair and shakes his head. "Audra, not again."

She goes over and sits on the edge of his desk. "Dad, it's different this time."

This time? What are they talking about? Their voices are soft, and I inch nearer.

"What now?" he asks.

"I think she's in danger. Someone's out to get her."

He sits up straight, and I'm on alert, too. "Did someone threaten her?" he asks.

"Sort of. Well, technically, no."

Sheriff Rafferty's posture loosens. "So it's another one of her stories."

"No," she says.

"So there's proof?" he asks.

Audra's face scrunches up. "It's a feeling."

"A feeling like that time she said the Arazadis' house was going to burn down on Super Bowl Sunday? Or that Fernando Perez was going to have a horrible car accident? Or that your principal was going to choke on his steak?"

Audra moves off the desk and onto the chair in front of it.

I sweep my way even closer to them. Probably too close. I know I should be more subtle, but I can't help it. I don't want to miss a word.

"Did you ever think," Audra says, "that all those things didn't happen because you showed up? Your warning about the fire probably made the Arazadis decide not to light a candle, or maybe made them check whether the kids were playing with matches."

The sheriff twirls his wedding band. He does that a lot. Maybe it's guilt. "All it did," he says, "was make the Arazadis and my officers miss the final touchdown of the game—and have me answering a lot of questions about how I'm using my resources."

"Dad," Audra says, "you know her hunches are good. She's helped."

"Not as often as she's wasted our time. If she has real reason to believe she's in danger, we want to hear it, but it has to be more than a hunch. Are there threats, someone following her, harassing her online?"

Audra shakes her head. "Forget it. I'll help her myself."

"Audra," he says.

"It's fine." She stands up to go. "You may not believe Cassie, but I do."

And, while no one asked me, so do I.

12

Hayden

The ten dollars of gas I put in over two weeks ago is not curbing Greta's appetite, so Friday after school I suck it up and stop at Grayson's before heading to the sheriff's office. My aversion to wasting fuel driving to a different gas station outweighs my aversion to running into Brody again.

I open the door to the market and whoa!

Brody is here, all right . . . in what appears to be meltdown mode.

Candy bars, boxes of cereal, diapers, and pain relievers are strewn over the floor. The place is a disaster. And Brody himself is standing back by the walk-in cooler pulling out a couple of six-packs, not caring that several cans fell to the ground. Not caring about anything.

"Brody, cut it out," the guy who I sometimes see working the counter says. "The deputy is on his way. You really want to be caught with that? This isn't bad enough?"

"This is nothing," he says, then walks to the register and takes a seat on the counter.

Now that was a good saunter, I think before snapping back to what's really important. Brody just trashed the market at the gas station. I'm a little at a loss for words.

I mean, I know the rich, I-can-do-and-have-whatever-I-want one-percenters in this town think they can get away with anything, and yeah, Brody loves toying with people—especially me. But publicly destroying a place just for kicks? It isn't the impression I get from him.

Obnoxious? Entitled? Jerk?

Yes.

Cheater? Future embezzler? Obnoxious prank puller?

Very possibly.

But juvenile delinquent? Vandal? Common criminal?

Not even close.

He sees me standing there, and there's a flicker of resignation in his eyes, but then it's back to that playful glint.

"Grim! Here to see my downfall? Have a drink. Let's toast to me." He tosses a can in my direction.

I catch it but look for a place to get rid of it. Quickly. Deputy Flemming, the officer who helped the sheriff chase me around the school after the Brooke incident, just pulled up, and I don't need him finding me with a beer. Our relationship is already a little rocky. He didn't exactly appreciate the added exercise I gave him that day, and he's definitely on team she-shouldn't-be-working-in-the-sheriff's-office.

I manage to set the can on a shelf right before he walks in.

"Grayson Brody the third," Flemming says, shaking his head while taking in the situation.

Grayson? The third?

"At your service." Brody jumps off the counter and does an elaborate bow, using his arms for extra flourish.

"All right, gas station is closed while we sort this out," Flemming says. "Frank, make sure no one else tries to come in." Then Flemming looks at me. "Aren't you supposed to be at work?" he asks, acknowledging me to my face for the first time since our run-in.

"I wanted to get some gas."

"It will have to wait," he says. "Go."

"You don't need a witness statement or something?" I ask.

"Are you asking me if I know how to do my job?"

Yeah, Flemming's patience with me is microscopic. "No."

"Good. Then go. I know where to find you if I need you."

I nod. Greta will have to wait. She's gone longer with less.

Brody calls out to me as I leave. "Don't disappoint me, Grim. I want a nice-looking cell. See what you can do."

The sheriff's department has only two. They're side by side and identical as far as I can tell. In the roughly two weeks I've been working there, I haven't seen anyone use them. I didn't even know people got put in jail in this town. I just assumed that if anyone did something bad enough, they'd be sent somewhere else.

But I guess I was wrong.

The station is getting a new tenant.

Brody.

Ray Brody.

Grayson Brody III.

A guy who, apparently, is full of surprises.

13

HaYDen

"Hayden, can you put on a fresh pot of coffee?" Sheriff Rafferty says when I get to the station. There's a frenzied tension in the air. "We're going to need it," he mumbles to himself, and rubs his temples with his hand.

"Sure," I say. "Anything else?"

"Pearson," Rafferty calls out, ignoring me—or maybe he didn't hear me. He seems in the zone. "Do you have the paperwork I asked for? And make sure the interrogation room is ready."

Okay, I know this town is not a crime hot spot or anything, and, yes, what Brody did sucked, but they must have seen worse than some bratty kid trashing a gas station. Everyone in the office is way too on edge over this. You'd think they'd be happy to take one of Lightsend High's golden boys down a notch.

I dump out the old coffeepot, even though what's in there is definitely drinkable, and put a fresh filter in the machine. Who needs Netflix when I'm getting paid to watch drama unfold right in front of me? I'm not saying I'm giddy to have a front-row seat to what's going on—giddy is not something I do—but I'm pretty close. Too bad we don't have snacks.

It's not long before the door opens and Brody, Flemming, and two other men walk in.

Showtime.

"Phillip, none of this is necessary," the taller man says, walking right over to the sheriff. He's obviously Brody's dad. It's not just the eyes. It's the air of assholey-ness that exudes from him. "I'm not pressing charges."

"I understand that," Sheriff Rafferty answers, "but we still need—"

Brody Senior cuts him off. "Are you forgetting who—"

"Nice, Dad," Brody calls out. Interrupting apparently runs in the family. "Nothing like a little threat among friends. Maybe toss some money at the problem? That's how we do it, right?"

"Ray," his dad warns.

It's weird to hear Brody called that. Even the teachers don't use his first name.

"Father," he answers, matching the tone.

The man next to Brody, who, from the suit, I'm guessing is either his lawyer or his dad's business buddy, puts his hand on Brody's shoulder. If it's an attempt to get Brody to back off, it's not going to work. He has that smug, crooked little smile plastered on his face. I know that look. It's the one that means Brody's up to something.

"Watch it," his father says, nostrils flaring, "or I'll tell them to keep you here."

I *knew* this was going to be good. I should be recording it. I can picture the TMZ headline. *Grayson Empire CEO and Son Lash Out in Sheriff's Office. We Have the Video.* They'll probably pay big for an exclusive. I'll lose my job and probably get in trouble for filming here, but depending on what they're willing to shell out, it could be worth it. I reach for my phone but think better of it. If I can't sell the video, then I'm out of a job for nothing.

Brody slaps his hand against his chest in mock horror. "And sully the family name? Oh wait. You already did that, didn't you? Maybe they have the wrong one of us in custody."

"That's enough," Brody Senior says. His voice is sharp, but his volume is level.

"Is it?" Brody asks. "Ever think maybe I want to stay here? That getting away from you would be a vacation?"

"If that's how you want it," his dad says, "that can be arranged." Brody Senior's voice is eerily calm, but those nostrils are gargantuan now.

The lawyer guy opens his mouth to speak, but Brody Senior puts up his hand and directs his attention back to the sheriff. "It looks like my son might benefit from a night in here. Teach him some manners and a little respect."

Brody snorts.

What am I watching? I can't help myself, I give Brody a what-are-you-doing-don't-be-ridiculous-apologize-to-your-dad look.

And what does he do in response?

Heed my advice?

Nope.

He winks.

Winks. Talk about messed up.

"Okay, why don't we take this in there?" the sheriff says,

pointing to one of the back rooms. If he thinks this is as absurd as I do, he's doing a much better job of hiding it.

I drift toward interrogation room A.

"I don't think so," Flemming says, holding out his arm so I can't get past. "You're not invited."

"But the prince said everyone's invited to the ball. All the single ladies in all the land." My Disney princess impersonation is pretty spot-on.

Flemming is not amused.

"Relax," I tell him, using my real voice once again. "I'm just doing my job."

He doesn't move.

"Emptying the garbage cans," I explain, and point to one at the end of the hall. One that is conveniently located right near the interrogation room. I emptied it earlier, but he doesn't know that.

"It can wait."

"Fine," I say. "But if I get in trouble, it's on you."

"A risk I'm willing to take," he says, not even giving a hint of a smile.

I knew my chances of listening at the interrogation room door were slim, but of course it had to be Deputy Flemming who ruined it for me. Things were just getting good.

"Aren't you supposed to be making coffee?" he asks.

The coffee. Crap. I didn't hit the button to start it. I mock salute him and head back to the machine.

After it percolates, I put the pot, some cups, and a bunch of creamers on a tray to take back to the interrogation room. Maybe I'll get to see the rest of the fireworks after all.

I pocket a few of the creamers. Not for me. For my mom. She likes her coffee light but won't waste our milk.

I turn with the tray and Flemming is standing there. Of course. Most people wouldn't care about some missing creamers, but Flemming isn't everybody. He is letter of the law, and he caught me stealing office supplies. I can't believe I'm going to lose my job over cheap dairy substitutes.

He's staring me down. I don't have a clever explanation. I just put the tray back on the table, take the five creamers from my pocket, and hold them out. It's not the biggest offense, but little things add up, and I *am* working in a sheriff's office. I wait, ready for him to ream me out.

Only he doesn't. Flemming doesn't even acknowledge the mini containers in my hand. "*I'll* take the coffee back there," he says. "Looks like we're having an unexpected overnight guest. Why don't you head out now and come back in early tomorrow instead? It will add up to extra hours. We can use someone here to babysit. Eight a.m. work?"

I close my fingers around the creamers and nod.

"Good, and pick up some McDonald's in the morning for our 'guest.' We're going to have to give him something."

I debate whether I should tell him I can't. I don't really have money lying around to buy breakfast for possibly the richest guy in all of Lightsend. I don't even have money to buy breakfast for my mom. But seeing as I'm still clutching the creamers, and Flemming will use any excuse to get rid of me, I'm thinking maybe I should just suck this one up.

Before I can figure out what to do, Flemming's handing over a twenty-dollar bill.

"Get something for yourself, too," he says.

"That's okay," I say. "I'll bring you the change."

"Don't worry about it." His face softens ever so slightly.

The look is a giveaway. He must have seen my file. That's why he's being so nice. He knows where I live. *How* I live. I don't want his pity *or* his charity.

"I'll make sure you get it all," I say.

"Nothing's ever easy with you, is it, Jefferies? Just get yourself breakfast. And don't worry, I still think having you here is a mistake." The annoyed tinge to his voice is back. "This is not a gift from me. I'm taking it out of the discretionary fund. The same one I used to buy those donuts you demolished the other day. No different. So get the damn breakfast, will ya?"

He takes the coffee tray and walks off, shaking his head.

"Thank you," I whisper once he's out of earshot.

Maybe Flemming isn't so bad after all.

14

cassie

"I'm staying," Audra says, stirring a brush around the jar of forest-green paint.

"I'm fine," I tell her, and study the background theater flat lying in front of me. I don't want her to see my face. She knows my expressions too well.

"After everything you've seen, I'm not going to leave you alone."

That horror vision in the restroom was the first of many. Each a different scenario, each ending with my life in danger. I squirm just thinking about it. When I have a vision starring myself, I'm not only seeing what happens, I feel it—and these last ones have really put me through the wringer. "I'll be okay," I tell her. I try to keep my voice steady, my nerves calm. I don't really want Audra to leave, but I also don't want to be the reason she flakes on her sister. She needs to be there. "I'm not alone. Ms. Warmack is sitting right over there." I nod toward the table below the stage, where my teacher is studying a slew of spread-out papers.

"I'm not going," Audra says, stabbing the paintbrush into the jar for added effect.

"You're going." I look up at her and force a smile. "I'm not having Delaney Lamont mad at me. If you miss Kendall's dance recital because of me, I won't have to worry about some mystery person with a knife. Your mother will kill me. And you."

"Don't make jokes," she says. "This is serious."

"I know." It's all I've been able to think about. I've barely slept in two weeks.

"Then come with me." She looks at the time on her phone. 5:21. She has to leave soon-ish if she wants to make it on time.

"I have to finish painting this. You know I promised Ms. Warmack I'd have it done tonight. It's Friday, and tech week starts Monday. We're already cutting it way too close by doing it tonight. Not that I had much choice." I finished the backdrops weeks ago, but when they were rolling out the car from the "Greased Lightnin'" number during rehearsal the other day, Emil Pritchard accidentally steered it directly into one of them. Tore it right in two.

"Your safety is more important than this. Paint during rehearsal. tomorrow or Sunday. I can come with you. Or Brody can. One of us will make sure you're covered. We were already planning on taking you."

They've both been so good. Except for class or when I'm home with my father, one of them has been by my side since these visions of me in jeopardy started. The awkwardness with Brody disappeared, too. I wasn't sure he meant it when he said he wanted us to still be friends, but this proved it. He's shown up when I needed him.

I wipe my hands on my smock. "There won't be room for me to work. Not on something this big. I'll get in the way of the cast."

"They can work around you," she says.

"Audra, they can't. Besides, I have other things for the show to do then. I have to finish painting now. I promised."

I can see her fighting back an eye roll. "Maybe it's not too late to get Brody here."

"He's at the gas station. He has to work today," I say.

I hate being in constant fear. I hate living this way. I need a little bit of normal. "I've got this," I tell her. "I'll be careful. I'll stick by Ms. Warmack. I don't need a babysitter."

She crosses her arms. "But you do need a bodyguard."

I double-check that Ms. Warmack isn't paying attention to us. She's not, but I whisper nonetheless. "I'm probably in the clear now. I've seen myself in danger five times these past two weeks, and none of them happened."

"Because you changed the circumstances," she says. "You didn't leave the journal in your locker, so you didn't come back here. You didn't get up at the butt crack of dawn and go out for air. You didn't run over those nails and get stuck on the side of the road. Whoever is out to get you could still be there."

I feel tears stinging my eyes. I can't keep doing this. "Or I was letting the stress get to my head. Am I supposed to stay locked up forever just in case?"

"Yes," she says.

"I haven't had a vision since Wednesday. Nothing telling me to watch out. It's a good sign. Maybe we changed things."

"And what if we didn't?"

I don't want to let myself think that way. "I can't live like that, Audra. I feel like a prisoner in my own life."

"You're not. You're just coming to a cute eight-year-old's dance recital." She looks at her phone again. "Please."

I don't know what to do. Do I go? *No*, I tell myself. I'm going to be fine. I'm not alone. This is not a big deal. "I'm going to stay. Go without me," I tell her. "I'm safe. Ms. Warmack is here. I parked right near her car. I'll make sure to walk out with her. Okay?"

"I don't feel good about this."

"Well, I do. And I won't let Ms. Warmack out of my sight. If she goes to the bathroom, I'll go with her. She goes to the water fountain, I'll go get a drink, too. Now go. Please. I'm not giving you a choice. I'm making you go to that recital. I'll have 911 ready to go on my phone. Any danger, I hit call. Will that make you feel better?"

"A little. You promise you'll be careful?"

"I promise."

"And you'll text me when you leave and as soon as you get home."

"Yes."

Audra eyes me, and I put on my bravest face. It must be convincing, because she nods at me. "Okay, but only if you really, truly think you're okay."

"I do."

She gives me a hug. "Fine, but don't do anything even the tiniest bit risky."

"I won't. I swear."

Audra leaves, and I wonder if I just did by letting her go. I glance back at Ms. Warmack. She's there. I'm being ridiculous. I focus on my breath and pick up the paintbrush. *Concentrate on the strokes. On the colors.* I somehow manage to get sucked in, and over the next two hours get the whole backdrop finished.

"Looks good," Ms. Warmack says. "Ready to call it a night?"

I nod.

We put the paint away and walk outside together. I feel a huge sense of relief being out of that building. I text Audra.

Cassie

On my way home now.

"Thank you for all your help," Ms. Warmack tells me. "You're a life sav—" Her phone rings, and she puts up her finger in a *one minute* gesture and answers it.

"Yes, it is. What?" she asks. "No. Hold on a second." She pulls the phone away from her mouth. "Cassie, I'm sorry. I have to take this. I'll see you on Monday. Okay?"

She goes and takes a seat on one of the benches near where we exited.

Now what? Do I wait? She told me to go. But she doesn't know what's going on and that I'd feel safer with an escort to my car.

I hover.

"You okay?" she mouths to me.

I nod.

I feel like a child. What am I going to say, that I'm worried about some rando jumping out of the bushes? She's still on the phone; I'm not going to explain it to her now. I'm being a fool. I didn't have any visions today, and I'm parked right outside the teachers' lot in the back. Two quick rights, and I'm there. Ms. Warmack is in screaming distance if anything happens. I can do this. It'll be like she's right beside me.

I suck it up and start walking. I make the first right. So far, so good. I count my steps as I go. Eighty-six.

One more right, then fifty feet, and I'm there.

Every single tree rustle makes me jump. I'm second-guessing my decision. I should have waited for Ms. Warmack. I should've listened to Audra. She's going to murder me. If someone doesn't beat her to it. My breathing picks up. It's not too late to run back to my teacher, but at this point that's farther away than my car.

Relax.

There's nothing to be afraid of.

The knife, the other attempts, they were just visions, and visions don't always come true. They can be changed.

Only I keep getting them. That never happens. Well, other than the Brody and Hayden ones. What if it means whoever's out to get me won't give up until they succeed? What if they can't be stopped? What if it's destined to happen no matter what I do?

A chill runs through me, despite the weather being uncharacteristically warm for this time of year. I should have worn a coat. Not that it would help. This feeling is now deep in my bones. I sling my backpack higher up on my shoulder and wrap my arms around myself, my phone gripped in my left hand.

Keep moving. Focus on your steps.

I never realized how dark it was over here. The streetlights cast a glow, but they don't illuminate the area, not very well, anyway.

I make the last turn. The area looks empty, but what if I'm missing something? Missing *someone*? "Hello. Hello," I call out.

This street is quiet. Too quiet.

"Hello," I say again, positioning my phone so my finger hovers over the call button. 911 punched in just in case.

No response.

A shadow moves in front of me.

I suck in a breath and stop in my tracks. This is it.

I'm about to dial for help, when the shadow on the sidewalk moves again. I look up and can't help but let out a laugh. It's a tree. A branch swaying in the breeze, catching the light.

I'm being absurd. No one's around. School let out hours ago. The street is quiet. The teachers' lot is empty except for a few parked cars. Same for the small students' lot right next to it, where my car is located. I sprint the rest of the way there anyway, my backpack smacking me with each step, and exhale as I put my hand on my door. I'm safe.

Still, I look underneath before getting in.

Nothing.

Paranoia is my new best friend.

I take off my backpack and lock myself inside the refuge of my car, tossing my things on the passenger seat.

"Get a grip," I mutter to myself.

I clutch the steering wheel. I need to relax. This is getting out of hand. I need to tame my imagination.

Inhale.

One, two, three, four, five.

Hold.

Release.

Dr. Mukherjee insists that these breathing exercises will help me, but he's never dealt with a case like mine. He doesn't understand what I can do. What I can see . . .

The breath work isn't calming me down, but it doesn't matter. I need to get home. I need to text Audra. I need to—

What the . . . ?

A shadow crosses my rearview mirror. It's not a tree this time. I didn't park under one.

I freeze.

This isn't happening. It's just another vision.

Please let it be another vision.

There's no one in your car. There's no one in your car.

My hands are shaking. I reach toward the seat next to me for my phone. Where is it? Where did I put it? There's a sound behind me. I turn to look. Everything goes dark. Something is over my eyes, my mouth. I try to scream. Nothing comes out.

I feel breathing through the fabric, a heat against my ear. And someone whispers, "You should have seen this coming . . ." before everything goes silent.

15

HAYDEN

"Great," Pearson, one of the nicer deputies, says when I walk in, McDonald's bag in hand. He's sitting at the front desk, manning the phones and doing some paperwork. "Just sit back there, and let me know if Junior needs to go to the bathroom or acts up or anything. If you need me—yell."

Then he leans his head toward the room where Brody is and calls out, "Touch her, try anything, and you'll find out what doing real time is like."

I appreciate the effort, but I can handle Brody. Especially a Brody behind bars.

I head back to see "Junior." The holding cells aren't in a special area, they're just smack in the back of the pit. It's mostly filing cabinets, but there are four desks—including one the sheriff uses all the time. He has an actual office but sits out here more often than not. It's either a morale all-for-one type of thing, or because it's closer to the files. I haven't quite figured out his MO yet.

Brody is sitting on a little cot in the first cell. I've seen one of the deputies take a nap in there, but it seems different with the bar door shut and locked. Especially with one of my classmates inside. Brody lifts his head as I get closer. He looks like he hasn't slept at all. His hair is mussed up, and he has the faintest trace of stubble forming. His eyes look almost green today, and they're piercing. I catch myself staring and look to the bag in my hand instead.

"They made the Grim Reaper my gatekeeper?" he asks. "That can't bode well."

"Mary Poppins was busy," I tell him, and push the bag through the bars.

He reaches over and takes it, then wrinkles his nose as he unwraps the Egg McMuffin. "I'm a vegetarian."

This surprises me, but I don't let it show. I put out my hand, and he returns the sandwich. I pull off the ham and pop it into my mouth.

And—Oh. My. God. It's heaven. It's even warm. I haven't had one of these since my mom and I made an emergency pit stop on one of our moves.

"Problem solved," I say, once I've swallowed, and hand the rest of the sandwich back to him.

"I'm not eating that," he says.

I shrug and pull it back through the bars, then take a big bite out of it.

"Or these." He holds out the hash browns I got him, like I smeared them in blood.

"Good," I tell him, and take them. "More for me." I didn't order anything for myself. I can make the rest of the twenty Flemming gave me go a lot farther at the grocery store than at McDonald's.

"Are you going to get me something else?" he asks.

If he's expecting me to go do a food run for him, he's got the wrong girl. "Does this look like Brennan's Bistro?" I ask him. "You get what you get. There's an orange juice in there. I promise you, golden boy, missing one meal won't kill you."

He gives me an exaggerated eye roll.

"Not even a coffee?" he asks.

I don't particularly want to play waitress to him, but I relent. "Fine." I walk over to the coffeepot and pour him a cup.

"That's been sitting there all night."

"Do you want it or not?"

"Just give it to me."

I ignore his tone and hand over the mug, and then go and pour myself a cup. It's definitely not the freshest, but while the department has enough ground coffee to last a year and can afford to buy more, I hate wasting it. There's something about dumping out a full pot that gnaws at me.

"Cream, sugar?" I ask him.

He nods, and I bring them over. His hand touches mine as he takes them. "Our first date," he says, sinking back onto his cot.

"You sure know how to treat a girl. No wonder they're all lining up for a chance at you."

"Interesting," he says.

I know I shouldn't bite, but I can't help it. "What?" I ask.

"Just you noticing all the people who want to be with me. Seems like someone may be a little bit smitten. Secret crush, maybe?"

I can't see his expression, the mug is covering most of his face, but I guarantee there's a huge smirk there.

"Uck." I shudder and hold my stomach. "Just because you're not having breakfast, don't make me lose mine."

"Protesting a little too much?"

"That's not the quote," I say.

He raises an eyebrow.

"Shakespeare."

"What about him?" he asks.

I groan and head over to the desks. I'm not here to educate Brody on famous lines from dead playwrights. I'm not quite sure why I'm here at all, frankly. Getting paid to hang around—and what? Make sure Brody doesn't try to break out of jail? Accidentally slip and hit his head on the bars? I'm not complaining. It definitely beats the busywork the deputies usually find for me, like cleaning the supply closet, but still it seems a little extra. I'll take it, though. Easy money and plenty of time to do my trig homework.

I put my mug down on the desk facing the sheriff's. They're butted up to each other, and I find myself taking inventory of his things. He keeps the space neat. A couple of files in his in-box, otherwise no loose papers around. There's a lamp, an office blotter, and a notebook that take up a good chunk of the desk space. My fingers glide over the picture frame of his family, and some little Star Wars figurines in front of it, but they rest on a medal with a ribbon attached to it.

Then it happens.

I'm still in the office at the desk, but it's no longer today, and it's no longer my eyes I'm seeing through. I'm not sure who they belong to, but they're holding the medal and looking at Sheriff Rafferty.

"This should be framed, hanging on the wall," a female-sounding voice says. "It's an honor."

"Not when you didn't earn it."

"You earned it."

He's spinning his ring around his finger, the creases in his forehead showing more than usual. "I don't want it. A medal of valor? Not after what I did. It's not right."

"Grim. Earth to Grim. Do you even hear me?"

Brody's voice brings me back to the present.

"What?" I snap. I make a mental note to ask the sheriff about the medal and see what I can find out. Maybe my Robin Hood days aren't over after all, just reaching bigger and better heights. And if need be, a way to keep the sheriff away from my mother.

"Where'd you go?" Brody asks. "Communing with your demon overlords?"

"Yeah," I deadpan, relieved that my back was facing him, so he couldn't have seen my vision face. "We conferred. They don't want your soul. They're way over quota on entitled rich boys."

He clucks his tongue, and it sets me off.

"What?" I ask. "You think basically begging to be in jail, knowing it won't stick or hurt your chances at college or a career or whatever it is you want, is normal?"

"You don't get it." He stands up.

"No, I don't." I walk back to the cell. "I don't get how you can act so righteous. Do you know what people would give to have a fraction of what you have? And yet you trash a store for fun. Throw a little temper tantrum to get daddy's attention. No consequences. You're not the one who has to pick up little pieces of trash from the floor, or clean ketchup off the walls, or lose a shift because the store is closed while new inventory comes in. Everyone else gets to clean up your mess. Literally and figuratively."

"I had a reason."

"Yeah, I'm sure."

His eyes are wide. "I *did*."

This I want to hear. "Okay, lay it on me."

Brody runs his fingers through his hair and sits back down. "Never mind. You wouldn't get it."

"Right," I say, and head back to the desk and my coffee. "Like I thought . . ."

"Things aren't always as they seem," he says, like that explains anything.

"And sometimes," I tell him, "a cigar is just a cigar."

"Huh?" he asks.

"Never mind," I parrot back. "You wouldn't get it."

I'm done wasting my time talking to Brody. He's not worth the effort. I hunker down and start my trig homework.

Forty minutes of excruciating problems later—ones that may very well be trick questions—the quiet of the office is shattered.

"Where is my dad?"

It's Audra Rafferty. And she's loud enough that she caught both my and Brody's attention.

If the deputy answers, I can't hear him.

Audra, on the other hand, is getting an A-plus in projection. "I need my dad," she says. It's a half plea, half demand.

She doesn't need to ask again. The sheriff appears out of nowhere. He must have raced from his office when he heard Audra's voice. I didn't even know he was in the office today. I guess when you have one of the town's elites behind bars, you stick around to make sure they're treated okay.

"What's going on?" he asks. "Are you alright?"

Audra shakes her head. "No. It's Cassie. She's missing."

Missing?

First Brody, now this? What is with all the drama in this town? It's like living in a private soap opera.

"Wait, what did she say?" Brody asks me. He doesn't wait for an answer.

"Audra," he calls out from his cell. "Audra!"

Looks like the show is coming straight to me. As soon as Audra hears his voice, she storms our way, followed by the sheriff. They stop at the doorway on the left, blocking my closest exit. Not that I'm looking to go anywhere. I'll admit it. I'm hooked. I want to hear what happens next.

"Cassie's gone. She never came home," Audra says. "I tried her all night." Tears are streaming down her face. She turns her attention back to her father. "I shouldn't have listened to Mom. I knew I should have gone over to her house and checked on her. What if it's too late?"

The sheriff puts his arm around her, and she sinks into him. She's sobbing while he strokes her back. I expect her to stop, but she doesn't. The entertainment factor in all this is gone. This isn't some juicy gossip, it's somber and raw, and it's making me feel antsy. Like I'm in a vision I shouldn't be seeing. One that's too personal and awkward. One that doesn't have any blackmail material and is just uncomfortable to watch. But unlike a vision, I can get out of this anytime I want. I grab my bag and scoot back on my chair.

84

"It's going to be okay," the sheriff tells her. "Calm down. I'm sure she's fine."

This snaps her back to attention. She straightens up. "You don't know that. You don't know what she's seen."

"Audra," he says.

"Dad!"

I head for the exit on the other side of the room.

"Get me out of here!" Brody yells right as I pass him. I jump at the sound of his voice. It's gravelly, raw, and scared. He's on his feet, gripping the bars. "Get my dad. I want out. I'll do whatever he says."

He's looking right at me, and I freeze. Do I keep going? Do I stay?

Audra runs over to him. "We were supposed to keep her safe."

"Okay, okay," Sheriff Rafferty says. He's holding out his hands as if that will calm anyone down. "Let's everyone take a breath. Audra, when was the last time you heard from Cassie?"

"Before the dance recital."

He shakes his head. "It hasn't even been twenty-four hours."

"It only takes a minute to disappear and not much longer for a missing person's case to go cold."

"Hold on there," he says. "We don't know if she's missing. You know she has a history of taking off." He says the last part quietly.

Taking off? Little Miss Perfect? Not someone I'd expect to have a track record of running away. In all the dirt I found on people, nothing ever came up on her.

Audra's pacing now. "I don't care. This is different. I know it. She would have told me if she was leaving."

"Hey," Brody says. "Will somebody get me out of here already?" It's more of a demand than a question.

I catch his eyes again.

"What?" he asks. "If he's not going to search for her, I am."

"Everyone, relax," Sheriff Rafferty says. "I'm sure Cassie is fine, but just to calm your nerves, I'm going to see what I can find out."

"Thank you," Audra says, wiping the tears from her face.

He gives her a squeeze on the shoulder and then heads out.

Audra takes a seat at one of the desks and Brody watches her, lips in a tight line. She looks back at him. They have some serious eye contact going on. Way more than what he and I had—this is like they're having a whole silent conversation.

Now seems like a good time to make that escape I was planning. I'm sure Pearson can find another closet for me to clean out or a hallway to sweep or some other mundane task that will take me away from these two.

"Not so fast," Audra says as I start my getaway.

I turn around, and that serious eye contact she was giving Brody before is now all on me.

Brody presses his body up against the bars. "No, Audra."

"You know what Cassie saw," she tells him. Audra's tears are gone; all that's left are the damp tracks on her cheeks, and in their place is a look of determination. "We have to."

He grips the bars. "And you know what I think about that."

"If it could save her, I don't care," Audra says.

"Is someone going to tell me what's going on here?" I ask, before deciding whether to bolt.

"I need your help," she says, her red, puffy eyes back on me. "*We* need your help."

Brody is shaking his head, his hands grasping the bars so hard, they're white.

I must be hearing things. There is no way Audra Rafferty is asking for my help.

"Me?" I ask. "Yeah, right."

"I'm serious," she says.

And I'm seriously regretting not getting out of here when I had the chance. I don't know what she's playing at, but I don't want any part of it.

"It's about Cassie," Audra says. "We need your help to find her."

The sound I make is somewhere between a snort and guffaw. "Sure, because who needs the sheriff to find your friend when you can have the sheriff's cleaning girl?"

"I know how it sounds," she says.

"I don't think you do." The look she's giving me says she means business. "Your dad says he's looking into it."

"It's not enough."

"Just let her go," Brody says.

"I can't."

Okay, she's getting way too intense on me. I don't know what this is all about, but I'm pretty confident the sheriff won't want me messing around in his business, and I'm not about to risk a decent-paying job—the best one I've ever had—to go searching for a girl who probably doesn't want to be found.

"Look," I tell her, "you have the wrong person. I didn't even know the sheriff was your father, or that *he*"—I throw my arm toward Brody—"was heir to the Grayson gas empire. Even knowing your last names, I still didn't put it together. I don't think I'm what you need right now."

"But I am," Brody says. "I need to get out of here."

Audra ignores him and keeps her focus on me. "We need *you*."

She is making zero sense. Just because I found out some dirt on a few people at school doesn't mean I know how to find a missing person. Her father is the actual sheriff, and between him and me—I'd put my money on him.

"You don't even like me," I remind her.

"So what? I don't need to like you to work with you." Well, at least she's honest. "This is about Cassie."

Audra pokes her head out to the main office, and then comes over to me and pulls me toward the back of the room, closer to Brody and the cells.

"Okay," Audra says, her voice low, and still gripping my wrist. "This is going to sound strange, but it's true. You have to trust me."

It's definitely strange, I'll give her that. Strange enough that I'm sticking around waiting for her to say her piece. There's a pause before she speaks.

"Cassie can see things," she says.

"Audra, stop," Brody warns.

"*See* things?" My whole body stiffens. I remember Audra telling her dad about Cassie's hunches. But hunches and seeing things are not the same. Not even close. Does Cassie have episodes too? Is she like me? "What do you mean, 'see things'?"

"Audra," Brody says again.

"She has to hear this," she tells him.

Audra drops her hand from my wrist and circles her own. Reminds me of her dad and his ring. "Cassie gets visions. It's not something she talks about. Not to anyone but Brody and me. But recently, she had some that you were in." Her eyes dart to Brody. "Both of you."

"Those damn visions," Brody mutters.

I ignore him and keep my focus on Audra. This is not something I ever expected to hear.

"This one was different," she says.

Brody is watching her now. Silent. Expressionless.

"She saw the two of you in school, sneaking into a classroom, looking in a desk for phones. When you got them, you said it could be the key to finding her."

Brody's eyebrows rise. I don't think he's heard this before.

"So you're saying she knew she was going to go missing and what?" I ask. "We were going to track her down?" This is a lot to process. Someone else with visions. Visions with me in them. I'm not sure what it means.

"No. Not exactly." Audra throws her head back and looks to the ceiling, like she's trying to find the right words. There's a hitch in her breath, and I'm pretty sure she's willing herself not to cry again, to stay strong. "She has seen herself in danger. A lot. Threats to her life. But this . . . this vision of you two happened before that. She didn't even say that she was the one you were looking for. She didn't know. I just . . ." She stops and collects her thoughts. "I got to thinking last night. It adds up. She's gone. You guys were looking for someone. All those attack visions she was getting. Doesn't it make sense that it was Cassie that you were trying to find?"

"You need to back this up," I tell her, trying to take in everything she just said.

Cassie has visions.

It still doesn't seem possible. Can there really be someone else like me? Here? "What threats? How many? What does she see in these visions? Does she get them a lot? How do they work?" The questions pour out of me.

"You shouldn't be telling her this stuff," Brody says, before Audra can answer.

"Yes, I should." Her voice is strong. "I don't care how you feel about her. And you might not think so, but this vision is the key to finding Cassie. I know it. If that means the two of you need to work together, then you have to work together. End of story. You said you'd do anything for Cassie. Prove it. Or was that all talk?"

He doesn't answer. Not immediately, anyway.

Just when I think Audra is going to ream him out, he starts speaking. "She gets the visions randomly." His voice, his expression, seem worlds away. "She was trying to control them. Sometimes she could, but it was getting bad these past months."

I want to know more. "Does she have to touch something for the visions to happen?"

He shakes his head. "They just happen."

That's not exactly like me, but still . . . this can't be a coincidence. Not two of us in the same town. "And she sees what? The future?"

"Yeah," Audra says, "and she's been seeing herself in danger." She goes on to explain some of the recent visions that Cassie has had.

I must have caught a glimpse of one of them when I picked up her journal in the bathroom at school.

"I don't know what you want me to do about it," I tell her. Even though they told me Cassie's secret, I don't tell them mine.

They don't need to know. It's not like I can magically pinpoint Cassie's location. My episodes don't come on demand. "Break into the school?"

"Yes, no, I don't know," Audra says, and squeezes her wrist. "I haven't figured that part out yet. I just know you're key to this. That you help, you and Brody, and it could be what gets her home. I need you to do this, and if I have to literally force the two of you into some classroom, or tie you together to go looking for Cassie, then fine, I will. I'll try anything. I have to get her back. This is my fault. I left her at that school. If I had stayed or made her go home, maybe I could have stopped this."

"This isn't on you." It's the sheriff, her dad. He's back.

"Did you find her?" Audra asks, forgetting about me.

"Found her car."

"That was fast," I say, more to myself than anyone else, but the sheriff hears and looks at me.

"It doesn't take long to find a car parked at the back of the bus station lot."

"No," Audra says. "She didn't take off."

"Her car is at the station. It's Cassie doing what Cassie always does," he says.

"Not this time," Audra protests. "You need to have people out looking for her."

The sheriff puts his hand on her arm. "We had search parties the first two times she did this. Now we have to wait. It hasn't even been twenty-four hours."

Audra shakes his hand off her. "That will be too late. You have to do something now."

"Honey—" he starts.

"No," she cuts him off. "Don't placate me. Do something." She runs to the door. "Pearson. We need an APB. Get Flemming. Get everyone. We need to find Cassie."

"AUDRA!" her father bellows. "Enough. It's time to go home."

She crosses her arms in front of her. "You mean time to look for Cassie."

"Don't get me started, Audra," he says, his voice low but firm. He knows I'm watching. "Go home now. I do not want you wrapped up in this. You're supposed to be watching your sister today. You know your mom has plans. Don't keep her waiting."

"But Dad—"

"Go," he says, "before you're grounded."

"Fine," she tells him, but not before turning to Brody and me. "You know what you have to do."

"Audra!" the sheriff repeats.

"Help find her," she mouths to me before she turns to leave.

I don't know what I'm supposed to do. I don't even know if Cassie wants to be found.

16

HayDen

The room is quiet. The sheriff left. Audra left. Brody is standing motionless in his cell. And I'm still taking in what just happened. It's a lot. Not only does someone else in this town have visions, but now Audra expects me to be part of some Scooby-Doo crew.

Sure. No big deal. "'Help find her,'" I mutter to myself.

"Will you?" Brody asks.

"Will I what?"

"Help find her."

Now he wants me to? "You're team Hayden all of a sudden?" I ask him.

"I'm team *Cassie*," he practically spits at me. "And if that means working with you, I'll do it."

Audra clearly got to him.

"Well, that doesn't mean I will," I say.

"You have to," he tells me.

I go and prop myself against one of the desks. What is wrong with these people? "I don't *have* to do anything. Did you not just hear the sheriff?"

Brody presses his head up against the bars and peers at me. "He's wrong. She wouldn't have just taken off."

"How are you so sure?"

"She would have told me."

"Right," I say, letting the sarcasm drip off my words, "because everyone tells their ex everything. That's totally normal."

Brody's brows furrow. "We're broken up, but we're still friends, and she trusts me. She knows I have her back. Always."

He seems so sure, but I'm not. It's Occam's razor. The simplest explanation is usually the correct one. "Isn't it possible she just ran off?"

Brody shakes his head. "No. She was scared of the visions she was having. Audra and I were constantly checking in on her to make sure she was safe. She wouldn't have just taken off and not said anything." He runs his hand through his hair and grips the back of his neck. "Cassie wouldn't have done that to us. She's not like that. She would have known we'd think the worst."

Even though I'm not a Brody fan, I can see how upset he is about this, so I tread lightly. "But she took off before."

"A few times, but she always gave us a heads-up."

"Where'd she go?" I ask.

He shrugs so slightly I almost miss it. "She wouldn't say. Not to me. Just that she thought she could get answers about her visions."

"Did she?

"I don't know."

I nod. I definitely want to know more about that, but Brody either doesn't have the answers or doesn't want to share them with me.

An awkward silence floods the room again. I wait for Brody to say something, but he's just watching me. I shift, not sure where to look. I wind up staring at the ceiling, but I can feel his eyes still on me.

"What?" I ask. "What do you want from me? Contrary to what Audra may think, I'm not Nancy Drew."

"Maybe not," he says, "but you've found a lot of information on a lot of people. Things they wanted to hide."

"It's not the same, and if it was, come on." I turn my focus back to him. "You and me working together? Vision or not, it's a bad idea, and I can't imagine the sheriff would be too thrilled with either of us poking into his cases."

"Then we have nothing to worry about. You heard him: This isn't a case. It hasn't been twenty-four hours."

"Brody . . ."

"Hayden, please." He didn't call me Grim. He used *please*. And for once, that little smirk of his is gone. Maybe he is serious about this.

"I can't risk this job," I tell him.

"You won't be risking it—we're not doing anything illegal."

"Just breaking into a classroom," I remind him.

"Again, that's nothing. No one's going to care."

Yeah, no one's going to care if *he* does it. I'm a different story. I could lose my job, and I like this one—as far as jobs go. On top of the pay, there's always donuts and coffee. He may not appreciate things like that, but I do.

"If—when—it comes to that, we won't get caught," he assures me. "And if we do, I'll take the blame. I'll say I forced you, that I made you do it."

When I don't respond, he keeps talking, refusing to let up.

"We can start with something easy. Something legal. We'll just go look at her car. What can that hurt?"

My gut reaction is to say no, but that's my gut reaction to anything involving Brody.

"What do you say?" he asks.

Before I can answer, Deputy Pearson, followed by the man from yesterday, comes in and unlocks the cell.

"You're a free man," Pearson tells Brody. "You can thank your lawyer here—and your dad. No charges. Now stay out of trouble. I don't want to see you back in this cell."

Brody nods.

Pearson turns his attention to me. "You can get out of here too. No need to stick around." I guess babysitting is over.

"Let's go," Brody's lawyer tells him.

"Actually," Brody says, and looks at me, that smirk of his back, "she's giving me a ride."

I open my mouth to object, but then I notice it.

Beneath the smirk is fear.

I cave. I guess it can't hurt to go look at Cassie's car.

17

HAYDEN

Brody follows me out from the station to my car. I hesitate before trying the door handle.

"Do we get in the front, or is climbing over the back the preferred entrance?" I knew he saw me at the gas station. He's back to his old self, dimple flashing at me as he waits for my response, and I'm already regretting my decision to help.

I glare at him over the hood, but the truth is I don't know the answer. It depends on Greta's mood.

Come on, you beautiful piece of rust, work for me, I silently beg my car. And by some miracle, she cooperates. My door opens with just one giant tug. I get in, reach over, and push the passenger side open for Brody before throwing my bag in the back.

I see his eyes trail over my mess of papers, books, and crumpled napkins. "If you don't like it," I tell him, "I'm sure your lawyer has a lovely, expensive ride you can take."

"I didn't say anything."

"You were thinking it."

"You're a mind reader now?"

If he only knew. I swipe the papers from his seat to the floor. "Just get in."

I can't believe I'm playing chauffeur to Brody. What was I thinking?

"Know where the bus station is?" he asks.

"Yeah, the opposite side of town." I glance at the gas meter.

He must have seen me because he says, "I'll chip in for the gas."

"Yeah, you will." I don't bother playing coy or pretending it's not necessary. He's rich, and his family owns a gazillion gas stations. He can take care of it. This wild-goose chase is his idea, not mine.

"Pull over at Grayson's," he tells me once we're on the road. I look over at him, and he winks. "I have a hookup."

"Yeah, with people who put you in jail?"

He waves his hand. "Yesterday's news. They love me."

"Guess somebody has to."

"Aww, come on, I'm growing on you. I can feel it." Brody puts his hand over his heart.

It's like this guy's favorite pastime is messing with me. "It's the gas fumes, they're getting to your head," I tell him as I pull up to one of the pumps at the station.

"Sure, that's what it is," he says, and gets out of the car, giving me another wink. I respond with an eye roll as he goes to fill up the gas. He pays inside and returns with a giant package of Twizzlers.

He makes himself comfortable on the passenger side, unzipping his jacket and readjusting the back of the seat. "Want?" he asks, holding a Twizzler out to me and twirling it like a wand, as I get us back on the road.

"Not one your hands have been all over."

"So picky," he says, and extends the bag. I take a piece. Chewing means less talking, but I don't really have to worry about small talk.

Brody is silent the rest of the ride, just staring out the window, the cockiness gone from his expression. I can't help but glance at him as I drive. He's lost in thought but snaps to when we pull into the bus station lot. "Over there, the red one at the end of the lot," he says, pointing to a car way off in the very last spot in the back row. The car is surrounded by woods behind it and to its right.

I pull up on the left, in the spot next to it, and Brody jumps out of Greta before I can put her in park. He walks around Cassie's car, examining it from all angles. I get out and watch him. He's inspecting every inch. Even crouching and looking underneath. "Doesn't look tampered with," he says.

No surprise there. The sheriff's office was the one to locate the car. I'm sure they checked for signs of a struggle or break-in.

"Good. Does that mean we can go now?"

He holds his hands up to his face like blinders and peers into the driver's-side window of the car. "No, not until I've checked everything."

Brody tries every door, but they're all locked. His mouth puckers and his nostrils flare, and then he heads into the wooded area.

"What are you doing?" I call after him.

He doesn't answer.

"Brody?" I yell again. I can't see him now. I move closer to where he disappeared. "Hello?"

I really don't want to follow him in there. That's how people die in horror films.

As I weigh my options, he returns, carrying a giant rock.

"What are you doing with that?"

"Getting into the car."

"Whoa," I say, grabbing it from his hand. "Do you like spending the night in jail? What happened to 'this will all be legal'?"

"I need to see inside. Give it back."

"You really think breaking the window and getting glass all over everything is the answer?" I sigh. "You're hopeless." I throw the rock back into the woods.

"Hey!"

"Just hold on." I can't believe I'm doing this. I go to my trunk and move some junk around. On the bottom is an old wire hanger that's already been untwisted into a long metal rod. Always come prepared, I say. You never know when you're going to need a helping hand. This isn't my first break-in, but I'm not exactly jumping at the chance to do it again. But it beats letting Brody cause a scene that could bring attention to us. No one is in our immediate vicinity at the moment, but the sound of a shattering window could change that. I go back to Cassie's car and slip the hanger in through the top of the passenger side window, carefully bypassing the rubber that surrounds the door. The hanger makes its way down, and I'm able to maneuver it to the unlock button. I push it, hear the click, and open the door. "Ta-da," I say, my voice flat.

"How'd you . . ." Brody holds up his hands. "You know what, it doesn't matter. Just look inside with me. Maybe you'll see something I miss."

All I see is me wasting my time and risking possible breaking-and-entering charges, but I move to the driver's side and get in anyway. The sooner Brody realizes this is nothing, the sooner I get to go home. My part will be done.

I sit back in the seat and instantly stiffen. This isn't right. My foot barely reaches the gas, and I'm taller than Cassie. The seat is way too far back for someone her height.

I look at the rearview mirror. It seems to be at the wrong angle, too. I don't reach for it. Not with Brody there. I got my first vision touching a mirror like that while trying to run an errand for my mom so that she didn't have to go out in public. I crashed Greta into a tree in the process. I was twelve at the time—too young to be operating a vehicle or to be having visions. I'm not about to chance another episode with Brody practically on top of me.

Besides, this doesn't mean anything, I remind myself. The seat can be back because Cassie dropped her wallet when she got out of the car and needed to get it, or was taking a nap, or eating lunch and didn't want the steering wheel getting into her food. There are dozens of perfectly normal explanations.

"I told you," Brody says, pulling something out of the glove compartment. It's a phone with a purple ombre case.

Cassie's phone.

It's off, which explains why Audra wasn't able to track it. Brody fixes that. A minute later messages from the night before come flooding in. "She wouldn't have left her phone here," he says.

"She would if she didn't want to be tracked." Although I'm not as convinced as I was before.

"I'm telling you, she wouldn't." He scrolls through her phone and text logs. "There's nothing here. Nothing unusual or that helps tell us where she is."

Brody throws his head back against the headrest and squeezes his eyes shut.

I'm not sure what to say, but I know what to do. I need to get my hands on the phone and hope for a vision. Brody didn't see anything, but maybe I will.

"Why don't you go into the bus station?" I suggest. "See if anyone saw her, remembers her. I'll look around here some more."

Brody nods. "Yeah. Good idea." His voice is low. Rough-sounding.

"I'm sure she's fine."

He nods again, looking more unsettled than before.

"Leave the phone," I tell him.

He drops it back on the seat and heads toward the station.

I'm alone. Just me, Cassie's car, and the sinking feeling I'm getting in my stomach that maybe Cassie was taken after all.

Brody isn't out of my sight yet, so I stop myself from grabbing the phone. I can hold off checking another two minutes. I do not want him turning around and seeing me go all zombie mode.

As I sit alone with my thoughts, the position of the driver's seat keeps gnawing at me. I reach down to move the seat forward, and my hand grazes something. I freeze and wait. No episode comes, so I lean down farther to see what I hit.

A shoe.

I pull it out to inspect it. A pink leather slip-on flat with a tiny bow at the front. It makes sense that it would be Cassie's shoe. But was it the shoe she wore yesterday?

I have no clue.

I'm observant, but that's not something I was paying attention to. Cassie was not a top priority for me that day—or most days. I reach back down to see if the other shoe, or anything else, is under there. I come up empty-handed. Her car is pretty much the opposite of mine. No sand, dirt, or crumbs on the floor and no junk whatsoever. It's spotless. I look in the back and under the seat next to me. No shoe there, either.

It could be a fluke. An extra shoe that fell out of her bag. Only I'm not so sure. Too many flukes are often not flukes at all.

It's time. I grab the rearview mirror. I get nothing.

On to the phone. I pick it up and hope I see something.

For once my visions don't let me down. The car, the parking lot, the sound of the wind rustling the trees, all slip away.

I'm in the school auditorium. A bunch of guys are onstage. "Try it again," Ms. Warmack says. "This is Kenickie's car. He's imagining how incredible it will be when it's all souped up. Let me see that."

I'm at a Grease *rehearsal, standing off to the side near the back, holding Cassie's phone. It vibrates. A text from Audra:*

Audra
Are you still mad?

I'm clearly seeing through Cassie's eyes. It's not just the phone. I can see the long, shiny black braid hanging over the light blue cashmere sweater, the pair of dark high-waisted jeans, the slim, athletic build, and the blue flats, identical to the pink one I found in the car.

"You!" It's Brooke, and she's storming in Cassie's direction. "This is your fault. I should not have to be here. You're going to pay for this." She knocks the phone out of Cassie's hand. She doesn't bother to make it look

like an accident. She outright smacks it and then keeps going to the last row, where she sits down in a huff.

"What the hell?" Valerie, who is standing nearby, says. She rushes over and picks up the phone. "Here." She hands it back to Cassie. "Ignore her."

"Excuse me?" Brooke says, and both Cassie and Valerie turn toward her. "Do you really want to get involved with this, Val? I don't suggest it."

Before I can hear the response, it's over. I'm back in the car at the bus station parking lot.

I put the phone in the glove compartment and replay everything in my head. Brooke threatening Cassie. Is there a reason I saw this specific vision? Is it relevant? Does it have anything to do with where Cassie is, or is it just another glimpse of how horrible the people are in this town? Obviously Brooke is evil—but evil enough to do something to Cassie? It's possible. Very possible.

Something glints in the rearview mirror. I jerk my head around to look. I don't see anything or anyone—not from where I'm sitting. I get out for a better view. No one's around. Yet I don't feel alone.

It's like the opposite of being in a vision. Instead of unintentionally creeping up on someone else, it's like someone is watching me.

I go over to Greta, while keeping my eyes peeled on my surroundings. I thank myself for not closing her door all the way and reach into the backseat for my bag. I pull out my bear spray. Living in the woods has given me a few close encounters with some of nature's wildlife. I've never had to use the stuff, but having it makes me feel safer. And right now, I don't feel very safe.

"Is someone there?" I call out.

No answer.

"Hello?"

I hear something in the woods.

A branch snapping. Movement. Something.

It's windy. That's probably it, but I move toward it anyway.

I keep the can out in front of me, finger on the nozzle, and remind myself not to stand downwind. "I said, is someone there?"

Still no reply.

This is your imagination, I tell myself. But I don't believe it.

My breathing picks up. I take another step forward.

"I'm warning you," I call out, "I'm armed. Come near me, you'll regret it."

"Whoa," Brody says.

I jump at the sound of his voice, my whole body twisting in his direction, bear spray still out.

He holds his hands up. "Easy there, Grim."

I lower the can. Was it Brody I heard? How long has he been there? He came from the other direction, from the bus station, but maybe my ears were playing tricks on me.

"What's the matter?" he asks.

I look back at the woods. I still don't see anyone, and the feeling of dread dissipates. "Nothing," I say, dropping the can back into my bag. "Just never know what will pop out of the woods. Any luck inside?"

Brody shakes his head. "No one saw her, no one remembers anyone like her here last night or this morning." He pounds his fist on the hood of Cassie's car. "I know she wouldn't just take off." He goes silent as his eyes catch on something inside. He swings the passenger door open. "Where did this come from?"

He picks up the shoe.

"I found it under the seat."

Brody's face goes ashen. "She was wearing this yesterday."

"Are you sure?"

"Yes. She wore that pink-and-gray sweater, and she has this thing about matching shoes." He grips the slip-on so tight, I think he's going to break it. "This proves it. She was taken. Maybe you leave your phone if you're running away, but you don't leave *one* shoe."

It could happen. She could have changed shoes and left one of the old ones behind. But the excuses about how she may have run off aren't ringing true anymore.

I don't say anything.

"Cassie was kidnapped," he says, studying my expression. "You believe it now, don't you?"

While I hate to admit it, hate to think it's true, I kind of do.

18

Cassie

What's going on? Where am I?

Everything is dark, and my head feels all groggy. What's happening? I was just in my car and—

The air rushes out of me as the memories come pouring in. A glimpse of something in the mirror. Someone in the back. Their hand over my mouth and nose . . .

No. This can't be real. It can't. Please, no. Let this be a vision like all the other times. *Snap out of it, Cass. Snap out of it. Come on. Please.*

My stomach drops and my whole body goes cold, each goose bump prickling my skin. My insides feel hollow. It's the same dread as all those visions, but I know this isn't one.

This is real.

This is happening.

What do I do? What do I do? What do I do? I reach up, but my hands jerk back.

Oh god. I'm bound. "No," I wail. "No."

There's something over my head. I can't see. I can't breathe. I feel like I'm suffocating. I need it off. I need it off now. I shake, lashing my neck back and forth, up and down violently. A pillow-case falls off my head.

I suck in some air and blink as my eyes adjust from the dark-ness. What is this place? Someone's basement? I'm on a dirty mattress, my arms wrapped around some sort of support beam or pole, wrists tied with a plastic zip-tie handcuff. My ankles encir-cled in ropes. How is this real? How do I get out of here? How do I get free?

"Help!" I scream. "Help! Help! Help me!"

No one answers.

My throat is raw from my cries, my voice strained, and I feel bile rise in my throat, but I try again. I don't know what else to do. "Somebody help me. Please."

Salty tears spill over my mouth, and I break down into sobs.

I want to go home. I don't want to die.

I hear a creak, and my whole body jolts. Is someone there? I push myself back into the corner as far back as the binds will allow.

What's going to happen? What do they want from me? Are they are going to keep me here? Hurt me? Kill me? Worse?

I look up, and my eye catches on a red blinking light mounted on the wall across from me.

It's a camera.

My legs, my arms, my fingers, my head, my *everything* feel numb. And something cold, something like horror, floods my insides. I close my eyes.

Someone is watching me.

19

HaYDen

"I told you Cassie wouldn't just take off," Brody says.

"Okay," I concede. "It doesn't look that way."

He's pacing now. "I'm thinking our first step should be talking to Warmack. She was the last to see her."

"Hold on there," I tell him. "Just because I agree that she's missing doesn't mean I'm volunteering to lead the search party. That's the sheriff's territory. We'll bring the shoe to him, tell him about the seat being pushed too far back—"

"The what?!" he cuts me off.

I forgot I hadn't filled him in on that part. Once I remedy the situation, Brody is even more insistent on my involvement. "Don't you see? The sheriff will say it's nothing. He'll say she dropped the shoe and pushed the seat back to look for it."

When he puts it that way . . .

"We can't waste time," he continues. "Cassie's gone, and the longer we take to find her, the bigger the chances are we won't. She saw us working together. *You* are a part of this. You may not believe it, but Cassie *does* have visions. They're real, and you were in them.

Audra's right. If there's even a slight chance you can figure out where she is, then I need your help. *Cassie* needs your help."

Her visions. Visions of *me*.

My mind wanders back to the bathroom and the glimmer I got of the knife at her throat, of her terror. That's not all that comes flooding back, though. The sound of her yelling at me that this was all my fault rings through my head.

Did she see something? Did I do something that altered her future?

Is she missing because of me?

No. There's no way. Unless . . .

Her accusations pulse louder and louder.

You did this. This is your fault.

I can't shake her voice.

You. You.

"Fine. I'll do it," I snap, more at myself than at Brody.

I'm not sure how much help I'll be, but if the sheriff isn't going to try, somebody should. Cassie deserves it. She tried helping me when I started at Lightsend High; I can at least try and help her now.

Brody doesn't thank me, but gives me a slight nod in acknowledgment. "Warmack, then?" he asks.

I shake my head. "Brooke."

His face scrunches up. "Brooke Tamison?"

"Yes."

"No way," he says. "She's not involved in this."

"Do you want my help or not?" I ask. "That's who I want to talk to." Cassie saw me as part of this in her vision, and I saw Brooke in mine. It's not a solid lead, I'm not sure if the two are connected, but it's the best I've got. Brooke told Cassie she'd pay, and I wouldn't put anything past her—not even kidnapping.

"Okay," Brody says, and pulls out his phone. "Brooke it is. We can check her social media. Or rather *I* can, since apparently someone here is from another century. You know, even my grandma has Instagram."

I raise an eyebrow. "Cyberstalking me?"

"Researching," he says, and begins swiping.

I actually do have an account. Only not as Hayden Jefferies. My fake persona is Charlotte Donovan. A character from some book I read, and she posts random things now and then—to make it seem legit. She follows Brody, Brooke, and most of the school. A bunch even follow back, and no one's ever questioned how they know her. Even the private accounts accepted "Charlie." They love more followers, and I love another way to spy on my classmates. It's kinda surprising how much information people put on social media, but it comes in handy—or at least it did before the sheriff shut down my operation.

"Jackpot," Brody says, holding the screen out to me. "We know where she'll be."

Brooke posted a picture of the *Grease* call sheet an hour ago and captioned it, *Another day, another rehearsal.* The sheet lists the cast and crew that are supposed to be at the auditorium today. Brooke's on it. So is Cassie.

Brody turns the phone back in his direction. "Warmack will be there, too. Two birds, one stone."

"Okay. Let's head over," I say.

"The rehearsal doesn't start for two hours," he says.

I shrug. "Then let's go straight to Brooke's house."

"Probably not a smart idea for you to go to the Tamisons'. They wanted you arrested."

Brooke did a good job of making sure everyone knew that.

"Better off cornering her at school," he continues.

He's right, but I'm not going to drop him off, then drive home, and then drive to Lightsend High. Brody may have paid for the gas, but I don't intend to waste it. "We'll get to the rehearsal early, then. Stake them out or something."

"No, I have a better idea," he says. "Come on, I'll give you directions."

"To where?"

"You'll see. Take Main," Brody says when we're in the car, his voice energized. It's almost like my agreeing to help in the search brought him back to life. "And just keep going."

He's back on his phone, but I can't see what he's doing. "Can I use this?" he asks, pointing to the charger I have plugged into the car's lighter. "They didn't plug it in for me. I'm almost out of battery."

"Aww, poor baby. You mean jail didn't cater to your every whim?"

"Can I use it or not?"

"You can try. It's temperamental."

"Wouldn't expect anything less from something of yours."

Just for that, I don't bother telling him the trick of holding it still at exactly a forty-five-degree angle while pinching the cord.

"And are you going to tell me where we're headed?" I ask him.

"Nope."

"I'm not your chauffeur," I remind him.

"No kidding. Our chauffeur would never keep the car looking like this." That annoying smirk of his is back.

I side-eye him. "You could walk, you know."

"You'd miss me too much," he says, dimple on full display. "Ooh. Take a left at the light and then an immediate right, and pull into the lot."

I want to respond, but I'm too focused on the road and not missing the turns to come up with a snappy comeback. Eventually, a restaurant comes into view. "Brennan's Bistro? That's your grandiose idea?" I stop the car.

"Uh, yeah. Some of us didn't get to eat today, thanks to a certain someone."

He opens the door and gets out. "Be right back."

"Hey," I call after him, "you're not going to ask if I want anything?" I don't, but that's not the point.

He turns back to me. "You picked breakfast, I pick lunch. Already ordered on my phone. No thanks to your charger. Had just enough battery left."

This I didn't expect, and it's an unwelcome surprise. Brennan's Bistro is super expensive and not where I plan to spend my money. "Not so fast," I tell him. "I don't want anything from here. Especially something I didn't choose."

"Know the feeling. The smell of that Egg McMuffin still haunts me, but don't worry, my taste is a lot better than yours."

"Not interested," I tell him.

"What?" Brody asks, poking his head back in the door. "You don't like decent food? McDonald's or bust?"

"How about I don't like paying twelve bucks or whatever it

costs here for fries when I can get them for ninety-nine cents." Or not get them at all.

"It's on me," he says.

"I don't want it to be on you."

"Fine, then you can pay," he says with a wink, and I want to throttle him.

"Brody . . ."

"I'm kidding," he says. "Come on, you're helping me. Lunch is the least I can do."

"Just get some for yourself. I'm not hungry."

He holds up his hands in defeat, and goes inside. Fifteen minutes later, he comes back, two huge white paper bags in hand. He puts them near his feet and says, "One more stop."

He asks me to take him to Shake Dream, a small place in town known for, as the name suggests, ice cream shakes. I don't argue. It's not worth it. It's on the way to the school, and we still have a bunch of time to kill.

"Sure you don't want one?" he asks. "They're really good."

"I'm sure." I've looked at the menu before. A small is six dollars. On sale you can get two half gallons of ice cream, plus toppings, at the grocery store for that price. Brody leaves me in the car again. This time, though, he doesn't leave my line of sight. Shake Dream is tiny. You can't even go in, there's just a window you order from. No one else is here. With no indoor seating, and the weather brisker today, that doesn't really surprise me, though.

Brody gives me a thumbs-up before picking up two huge milk-shakes and making his way back to the car.

He puts them in the cup holders between us. "Couldn't decide between two flavors," he says, "so I got both." Of course he did.

Go big or bust. The rich can play like that. He does another once-over of the inside of my car, this time in an exaggerated fashion. "I take it from the looks of things you're not opposed to eating in here?"

"Ha ha, soooo funny." I gesture for him to go ahead and eat. "Another dirty car joke. How do you come up with them?" I ask.

"Just born with it." He picks up one of the bags and opens it. An incredible smell wafts in my direction.

I try not to show any interest as he pulls out the oversize cartons one by one, opens them, and puts them on the dashboard, naming them as he goes. "Truffle fries. Sweet potato fries. Onion rings. Portobello burger. Veggie burger. And the pièce de résistance, macaroni-and-cheese balls. You know," he informs me, "they changed the recipe on these just for me. Used to make them with chicken broth."

"Well, aren't you special," I tell him.

He nods and gives me that cocky little smile again. "Yeah. It's kind of a burden. Everyone wants to do things for me, hang out with me, sit next to me in a car and watch me eat."

"You caught me," I say. "All of this was an elaborate plan to have lunch with you."

Brody's eyes cloud for a moment, but the look disappears as quickly as it arrived. He turns his attention to the shakes. He pulls out one of the straws, holds it over his mouth, and lets the thick mixture drip in.

"Now this is how you do a milkshake," he says, his face now filled with a look of euphoria. "Triple-Chocolate Mint Explosion. Want to try?" he asks, and points the straw at the cup.

"Eww. No. If I didn't want a Twizzler that you merely touched, do you really think I'm going to want to drink after you? Hard pass." I shudder for added effect.

"You're missing out." He pulls a packet of plastic utensils from the Brennan's Bistro bag and takes out the spoon. "Here," he says, holding it out to me. "Haven't even put the straw back in yet. Saliva-free. The spoon should meet your standards."

It does look good, and I've driven by this place so many times and always wondered what their shakes taste like, so I say okay before he rescinds the offer. "What are the choices?"

"The chocolate mint one or Grandma's Apple Pie."

Okay, I can see why he had a hard time choosing. I go with the apple pie. It sounds homey and comforting. And oh my god. It's like a creamy, rich, apple-cinnamon explosion in my mouth. This is by far the best thing I've ever tasted. Pie, ice cream, spices, with just the right amount of sweetness. This could win awards, it's that good.

"It's all right," I say, keeping my face neutral.

Brody raises an eyebrow. "Just all right?"

I try not to salivate as he puts his own spoon in. "Yep."

"I forgot," he says, "your Mickey D's palate is only used to the best."

"Yeah, well, Ronnie M., the Hamburglar, and I go way back. Eating elsewhere feels like cheating."

"You and 'Ronnie M.'? Hanging out with a clown, huh?" Brody asks.

"As a matter of fact, I am. He's sitting right next to me."

Brody looks like he's holding back a laugh. "I walked right into that one."

"You make it easy."

"Okay," he says, "kidding aside, you're going to have to eat some of this stuff with me. Take a shake, take everything. This is a sick amount of food. There's no way I'll finish it by myself."

It is an obscene amount for one person.

"Will you please have some?" he asks.

I shake my head.

"If you don't, it's just going to get thrown out, and it's too good for that. Have you ever tried Brennan's food?"

I shake my head again. Although it's a lie. I have. I cringe a little thinking about it. Some of my classmates order from Brennan's for lunch, eat two bites, and chuck the rest. On a few occasions, I waited until the lunch period was over and took the containers out of the trash. One of those times was right before Brody grabbed my bag in study hall. It was why I was extra pissed. I didn't want him to see what was inside.

"Then you have to try," he tells me. "Everyone who lives in Lightsend should have Brennan's Bistro at least once."

There really is no way he'll be able to finish it all on his own. "Fine," I say, like I'm doing him a favor. I can't bring myself just to say thanks, even though I know I probably should.

I take one of the truffle fries.

"See," he says, after I eat it. "What did I tell you?"

"It's good," I concede. It really is, and it's even better hot, and not having sat in my bag for a few hours.

"Just think of it as bribery to help find Cassie," Brody says.

"I don't need bribery. I already said I'd help."

"I know."

His eyes are soft when he says it, and they're trained on me.

It's weirding me out, so I look away and stuff a macaroni-and-cheese ball in my mouth.

And. Oh. My. God. It. Is. Scalding.

My tongue is on fire. I open my mouth and let the food fall into my hand. "So hot. So hot."

"Yeah, *real hot*," he says, laughing. He's making fun of me, but it's not cruel. His tone is playful.

Did I really just spit out my food in front of Brody?

Yeah, that's me, all class.

He takes a napkin and a bottle of water out of one of the bags and hands them to me. "Here," he says, "drink."

I do. It helps.

"You okay?" he asks.

"Peachy," I say, but I refuse to be embarrassed. That thing was way too hot.

"Cassie always says the mac and cheese should come with a warning label. You have to cut it open and let it cool."

Brody gets a faraway look.

"We'll find her," I tell him. I don't know if it's true, but it seems like the right thing to say.

"Yeah." His voice is low.

I squeeze my macaroni-filled napkin in my hand. "I wish we knew what she saw in that vision, so we could just make it happen already."

His mouth quirks into a half smile. "Doesn't work like that. If you don't play it out, you could change everything."

"Huh?" I ask.

"That's what she would always tell me. Visions aren't set. You can alter them. Sometimes."

"Only sometimes?"

"Seems that way. Cassie calls it the catch-22. Do the visions happen so that she can try and alter the future—or do they already take her actions into account?"

"Which is it?" I ask. I never really thought about my visions being a way for me to change things—well, other than my financial situation.

"A little bit of both, I guess. She researched it a lot. She was trying to find answers but wound up with more questions. Most people wouldn't be able to handle all the things she's seen. But Cassie . . . she . . ." His voice trails off.

I'm not sure what to say, so I let the silence breathe.

"I didn't dump her, you know," he finally says. "I know you think I'm some player who dumped his girlfriend to see what else was out there, but I'm not. It wasn't like that."

I don't confirm his suspicions, but he's right, it's exactly what I thought. Everyone in school gossiped about it.

I'm not exactly sure why he's telling me this. Maybe he thinks it will help in the search or maybe he just wants it off his chest. But I'm curious to know more, so I encourage him to go on. "What was it like?"

Brody picks up a fry and drops it back down.

"She ended it." His voice is throaty. "And there was no cheating or anything. We were together since fifth grade and then one day she says we're meant to be friends, says I'm not the one for her. That there's someone else for me." He rubs the back of his neck.

"Hard to argue with a girl who sees the future when she tells you she doesn't see the two of you together in it. No changing her mind."

"I'm sorry." I feel a twinge of guilt. Brody is certainly no angel, but maybe he's not quite the devil I've made him out to be in my head. He has his okay moments.

He shrugs. "We were making headway moving to the friend zone. She's like family to me. Always will be. I need her to know that. I want her to know that even if we're not together, she'll always be a part of my life. I want to tell her. I *need* to tell her."

I nod.

Silence fills the car again. After a few minutes he picks up the portobello sandwich, and I make a second attempt at a macaroni-and-cheese ball. We polish off a good chunk of the food. We don't say anything, we just eat, but it doesn't feel awkward. It just feels quiet.

Pretty soon it's time to go.

"Ready?" I ask.

"Yeah."

So am I.

I want to find her. I want to help. I'm not sure how, but I'm going to make sure Brody sees Cassie again.

20

HaYDen

finish circling the auditorium for the second time. "I can't find Brooke," I tell Brody. "She wasn't backstage, either."

The room is buzzing with cast members and crew, but no sign of the one person I want to talk to.

"I wouldn't put it past Brooke to blow the rehearsal off," he says.

Not what I want to hear, but Brody doesn't seem too concerned. He doesn't believe Brooke is behind all of this.

"Warmack's finally here," he says, and juts his chin over to a table in front of the stage. The drama teacher is standing there, looking more frazzled than usual. In the span of twenty seconds, she's looked at her phone more than a half-dozen times.

I reposition my bag on my shoulder. If I can't get what I came here for, I can at least get something. "I need you to distract her."

"What?" he says.

"Ms. Warmack."

"Why? She'll talk to me. We don't need to pull some trick.

The woman loves me. She was practically begging me to be in her show."

"Yeah?" I ask. "You think she'll just hand over her phone, too? Because that's what I want. I need to see it. When she lays it down on the table, you need to get her attention, enough for her to leave that thing unattended."

"Now you know how to crack an iPhone, MacGyver?" he asks, his eyebrows rising. "Wait, is that how you got the stuff on Ollie and everyone?"

"Caught me. Hayden Jefferies, superspy." I swat the back of my hand on his forearm, and then instantly wish I hadn't.

Why am I touching him? I should *not* be touching Brody. And why is he so toned?

"No," I say, making sure my hand stays firmly by my side. "I'm just hoping you'll do such a great job of catching her attention that I'll be able to get there before it turns back off."

At least that's what I tell him. While it would be great to look at Ms. Warmack's call log and search history, what I'm really hoping for is a vision. You can clear your search engine, but you can't clear one of my episodes. Warmack was the last one to see Cassie. Maybe she saw something she doesn't even realize she saw. Or maybe she's in on what happened. I can't rule anything out.

"This, I can do," Brody says.

I have no doubt. I've watched way too many teachers let him get away with crap because he's given them that dimpled smile and some kiss-ass compliment that they eat right up. It's like he erases their memory of what he just did with a look and a few simple words.

"Places," he says after he tells me his plan.

We move toward Warmack. Me hovering behind her trying not to be noticed, while Brody stands in front of the stage, facing the curtain.

Ms. Warmack puts her phone back down.

I let out a cough. "Go," I say underneath it.

It's showtime.

"Cassie," he calls out. "Cassie."

Right on cue, Ms. Warmack rushes over to him. A few people look up, but then they go right back to their phones and conversations.

"Brody," Ms. Warmack says, "I'm so sorry, she's not here."

He turns to face her. "I figured, but I had to try. Ms. Warmack, Cassie's missing. The sheriff's office found her car by the bus station. You were the last to see her."

"Oh my," she says. "Cassie was supposed to be here today to make sure everything looked up to par and to take care of any last-minute hiccups. She didn't say anything about going somewhere."

"No," he says, "I don't think she left on her own. I think she was taken."

"What did the sheriff say?"

I can't see Warmack's expression, but Brody's is intense.

"That she probably took off, and that he can't do anything because it hasn't even been twenty-four hours. Which is why I'm here. When you saw her, did you see anything strange? Anyone in the area?"

She shakes her head. "I'm sorry. No."

"Can you walk me through everything? Tell me what happened when you last saw her, just in case there's something that may help?"

I'm so wrapped up in their conversation, I almost forget my part in all of this. I grab her phone.

Come on, visions, don't fail me now. I want one so bad, I don't even care if it happens in front of all these people.

"I'm sorry," she says, "but I wasn't really paying attention. I didn't see where she went. I got a call after Cassie and I left the building, and I took it."

"From who?"

She pauses, debating how much to tell him. But I'm seeing what she's seeing. Brody's desperate, hopeful face. He's not trying to stall for time, he wants answers, and the concern for Cassie is written all over him. She'll talk.

"The credit card company," Ms. Warmack tells him. "They called to tell me there was suspicious activity on my card. Someone tried to use it at Mac of All Trades. Thirteen hundred dollars. They wanted to know if it was me. It wasn't."

I'm still not getting a vision.

I try to tune Brody and Ms. Warmack out and focus on the phone. I turn it over in my hand. Close my eyes. Toss it up slightly and catch it. Nothing is triggering an episode.

"Excuse me," Ms. Warmack says.

I open my eyes, and she's storming in my direction, Brody right behind her.

"What do you think you're doing?" she asks.

I've dealt with enough angry authority figures to know how to stay calm when caught red-handed. "Trying to find Cassie. I work at the sheriff's department, and I'm trying to get a jump on the case. Why wait twenty-four hours when you can start now? I thought if I could see who called you, it could help."

"And how will that help?"

"Well—"

"I wasn't looking for an answer," she says, cutting me off. She snatches her phone back. "It was rhetorical. I do not need *you* snooping around my belongings, Miss Jefferies. I've heard about the things you've done."

I almost say, *Then you know not to mess with me, that I know things*, but Brody slides between us before I open my big mouth.

"She's just worried about Cassie, too," he says. "She didn't mean anything by it. Hayden was in the sheriff's office when I spoke to him about Cassie. She's trying to help me and went a little too far. We're just scared. *I'm scared*."

Her face softens, and she nods.

Seriously, charming teachers may be Brody's superpower.

"Have you seen Brooke?" he asks her. "I was hoping to talk to her, too."

"She's probably around here somewhere. Hard to keep track of all the crew. So many moving pieces to this show."

Ms. Warmack seems to have forgotten about me, so I slip away as she continues ranting to Brody. No need to stick around and chance her changing her mind and deciding to turn me in to the principal—or worse, the sheriff—for trying to take her phone.

I decide to do a quick sweep of the halls, in case Brooke is wandering around or went to the vending machines or something. And, wow, the school is busy.

I had no idea how many people spend their weekends here. Walking from the auditorium to the cafeteria, I pass a choir practice, a volleyball tournament, a couple of random people doing I-don't-know-what, and almost smack into Coach Hill, the head of the school's athletics program and boys' gym teacher. Which means there's a good chance the football team is around, too.

I never joined a sport, or any activity, really. Tried once. Soccer, but then I found out how much it was going to cost me. Schools like to pretend extracurriculars are free, but they're not. Uniforms, presents for the coach, team-building excursions, and so on and so on and so on. I don't have money for that. In my home, a cell phone is a luxury—and even that's partially subsidized by the state.

"Sorry," I say as I swerve to avoid the coach, despite the fact that he should be the one apologizing, not me. His face is glued to his phone, he's not watching where he's going, like pretty much everyone at Lightsend High. But since I have enough problems with the staff at this school at the moment, I suck it up.

He doesn't look up or slow down. "Yeah," he grunts as some sort of acknowledgment.

Whatever, at least he's not reminding me that he knows about all the things I've been up to, like Ms. Warmack.

I make it to the cafeteria, and no sign of Brooke at the vending machines or anywhere. I check her Instagram. No new posts, but there is a new story from a couple of minutes ago. It shows a giant TV and some words written over it. *True crime binge watch. Who's ready?* She's not at rehearsal. She's home. Watching crime shows. Probably getting ideas. I knew I should have just gone straight there. What a mistake to wait. I don't care if it means running into her parents, I need to go now.

I exit through the door near the cafeteria and jog to Greta.

I'm almost there when I hear my name being called out.

"Hayden, what the hell?"

It's Brody.

Crap. Forgot about him.

He's walking over to me, and the look he's throwing my way? You'd think I was the one who kidnapped Cassie. "You were just going to leave me here?" he asks, his eyes narrowed into slits. "Nice. Just when I was thinking maybe you weren't so bad . . . I should have known. First impressions. Stick with them."

I was going to apologize, but now . . . ? Screw him. "Like you wouldn't have been able to figure out a way home? I'm sure calling Lyft is so difficult for you. How will you ever afford it?"

"Well, it *is* difficult when you have no battery left on your phone."

I feel a twinge of guilt but push it aside. He doesn't get to play victim here, not with the way he's talking to me. I almost left him at school, not in the middle of the Atlantic Ocean. "And I'm sure no one inside would let you borrow their charger or give you a ride."

"That's not the point." He shoves his hands into his jacket pockets and shakes his head. "And I thought you were serious about helping us find Cassie."

I cross my arms in front of my chest. "I am."

"Really seems that way."

Seriously?! "Where do you think I was going?" I ask.

"How would I know? You left me here."

"I didn't leave. I'm still here." I take a breath. Fighting with him isn't going to help anything, and he's right. I'd be pissed if he tried to ditch me. I didn't do it on purpose, but I guess that's not a good excuse. "I realized Brooke is at her house, and I wanted to ask her about Cassie," I explain.

"This was all about *Brooke*?"

My explanation doesn't help; he just seems more pissed.

"Yes. She *threatened* Cassie."

"*When?*"

"Sometime during one of their rehearsals. A crew member told me," I lie. "They said Brooke was out for blood."

"Look," he says, "Cassie and I have known Brooke forever. I know you have your issues with her, and yeah, she can be ruthless, but she's not dangerous. Not physically, anyway. Brooke's weapons are her words."

"Tell that to Leighton," I say. Brooke set her up, made it look like Leighton stole things from people, cheated, lied. Turned everyone against her. They all knew the truth, but no one said a word. Too afraid of Brooke's wrath.

"Yeah, that was messed up, but it's still a big jump from that to kidnapping."

"Maybe, maybe not."

"So your big idea is to go to Brooke's house and what? Demand she give you answers? Sure, that'll work. Her parents will just call the sheriff on you and have you locked up for trespassing. Wait until you see her at school."

He's using that condescending, I-know-what's-best tone, and it's taking everything in my power not to just get into Greta and really leave him here this time. "Do you want my help or not?" I spit back. "You said you wanted me to look for Cassie. This is how I'm looking. You don't want to come, then don't. I don't care. I don't need you. You're the one who jumped into my car, not the other way around."

"You know what?" he says. "Sure. Let's do it, let's go to Brooke's.

Let them arrest you, get you expelled. Don't know why I care. Would probably make my life easier."

"Anything to help you," I say, and tug violently at my car's door.

Stuck again—mine anyway. Brody's pops right open. "Traitor," I growl at Greta.

Before I have to go through the back, Brody pushes my door open from the inside. I don't say anything; I just get in.

Neither of us says anything. We sit in silence. I don't even ask him for directions to Brooke's, even though I'm sure he knows the way. I google it on my phone instead. He sees what I'm doing but doesn't offer to help.

I cannot believe I am stuck with him. I don't need this. But Cassie does. And if I'm responsible for what happened to her, or connected to it, I have to do this. I take a breath. Who am I kidding? Even if I wasn't, I'd do it anyway.

The ride takes forever. It's like I can feel Brody's resentment circling me. I feel like gagging up all that food I polished off. Eating something that Brody bought? What was I thinking?

I pull up in front of Brooke's house, although I'm not sure you can call it that. It's like the size of the high school.

I get out of the car and Brody follows.

"Well?" he says, when I don't move.

I'm just taking it all in. I can't imagine living in someplace like this. My cabin is smaller than Brooke's garage. Brody doesn't seem to think much of it. His place is probably just as big.

"I'm going." I take my phone, hit record, and put it into my jacket pocket before heading up the cobblestone walkway to the door, Brody right behind me. It's just a house, nothing to be intimidated by. Then I roll my eyes at myself for needing the reminder. Who cares that it's huge? Probably compensating for something. Or showing off. Or just a way for the Tamisons to never have to see one another. There is no reason for a single family to have something this size. I wouldn't even want it if I could afford it.

I jab my finger in the doorbell.

"Nervous?" Brody asks.

"No," I say. "Why would I be?"

He glances down at my foot, and I realize I'm tapping it. I stop and turn back to the door.

No answer. I try the knocker. "Come on," I mutter.

A minute later a woman comes to the door. It's not Mrs. Tamison. I don't know who she is. "Yes, may I help you?" she asks.

"I'm here to see Brooke," I say.

"And who may I tell Ms. Tamison is here to see her?"

Of course. The Tamisons have people to answer their door. Why deal with commoners if you don't have to? I hold back another eye roll.

"Taylor Swift," I say. Let Brooke come see for herself.

The woman raises an eyebrow.

"My parents have a sick sense of humor," I tell her.

"And you, Mr. Brody, I know," she says. "I'll let Ms. Tamison know you're here. Come wait in the foyer. I'll be right back."

I side-eye Brody. Does this woman recognize him because of his standing or because he actually hangs out with Brooke? Either one lowers my opinion of him tenfold. Not that it had much lower to go.

We step inside, and I feel like I'm on the set of a movie. The foyer or whatever she called it is like a giant lobby. There's even a bench to sit on. Marbled white floor with an actual family crest in it, a table with a massive vase and bouquet of fresh flowers—and not the kind you buy at the gas station: This is a lavish display, with blooms I don't know the names of, and a giant spiral staircase so big that I can't see where it disappears to.

A minute later, Brooke makes her way down the stairs. She stops midway when she sees me. "No. Uh-uh. Out. You are not welcome in this house."

"Such a charming hostess you are," I tell her. "Did you learn that in finishing school?"

"What do you want, Hayden?" Then she turns her attention to Brody. "And what are *you* doing with her? You break up with Cassie and this is what you wind up with? Forget lowering your standards, it's like you destroyed them altogether."

"Aren't you so clever, Brooke," I say. "With witty lines like that, you should be on the improv team. Then maybe people will laugh at something other than how desperate you are to be valedictorian."

"Out," she says, and points her whole arm toward the door. "Do I need a restraining order?"

"You're not helping," Brody says to me through gritted teeth. Then he turns his attention to Brooke. "She didn't mean it," he says, and keeps talking before I can interrupt with a *yes, I did*. "Please. We just want to talk to you for a minute. It's important."

There's a long pause, but it's all an act for dramatic effect. She's going to hear us out. I have no doubt. We've piqued her curiosity, and she wants another story for her friends about the "criminal delinquent" Hayden Jefferies.

"Only for you," she tells Brody, and continues down the stairs like she's making a grand entrance. I knew it.

"Out here," she says, and grabs a coat from a closet by the door and puts it on. Brooke walks outside, waving her hand in my direction. "Don't want that one stealing anything."

"Well, I don't want that one," I say, mimicking her, "planting anything on me."

"Enough," Brody says.

Brooke and I wind up standing face-to-face, staring each other down.

"Fine, you wanted to talk to me, I'm here," she says. "What's this all about? Trying to extort me again, because it went so well the last time?"

"I want to know about Cassie," I say.

"What about her?" she asks.

I put my hands on my hips. "Like you don't know."

Brooke turns to Brody. "Am I supposed to know what she's alluding to?"

"Cassie's missing," he says.

"Again?" she asks with a sigh. She doesn't seem particularly disturbed by the news. "What is this, like, the fifth, sixth time she's taken off? I'm surprised her dad hasn't chipped her yet."

Before this school, I thought that only happened to dogs, but apparently some rich people do it to their kids, too, in case they get taken. Too bad Cassie wasn't one of them.

Brody shakes his head. "It's not like that, not this time. She was taken. Forcibly."

"Yeah, okay. Like the time she ditched school for a week and a half."

"I'm serious," Brody says. "It's not the same." His tone is so intense that she holds up her hands.

"Fine, but what does any of this have to do with me?" she asks.

I will admit, Brooke is doing a pretty good innocent act.

"I know you threatened her," I tell her.

Brooke throws back her head and laughs. "Oh my god. You think I had something to do with her disappearance? You really are a piece of work. Trying to frame me again for something I didn't do. I may need to tell the sheriff about this little excursion of yours."

She's lying about what happened between us; maybe that means she's lying about Cassie, too. "Good," I say, "and you can tell him why you were after Cassie."

"I wasn't after her," she scoffs.

"People heard you threaten her, Brooke," Brody interjects. I'm surprised he's coming to my aid and not sticking by her.

She shrugs, and her nonchalance makes me so angry, I want to jump out of my skin. How can she be so blasé about threatening someone? What else is she capable of? Did Cassie find out something she wasn't supposed to? Did she confront Brooke? How far would Brooke go to keep her lies under wraps?

"Cassie told me everything," I lie. "She saw what went down between us and let me know everything she had on you. So if you think holding her somewhere keeps you safe, it doesn't. Might as well let her go."

"You really are as messed up as everyone says," Brooke tells me, rolling her eyes. "Yeah, okay. Let's go get Cassie. You caught me, Hayden. I've been driving around town with her locked in my Porsche. But oh no." She holds up her hands and pretends to shake them like she's nervous. "Now that you know my big secret, maybe I should put you in there with her. Hmm . . ." She shrugs again. "It's going to be hard to fit you both in the trunk. May have to throw Cassie over the cliff. Or should I just send the whole car into the falls and get a new one? Decisions, decisions," she says, twirling a strand of her hair.

"Enough, Brooke," Brody says.

"*Me?* She's the one accusing me of what? Kidnapping? Come on."

As much as I want this to be over, for it to be Brooke, for us to find Cassie hidden in one of the Tamisons' guest rooms, we won't. Brooke is telling the truth.

Her tone was too spot-on. There was no break in her expression, no quirks, not even the tiny flinch she does when she's lying. Brooke may be evil incarnate, she may have threatened Cassie, but Brody was right—she's not the kidnapper.

"Fine, okay, I get it. It wasn't you," I say, "but you still threatened her."

Brody looks as angry as I feel. "What did you do, Brooke?"

At first, I think she's going to deny everything, but she actually admits it. "It was nothing. It didn't mean anything."

"Tell us what happened," Brody insists.

"Fine, whatever. Like I said, it was nothing. It was all about those tedious *Grease* rehearsals. I signed up for crew, thought it would look good on my college applications, but god, it was *sooo* boring. So I stopped going. I had Twyla sign me in on the call sheet, but someone ratted me out."

"Cassie wouldn't do that," Brody says. "She would have talked to you first."

"Yeah, I know that now," Brooke snaps back. "Valerie owned up to it. Guilty conscience, I guess," she says.

Brooke must have done some pretty crappy stuff to Cassie, in order for Valerie to come clean. I can only imagine what she's doing to Valerie now.

"We worked it out," she continues. "Val told Ms. Warmack she was mistaken, that I had just been in a different part of the auditorium, and all is good again. So is this little inquisition over?"

"Hardly," I say. She may not be guilty of taking Cassie, but she's still guilty of inflicting pain on so many people—Cassie probably included. She needs to pay.

"When you thought it was Cassie," I ask, "what'd you do? Make fun of her? Lie, cheat, steal?"

"Go to hell, Hayden," she says.

"I'm talking to you," I tell her. "I'm already there. Don't forget I know what you did to Fiona, to Leighton, to half the school."

"Big deal. You think that scares me?" she asks with a laugh. "No one would believe it. You're not trustworthy, remember?"

"But I am," Brody says.

"Yeah, about that . . ." Brooke shakes her head. "You don't think word got around that you were just in jail? And you're running around with this one. Guilt by association. If it's me or you, people are going to believe me."

"Not if others come forward, too," I remind her.

"It's cute that you think they'd do that," she says, that evil smile of hers lighting her face. "Now, I've had enough of you. *Both* of you."

She turns and stalks back inside her house.

Brody starts to say something, but I put up my hand and stop him. It's not worth it.

"If you're not gone in three minutes, I call the sheriff," she says before slamming the door shut.

"That went well," Brody says. "She's—"

"Yeah, I know," I grunt, and head for the car. I take out my phone and stop the recording. I may not have found any tie between Brooke and Cassie's disappearance, but at least I sort of got her admitting to some of the crap she's pulled. It probably won't amount to much, maybe won't even get her a slap on the wrist, but it's a start at proving what she's really like.

"You really thought it was her," Brody says. "At first, anyway."

"Yeah, I get it, I was wrong," I say. "You were right. Is that what you want to hear?"

"That's not what I meant. It's just . . ." He rubs the back of his neck. "You thought Brooke took Cassie because of what she knew, and then you told her you knew the same stuff. That was . . ."

"What? Reckless? Dangerous? Impetuous?" I ask.

"No, I mean, it was, but it was also . . . nice. More than nice. You were going to risk yourself for Cassie. That was—"

"Just get in the car," I say, cutting him off. I'm not sure what to do with contrite, complimentary Brody. It feels weird. I try to open the door, but Greta is apparently out to get me today. Once again, Brody's side opens and mine doesn't. "Really?"

Brody lets me in.

"You know," he says as I start the car, "I could help you with that if you want."

"Huh?"

"The door. I can take a look."

"*You* know how to fix cars?"

"It's not that shocking," he says, but yeah, it is. "Stop looking at me like that," he protests.

"What? I just find it hard to believe you don't have someone who takes care of all that stuff."

"You do remember I work at the gas station, right?"

I shrug and he continues. "Practically grew up at the place. There's a garage in the back. My grandpa would take me there to 'tinker on the cars,' as he would call it. He loved it. He restored some beauties. I still go sometimes. Not as much since he's gone."

The look he gets when he talks about his grandpa keeps me from making a snide comment, like that a hubcap on one of his renovation projects probably costs more than my whole car.

"So anyway," he says, "if you want me to take a look, I will."

"Maybe," I tell him. "After we find Cassie."

"Yeah. So where to next?" he asks.

"I don't know. Did you get anything from Warmack?"

"You mean after you ditched me?" he asks, but the disgust from earlier is gone; this sounds almost playful.

"Yeah, that's what I mean." For some reason, I find myself wanting to smile, but I force myself not to.

"It was pretty much a bust. Warmack was so concerned about her credit card, she barely paid any attention to Cassie."

"So she's in the clear?" I ask.

He leans back on the headrest. "Doesn't seem like she's involved."

"Yeah, but she's also a drama teacher," I remind him. "Knows a thing or two about acting, could be fooling us."

"Possibly. I didn't get that feeling, though."

"So what are we supposed to do now?" I ask.

"Maybe you were right before."

"Say that again," I say.

He smiles. "I said maybe you were right, that we should just head back into the school and try breaking into one of the classrooms."

"I like being right and all—"

"You? No," he says, mocking me.

I ignore him and continue. "But somebody told me we can't rush the process. Catch-22 and all that."

"Sounds like somebody very smart," he says.

I hold out my hand and wave it back and forth. "Meh," I say. "Low to average seems more accurate."

He shakes his head. "Doesn't seem right to me. I think borderline genius."

"Mmmm . . . No, borderline genius would have already come up with a plan for what to do next."

He nods, his expression getting serious. "Yeah, I should have a plan to find her. I should have *something*. You're right again."

Only when he says it this time, it doesn't have the same effect. He's chastising himself for not knowing what to do, and I feel a little guilty for making him feel that way. It's not his fault Cassie's gone. If anything, it's mine. "If you want to go back into the school, we can," I say.

Brody shakes his head. "No, I have a better idea. Let's go to her house. Talk to her dad, check out her room, see if we find something."

"That's a good idea." It really is. Better than he knows. If I can get in there, maybe I can get a vision, see something useful.

He gives me directions, and pretty soon I'm on yet another street with massive houses. "That's hers," Brody says.

It's not the biggest on the block, not as big as Brooke's, but it's still giant, and the lawn, the hedges, the walkway, everything is meticulous.

"No one's home," he says. "Her dad always parks in the driveway. Can I use your phone? I'll call him, see where he is."

"You know his number by heart?"

He gets a faraway look in his eyes. "He made Cassie and me memorize it when we were younger in case we lost our phones and needed him. He said"—Brody stops and clears his throat before talking with a deeper voice—"no one would know what to do without their phones nowadays. No one remembers numbers anymore."

He's right. No one does.

"Here," I say, and hand him my phone.

He dials, and I wait and listen to his half of the conversation.

"Hi, it's Brody. How are you? I'm sure she'll be home soon. A friend and I were hoping to talk to you about that, see if maybe we can track her down. Tomorrow? Noon?" He looks over to me and raises his eyebrows.

I shake my head. "I work until two thirty," I whisper. I've been taking every single hour the department offers in hopes of making a dent in the stack of bills my mom has piling up.

"Can we make it three?" he asks. There's a pause and then, "Great, see you tomorrow."

"What now?" I ask after he hangs up and hands me my phone.

"Relax. Get some sleep. Regroup. I'm exhausted."

"Prison cot not the Four Seasons?" I ask.

"Surprisingly not," he says.

I turn the ignition on. "Where do you live?"

"I'll walk from here," Brody says. "I'm just two blocks over. Could use the air. Meet you here tomorrow?"

I nod.

"Wait, give me your phone back. I'll put in my number. Audra's, too," he says, holding his hand out, "in case something happens." I give it to him and he fills in his contact info. "I added us on Find My Friends, too."

"I don't want you tracking me," I tell him.

"Because of all the exciting places you go?"

"Because I don't need you in my business."

"It's not like I'm going to be looking at it all the time, it's only if we need it. You never know, it could help."

"Whatever," I say as he passes my phone back.

"Text us, too, so we'll have your number."

I don't know what to write, so I just type:

Hayden
Text.

"Done," I say as he gets out of the car.

"Thanks," he says. "I'll meet you here tomorrow."

"Wait," I say before he shuts the door. "Your leftovers."

"Oh, want me to trash them?" he asks, reaching down and picking up the bags on the floor.

"What? What do you mean trash them?"

"I mean," Brody says super slowly, "I walk them over to the garbage can right there and put them inside."

"Why would you do that?"

"Because that's what you do with trash."

I can't believe I have to explain this. "It's food. It's not trash."

"It's been sitting out."

"Not that long, and the air is cold."

"Okay, fine," Brody says. "I just don't do leftovers."

"That's not a thing," I tell him.

"Pretty sure it is," he assures me.

"'Trash them,'" I mimic. "What a waste. Just leave them here."

"All yours," he says, dropping the bags back down. "See you tomorrow."

"See ya."

I open the bags and consolidate them into one. There're still some macaroni-and-cheese balls, an almost full thing of onion rings, and a scattering of both types of fries. My mom will love this stuff. Fried is her favorite food group.

And maybe it will buy me a little goodwill and leverage. Brody may be done looking into Cassie's case for the day, but I'm not.

I need to grill my mom.

Obviously not as a suspect. She can't even leave the house without breaking down. But she may have some information about whether there's a link between Cassie and me. Whether these visions, these abilities, whatever you want to call them, are connected.

Maybe she knows something I don't, something that can help.

21

HAYDEN

I pat the steering wheel and sigh as I head to the cabin. "This is going to be fun."

Mom is not going to want to have a conversation about visions. She does everything she can to avoid talking about our abilities, but it's time. I need to know.

I wonder if she'll tell me anything. Mom may be an empath, but she is not a master communicator. She tends to shut down when she doesn't want to talk about something. When it came to my episodes, the only thing she ever said was to be very careful, and that I shouldn't tell a soul.

When I asked more questions, tried to figure out why these visions kept happening, why she could feel people's emotions, she would just say she didn't know. I didn't believe it then, and I don't believe it now.

I turn off the car and do my ritual mind cleanse before heading into the cabin. I even shake out my whole body, trying to get rid of the tension from the day. I need happy, open thoughts, because I need her to have them if I want to get any answers.

Mom shuts her beat-up old laptop as soon as I walk inside.

"Didn't expect you home so early," she says.

It's not early, but I don't correct her.

"Got you some food," I say, and dangle the bag before dropping it on the counter and taking off my jacket. "What are you working on?"

"Nothing. Just one of my articles."

I take a seat next to her on the couch. "About what?"

"The usual."

She's being cagey. First the whole situation with the sheriff and now making sure I don't see what's on her screen? Something is up. I want to press, but it will have to wait. I don't want her to put up a wall, not before I get to what I really want to know.

I'm not quite sure how to begin this conversation, so I just jump in. "I want to talk about our abilities."

I'm an open book, I want to share everything, I think.

"Hayden . . ." Mom shakes her head.

I have so much to share, I'm a little chatterbox, chatterbox, chatterbox. I love talking about my past.

"I know what you're trying to do," she says.

I lay my head on the back of the couch. "I wouldn't need to try to get you to open up, if you'd just talk to me."

"There's nothing to talk about. You know what I know."

I turn my head in her direction. She doesn't have to be an empath to know I think she's full of it. "Please, Mom."

She lets out a sigh.

I take that as an invitation to proceed. "Are there others like us? Others with abilities?"

"It's a big world, Hayden. Do you really think we're the only ones? We're not that special."

Her words, her tone, feel kind of like a gut punch, but I guess they are warranted. Thinking it was just her and me was pretty self-absorbed, but how was I supposed to know?

"Do you know them—the others?" I ask. "Or some of them, anyway? Are they related to us?"

There's a pause. "No."

"You're lying."

She stands up. "What do you want from me, Hayden? I'm telling you what I know."

"You're not." Now it's my turn to stand. "Why did you pick this town? Was it because of the sheriff? Does he come visit you when I'm not here?"

"What? No. I chose here because the cabin is cheap and it happens to be in an exceptional school district."

"And it has nothing to do with a psychic living here?"

She snatches up her laptop and hugs it to her chest. "Every town has a psychic, Hayden. We've seen the signs in how many windows over the years?"

"That's not what I'm talking about. You know it. I mean a real one. I mean the one in this town."

"I *don't* know a psychic in this town."

This is getting nowhere. I decide to change tactics. "My ability, my psychometry, it's nothing like what you can do. What does that mean? Was it my dad? Was he like me?"

"No," she says, her voice firm. "I can't explain why you are the way you are. I'm not a scientist, Hayden. I don't have the answers. Maybe things morphed. Maybe I have a gene that you inherited and it affects you differently than me. I don't talk about it because I don't know."

I'm not sure if it's her frustration coming out or mine, but we're both getting worked up.

"How come we never talk about your family?" I press. "*My* family?"

"Because there's nothing to say. They couldn't help me with my ability. They wanted to muzzle me, so I left."

"Muzzle?"

"Enough, Hayden, please."

She walks toward the kitchen. I follow. "What about my dad?"

"Just a guy."

"What guy?"

"Just a guy," she repeats, only this time her voice is a lot louder.

My phone dings, and I flinch. The sound catches me off guard. The only person who ever texts me is my mother, and she's standing right in front of me.

Mom breathes in so deeply it sounds like wheezing. She lets the breath out slowly. "You have a message," she says. "Why don't you answer it, because this conversation is over."

Then she turns and walks away. She doesn't even wait for me to reply or object. She's just done.

I want to scream. She gave me nothing. Like always.

I check the phone. It's a text from Audra to me and Brody:

Audra
SOS.

22

Cassie

don't know how long I've been down here. Hours? Minutes? Days?

I must've somehow fallen asleep at some point, because there's now a cup of water and a peanut butter sandwich next to me. My stomach lurches as I think about what this means. I'm a prisoner. I'm trapped. They're not planning on letting me go.

I pull at the plastic tie again. All that does is make it cut into my skin, but I keep trying.

"Hello," I scream. "Is anyone there?" My voice cracks, followed by a sob. "Please let me go."

There's no answer.

I can feel my heart racing, there's a hollow pain in my chest, and my skin feels clammy, cold. I'm going to die here.

Stop it, Cassie.

Panicking isn't going to help anything. Think. There has to be something I can do.

I take in the room. Maybe there's something I missed. A furnace. Tons of boxes. A couple of filing cabinets. An open door in the corner, showing a bathroom with a tiny window—it's the only natural light coming into the room, and it's not much. There's not a lot of artificial light either. There's just one light bulb overhead and an old lamp in the corner opposite me. It's enough to see by, but it's still on the darker side. Another door, this one closed, is at the top of a flight of wooden steps. It must lead to the rest of the house or building. Other than that, I don't see an exit.

Nothing close enough to help. I'm going to be trapped here forever.

Unless I can get this binding off.

Come on, focus.

I maneuver myself to my knees. If I get the right angle, the right force against the pipe, maybe I can break it apart.

I lift my arms, whipping them back as fast as I can. The plastic bites into my skin, which is red and raw. The top of my left wrist is bleeding. It hurts. I want to stop, but I can't. *Keep going, get them off.* I raise my arms again.

There's a crackle. It's coming from the camera, an intercom. "Stop," a voice says.

I freeze.

Someone's there.

"Hello," I say. It's the first time they've spoken to me.

"You don't have to do this," I plead. "You can set me free. It's not too late. I don't know who you are. You can just drop me somewhere, and it will be like it never happened."

They don't answer.

"You can't just leave me down here. Please."

Why won't they answer?

Do something, Cassie.

Grey's Anatomy. I saw some old episode where one of the characters said that if you tell a shooter personal details, they're less likely to kill you. I don't know if it's true or even works in real life, but I have to try something.

I look right at the camera and start talking.

"My name is Cassie Lee. I live with my dad, and if I don't get back to him, he's all alone. I'm all he has. My mom, Kelly, died giving birth to me. She was the love of his life."

I don't have many details about her. My dad doesn't talk about her much—doesn't talk much at all—but it's like his heart breaks every time he mentions her.

I force myself to give the camera a small smile. "I look like a combo of both my parents. But my smile," I say, and point to it, "it's a ringer for my mom's." That one he told me. He had no choice. He scared me when he'd freeze and just stare at me.

I let out a breath. *Keep talking, Cassie. You can do this.* "I love to paint, to draw, to write." I hear my voice shaking, but I push through. "I'm working on a graphic novel. I want to finish it. I want to see it published. I want to see people reading it."

I swallow. My throat feels dry and like there's something caught inside. I continue anyway. "I want to graduate. I want to go to college. I want to see my friends. I want to fall in love again. I want to make sure Audra and Brody and everyone know how much they mean to me. I want to tell my dad I forgive him. That I love him."

I stare at the camera, trying to make my case with my eyes.

Still no word from my captor.

"Are you still there? Hello? At least let me use the bathroom. Please."

I sink back down.

What if they don't come? Will I rot here? Will anyone ever find me? Find my body?

There's a creak by the door at the top of the steps, and my head whips in that direction. This is not like the sounds I've heard before; this is someone nearing the basement entrance.

Is someone actually coming?

For a brief moment I feel a surge of hope, but it quickly turns to fear. Someone is coming. Someone who is holding me captive. Someone who may have every intention of killing me.

The door swings open, and I hold my breath.

Who is it?

Who took me?

I see a black boot on the first step, and then they slowly come into full view. It's Darth Vader. Well, someone in a Darth Vader costume.

If the goal is to hide their identity, they're doing a good job. I can't tell if they're a man or woman—or any feature about them, really. Maybe height. They're about five-eight, I think. My vantage point skews things, and I've never really been good at guessing that stuff.

"Hello," I say.

"No talking," they say once they get to the bottom of the stairs. They're using a voice changer.

I nod to show I understand.

With a gloved hand, they reach into their cape. I'm half expecting to see a lightsaber, but what they pull out is worse.

It's a gun—and it's pointed at me.

My whole body shakes uncontrollably. This is it.

I brace myself, but they don't pull the trigger.

"I am going to let you go to the bathroom. You are not going to try anything funny," they say. "You are not going to even think about escaping. If you try, I *will* shoot you. I don't want to, but I will. Do you understand?"

My whole body is still trembling, but I manage to nod.

They take out scissors from one of the filing cabinets and come closer to me. "Move back as far as you can, arms straight out, taut."

I do as I'm told.

They keep the gun trained on me with one hand while using the other to cut off my wrist bind with the scissors. My hands come apart, and I shake them free.

My eyes go to the gun. Should I reach for it, should I grab it? If I can catch them off guard, it's possible I can get it. It's also possible I could get shot in the head. Fear keeps me from moving.

"Bathroom's over there," they say, and gesture with the gun. "Hurry up."

"My feet," I whisper, and touch the rope.

"Figure it out. I'm not untying you."

I kick off my shoe—I'm already missing the other one—and manage to stand. The ground is cold to the touch. I hop to the bathroom. It's not that far, but getting there this way, with a gun pointed at my back as I go, makes it seem like miles. What if they shoot me in the back? What if this is part of the plan?

I make it there and pull the door closed behind me, my fingers trembling. The knob is missing. There's a hole in its place, big enough to see out of—or for someone to see in if they wanted.

My eyes dart around the room. Is there something that can help me? There's not much in here. Bare minimum. Toilet, half roll of toilet paper, sink, bar of soap. Not even a towel, or a mirror, or a plunger. Any of those could have given me a chance. Shattered mirror to make a weapon. A towel to protect my hand when smashing glass. A plunger to break open the window.

My eyes fixate on the window. Is it a way out? It's small, high up, and tiny. It's not designed to open—like the ones on tall buildings to keep people from falling or jumping. As much as I want it to be an escape route, I know it's not. Even if I somehow manage to get it open, there's no way I'll be able to fit through.

"Hurry up," Vader calls. "One more minute and I'm coming in."

The sound of their voice makes my whole body convulse. I finish and open the door.

I gasp at the sight of the gun trained on me. My head feels dizzy.

"Back over there now," Vader says.

I do it, and they throw another plastic bind at me. "Put it on, arms around the pole."

I try, but my fingers are still shaking.

"Faster," they say.

All I can see is the gun.

They take a step forward.

I fumble more, but somehow get the plastic tie to latch. "It's on, it's on," I say, holding my arms out. "Don't shoot. Please."

They don't say anything. They leave without a single word. They don't even look back.

And just like that, I'm alone.

23

HaYDen

"Come on, Hayden, you have to help. I can't do this without you." Audra corners me outside the sheriff's office right before my Sunday morning shift. It's not even nine o'clock. I'm not ready to deal with Audra.

I already texted her back yesterday that this was a mistake, and I was not taking part in her scheme. Her big SOS was that her father got a call and raced out of the house. "Look, you don't know it was about Cassie," I say. "He's the sheriff. There could be a ton of reasons he had to go."

"I *know* it was about her."

"No. You don't. You *think* it was."

She grips her left wrist with her right hand and holds it so tight that her fingers pulsate. "I know my dad, I know Cassie, I know this town. I'm telling you, it was about her. We need to get a look at his files."

I lean back against Greta. This is ridiculous. I've said maybe ten words to Audra before this week, and now here she is trying to get me to go in and steal from the sheriff's office like I'm her henchman or partner in crime or something. I'm pretty sure what she's asking is a felony. Or at least a pretty serious misdemeanor. Forget getting kicked out of Lightsend High, this could land me in jail, and not some quaint one where they bring you McDonald's every morning and supply you with coffee. I want to find Cassie, too, but not like this.

"How about you try talking to your dad first?" I suggest.

"You don't think I tried?"

I shrug. Honestly, I'm not sure. The people around here are so extra, the idea that they'd jump right to breaking and entering without entertaining other ideas or worrying about the consequences, seems like a fair assessment.

"Well, I did," she says. "He wouldn't give me anything. Just said try not to worry. If it wasn't about Cassie, he would have tried to calm my nerves. He would have said this has nothing to do with her. He would've given one of his she-runs-off-this-is-just-Cassie-being-Cassie speeches. He didn't. I told him, 'I know it's about her. What did you find?'" She loosens the hold on her wrist and tightens it again. "Know what he said? That he had to go. He'd talk to me later."

"Wow," I say, "you mean the sheriff doesn't want to give his teenage daughter info on what might be an active missing persons case? Shocker."

"I don't need the sarcasm," Audra says. "This is serious."

"And so is breaking and entering," I shoot back.

"It's not so much breaking. You work here."

I throw my arms up. "Do you even hear yourself?"

"Okay, I'm sorry. It *is* a big deal. I know that, and I would do it myself, but my dad knows I'm flipping out about Cassie. He's not going to leave me alone in a place where I can get my hands on his files. *But* I can distract him long enough so that you can."

"And what's your great plan for when he catches me? Or for when Flemming or Pearson or one of the other deputies does?"

"They won't. You'll be careful, and I'll be keeping an eye out."

I don't want to admit it to her, but I am tempted. Not just because of Cassie, but maybe I can find something about what's going on between the sheriff and my mom. "It's not that easy," I tell her instead.

"For you? Come on." She's clearly trying to butter me up. "Karina Dulinkas told me you managed to break into her email account, and she claims she has one of those ridiculously complicated passwords. If you were able to do that and slip a copy of what you found into her bag without her noticing, and then manage to get her to pay you, I'd say you're up for this."

I'm surprised Karina told her. Bet she didn't go into details. But the whole Karina thing was easy. She hadn't fully logged out of the library computer. A lot of people don't and never realize it. I found a draft of a peer recommendation for Brown that she wrote for her supposed best friend, Lynsey, which she emailed to herself. It was brutal. A whole page about how her so-called BFF would be such a fun addition to the school, and it went on to describe how Lynsey got blackout drunk at a party this summer. Highlights included belting out Taylor Swift songs while tossing cheese puffs at people and leaving bright red lipstick stains on Luka, Kristoff, and a bunch of other football players' faces.

So yeah, I managed to get a copy of it into Karina's bag without her seeing, but so what? It doesn't mean I'm invisible.

"Not even close to the same thing," I tell her. Karina came and found me after reading the little note I attached. She claimed the essay was a joke. When I suggested we share it with Lynsey, all of a sudden it wasn't so funny. I took her money, but I also made her agree to either write a decent recommendation or tell Lynsey she couldn't do it.

"Karina couldn't ruin my future. Your dad can."

"How about this? Any sign of problems—you stop. Even a hint of someone coming by, you hit the brakes. And if all that fails, blame it on me. He won't be able to lock you up without also putting away his own daughter, and he'd never."

I'm not so sure about that, but even so, it doesn't solve all my problems. "And that will save my job how? You think he'll keep me here if I go through things I'm not supposed to?"

"That's why you stop at *any* sign of a problem. And I promise, if the worst-case scenario happens and you do get fired, I will make it up to you personally. I will give you my allowance. I will get a job and give you the money."

Maybe I should do it and try to get caught. Same pay, no sweeping. Too bad my conscience would never let me. I shake my head. I hate my sense of right and wrong. Sometimes it really screws me over.

"Can I get that in writing?" I ask anyway.

"If you want. I'll do anything. Look, it's my fault Cassie's gone. I knew I shouldn't have left her at the school. I didn't have a good feeling, but I listened to her. I let it go. If I had just stayed, she'd still be here."

"Or you'd both be gone."

"At least then I could help her. We could figure something out together," she says.

"You don't know that."

"What I do know," she says, her eyes wide, "is that I could have helped my best friend, and I didn't. Maybe I'm not responsible, but I feel that way. Do you have any idea what that's like?"

"Yeah, I do." Cassie's words come tumbling back to me again. *You did this. This is your fault.* "It's not you. You're not the one responsible for this," I tell her. "But I may be," I mumble.

"What?" she asks.

"Nothing," I say. It's not worth repeating. We both heard Cassie accuse me, and I'm not about to explain why she might be right. Not to Audra. "Just tell me your plan."

I can't believe I'm agreeing to this. I'll just look quickly, I tell myself. See if I spot anything about Cassie. Any mention of my mother. And Audra's right, any sign of trouble and I'll stop. It's not a big deal.

Her face breaks into a huge grin now that I've agreed to help. "It's easy. I'll keep him busy while you snoop around. The files will probably be in his office. If he's in there, I'll draw him out, so you can go in. And if he's in the pit, I'll make sure he stays there. But you should check around in there, too. Just in case."

"That's it?" I ask. "That's the whole plan?"

"What did you want? *Ocean's Eight?*"

I'm pretty sure that's a movie, but I'm not positive. I don't care enough to ask. "I wanted *something.*"

"There's this." She hands me a piece of paper with a bunch of numbers and letters scrawled on it. "I think it's my father's computer password."

"You *think* or you *know*?"

She shrugs in apology. "Think. I've watched him type it in so many times that I'm fairly certain I caught it, but it wasn't like I was trying to memorize it, so it could be wrong."

Great. This just gets better and better.

I know I am going to regret this. "Let's go," I tell her.

"Hi, George," she says to Deputy Flemming once we're inside. George. I've never heard anyone call him that before. Everyone here refers to him as Flemming. "Where's my dad?"

"Office," he tells her, and then turns to me. "Whole two minutes early."

I knew he was keeping tabs. Two minutes happens to be late for me. I make it a point to head to each shift early, in case of any unexpected holdups like Greta stalling or apparently getting cornered in the parking lot by Audra. I'm not giving them any reason to fire me. Well, until now. "Yeah," I tell him, "figure I should eat the staff donuts on my own time."

He actually snorts.

He's waiting for me to say something else, but it's hard to focus when Audra is standing close behind me, nudging me to head to the pit.

"Can you tell my dad that I'm here?" Audra asks Flemming.

Fine, while she tries to get him to come talk out here, I head over to the pit, drop my jacket and bag on an empty chair, and do a quick check of the room.

The sheriff's desk is clear. No files in his bin, and it's as neat as ever.

I grab a fritter from the box by the coffee machine—don't want to raise any suspicions with Flemming, plus I'm hungry. Mom didn't finish the leftovers, but I wanted her to have the rest, even though I'm still annoyed with her from yesterday.

I wait. Still don't see the sheriff, but after stuffing the last bite of doughy goodness in my mouth, I move into action anyway. I grab the broom and dustpan and start sweeping the hallway by his office.

A moment later he storms out. He doesn't even say hello. His lips are in a tight line, and he makes a beeline down the hall. I'm not sure if he's heading to Audra, but if he is, I don't think she's going to be able to distract him long. He is all business right now.

Shoot. He shut the office door behind him. Why did he have to do that? It would have been less conspicuous if he hadn't.

I put my hand on the doorknob. It lingers for a minute as I debate whether I'm really going through with this. Part of me thinks I'll regret it, but the other part thinks Audra is right. This is about Cassie. And I want to know what's going on, too. I open the door, sweeping as I move closer to his desk. If anyone comes by, that'll be my cover. Just cleaning. They may not buy it, but they can't really prove that it's not true.

Unlike the sheriff's desk in the pit, this one is a mess of papers. Nothing sitting out catches my eye. Nothing that screams *this is what you're looking for*. I glance to my left at the door. Coast is clear, but that can change. I don't shut myself in, because while I'm more likely to get caught if the door's open, I'll have a harder time explaining it if it's shut.

Just do it, I urge myself. *Go through his things.*

My heartbeat quickens as I shuffle through the papers.

Come on, be here.

So far nothing. Nothing good. A retirement letter for one of the deputies. Town ordinances. Some traffic violations. No mention of Cassie. No love letters to my mom. No vision, either. I'm a little grateful for the last part. Now would not be the best time.

The desk seems a bust, but there's one thing I haven't tried. One thing I really shouldn't try. The computer. The sheriff will have my head if he thinks I hacked his password, but I didn't come this far for nothing. I move to the other side of the desk, so that I'm facing the monitor. I take another sideways look at the door and move the mouse.

The screen comes to life. I don't have to try Audra's password guess. The computer hasn't fully gone to sleep yet. Everything is right at my fingertips. The fear I was feeling before is gone; it's been replaced by a bolt of energy. Like when I get the goods on one of my classmates—it's that rush of excitement when you find out something you aren't supposed to know.

"Dad!"

It's Audra. She's far off, but I can hear her. That's her warning to me. He's coming.

I should leave, get out of there, but I don't. I'm already in.

The sheriff's screen has a lot of stuff on it. There are so many open documents. I click on them, one by one, bringing them to the forefront.

No mentions of Anastasia Jefferies and none of Cassie Lee.

Come on, don't let this be for nothing.

I click through a few more.

Yes! Touchdown. Ninth try, I see something titled "Gale Warmack—Statement and Follow Up."

The sheriff will be here any second, but I want to know what it says. Warmack told Brody she didn't have any information. Was that a lie? Or did she remember something afterward?

I decide to risk it, but clutch the broom so that I have my excuse ready just in case.

I skim the page, and that adrenaline rush I was feeling disappears.

Whoever Ms. Warmack had been on the phone with, it wasn't the credit card company. It was a scam. Someone called to find out her PIN, and possibly to keep her distracted. She was a pawn.

I hear footsteps approaching, but I force myself to take in all the details of the report.

Warmack noticed a random order on her Amazon account after the rehearsal. One-day delivery to a house on Sunset Lane near the school that belongs to John Odell, a retired Lightsend High teacher. He and his wife are snowbirds now and go to Florida six months out of the year. They left last month, and the house is empty.

"Dad, please wait," Audra calls out.

They're close. I don't stop.

The order was placed Friday night, right after Cassie was taken, and delivered last night. A deputy went to Sunset Lane to look for the package. It wasn't there.

Whatever last remnants of energy I had run cold.

The order consisted of chains, rope, ties, cement, and a shovel.

"Hayden!" the sheriff says in a voice harsher than I've ever heard him use before.

"Dad, it was me—" Audra starts.

I put up my hand and step out from behind his desk. "Stop."
This isn't the time for excuses. Not from her, and not from me.
Not with what's at stake. I don't lie about the sweeping.

Cassie is in serious danger.

It's time for the truth.

24

HaYDen

I tell the sheriff about going to Cassie's car, about finding her phone, her shoe, about the seat being pushed too far back for someone her size, and he listens without saying a word.

When I stop talking, he looks from Audra to me. I'm expecting him to ream us out, to yell about me being in his office, but his voice is calm. "I know you're both worried about your friend, but I need you to stay out of this."

"Someone has to do something," Audra says.

"We are." The sheriff grasps his ring. "We've opened an investigation."

"Why?" Audra steps closer to her father. "What made you change your mind?"

He doesn't tell her about Warmack and the Amazon purchases, and I don't volunteer the information. Not yet. There's a chance the sheriff doesn't know just how much I snooped, and I'm not about to confess.

"We have reason to believe she didn't just run off."

I can see Audra's throat tighten. "What kind of reason?"

"A reason that you don't need to worry about. I need you to go home, Audra, but if you notice anything out of the ordinary, do not get out of your car. You call me. *Anything.* Keep your eyes open, your phone on you, and the location services on at all times."

"You're freaking me out, Dad."

He pulls her in for a hug. "It will be okay. I'm just being cautious. You're my kid. We're going to find her. Now please, go home. I have work to do here."

"But—"

"Audra, please. Let me do my job."

She nods, and I follow her out, broom and dustpan in hand.

"Not so fast, Hayden," the sheriff says before I even set foot in the hallway. I should've known it was not going to be this easy.

He crosses his arms in front of him. "My office is off-limits. I know my daughter probably put you up to this, but that's not an excuse. If I catch you in here again without permission, this little arrangement of ours will end. Understood?"

"Yes."

"Good." He goes to take a seat behind his desk. He looks from the computer screen to me. Crap. It must not have gone to sleep yet; the file I looked at will still be on top. I'm busted. "You went on my computer?"

I refuse to meet his eyes and focus on the bristles of the broom instead.

I hear him suck in a deep breath. He doesn't speak, and I peek over. He's gripping his desk. "This is your last warning," he finally says. "Back to work. Now."

I don't need him to tell me twice. I book it out of there and head right for the pit.

Audra is there waiting for me. "Finally," she says. "Everything okay?"

In relation to me not getting in trouble, yes. As for Cassie . . . I lean the cleaning supplies against the wall and fill Audra in on what I saw on her dad's computer.

"No, no, no, no, no, no, no," she says on repeat, her voice trembling. "They're going to kill her."

"It doesn't mean that," I try to reassure her. "Look, she's more an asset to them alive than dead. If they know her secret, they'll want things from her. And if they don't know it, she's smart. She'll use it to her advantage."

"Maybe," Audra says. She lifts her red metal water bottle to her mouth, but her hands are so shaky that some of the liquid spills onto her hand.

"Definitely," I tell her. "She just needs to give a winning lottery number or some other tidbit that can profit them, and she's bought herself time and goodwill."

Audra nods but doesn't look relieved. She tries to put the cap back on her bottle, but her hands still aren't steady. She drops it, and I reach down to pick it up.

When I stand back up, I'm in the same room, but it's no longer the present.

"Will you please leave this alone?" Audra says, slamming the water bottle onto her father's desk. "Don't you realize what this could do?" Her voice is a harsh whisper, and she looks half-angry, half-scared.

I'm not sure who she's talking to yet. I can't tell whose eyes I'm seeing through. They're 100 percent focused on Audra. I'm pretty sure it's not the sheriff. I don't see Audra talking to her dad like that; the tone is off. The angle, too. This is someone much shorter than Audra.

"Say something," she says.

"I've already said everything I have to say."

It's Cassie.

Audra steps closer. "If you do this, I will never forgive you."

"Audra, that's not fair. He's paying him off. Even forgetting how unethical that is, this can help. I need to do this."

"No, you don't. It's my father, Cass."

Her father? What was the sheriff up to? And what did Cassie need to do? Why can't visions come with a translation kit? I have no idea what they're talking about.

"Then let's go to your dad," Cassie says.

"No," Audra tells her. "You have no proof. It was a vision. You said it yourself, they're not always right. Let it go. If you don't, you'll regret it."

I don't hear the response. The vision is over. I'm back, and Audra is staring at me, her eyes huge.

"No way. You have vis—"

"Shhh," I hiss over her, and look around to make sure no one else came into the room while I was zoned out. "No. I don't know what you're talking about. Just stop." I can feel my heartbeat quicken.

Audra stands firm, her arms crossed in front of her. "I know what visions look like. I've seen it enough with Cassie. That frozen, rigid stance, eyes far away with a deer-in-headlights look. You totally just had one."

She's right. I used to wonder what I looked like when I was having a vision, so a few years back, I set my phone up to record myself as I flipped through library books. Took two and a half weeks, but I finally caught myself having an episode. The vision felt like ten minutes, but according to my phone it had just been about thirty seconds. That tends to be the average, but there's no hard-set rule. In general, they're just long enough to screw things up. To get into a car accident, to have a teacher think I'm not paying attention, to have Audra figure out my secret. "I don't know what you're talking about," I tell her, walking away in a huff. I take a seat behind one of the desks and fiddle with the water bottle cap. I'm not the one who should be answering questions here. She should be doing the talking.

"Why didn't you say anything?" Audra asks, pulling herself up so that she's sitting on top of the desk, totally ignoring my denial. "This is good. We can use this." She sees the look on my face, and her eyebrows knit together. "You know you don't have to worry, right? I've kept Cassie's secret. I can keep yours. I won't say anything."

I don't remind her that she blabbed about Cassie to me. It won't do much good; she saw me in the midst of an episode. She knows. I just have to hope she'll keep her mouth shut. "Not a word to anyone," I tell her. "Not even Brody."

"I promise," she says, and her whole face lights up. "This can help us find Cassie." She looks sincere, like she really wants her friend back, but my vision has me questioning that.

"Look," I say, my voice low, "don't get your hopes up. My visions don't work like Cassie's. She sees the future. I see the past, but things don't just come to me. I'm not going to all of a sudden see who took her. I don't get to pick what they're about. Besides,

I only have episodes when I touch things, and even then it's not a guarantee."

"Still . . . ," she says.

"Still," I repeat, "you're right. I do sometimes get something. Like Cassie's best friend warning her to leave it alone or she'll 'regret it.'"

That sanguine look disappears from Audra's face. "Friends fight. It's no big deal."

"Usually they don't go missing afterward," I say.

She jumps off the desk. "First of all, that was months ago. Second, you don't seriously think I had anything to do with her disappearance, do you? I'm the one trying to find her."

I don't say anything.

She grasps her wrist. "I don't believe this. I love Cassie. She's like family. I want her home."

"What were you fighting about?"

"Nothing."

I stand up to help close the height gap. What is she keeping from me? "I wouldn't call your father nothing."

Audra shuts her eyes and opens them again. "This is none of your business. It has nothing to do with Cassie's disappearance."

"Fine. Then where were you when she went missing?"

"This is ridiculous."

"Are you saying you won't tell me?" I ask.

She shakes her head. "You know this. I was at my sister's dance recital at Lightsend Elementary. With my mom *and* my dad. There were a bazillion witnesses."

"Were you inside the whole time? Was there an intermission? Were you together?"

"What is this?" she asks.

"Just answer."

"Yeah, there was an intermission. I went outside for some air. Alone. But it was only like fifteen, twenty minutes."

A lot could happen in that amount of time. The elementary school and high school are only five minutes from each other by car. Close enough for someone to slip away unnoticed. Someone like the sheriff.

"Where was everyone else?" I ask.

She lets out an irritated sigh. "I wasn't keeping tabs on them. My mom was in her seat when I got back, and my dad came in maybe a half hour later. He may have missed a little of the show, but don't get any ideas. That's normal. He's the sheriff. He gets calls he has to take all the time."

I study her face, and she studies mine right back. "Did my answers meet your standards, detective? Are we done?" she asks. "Can we get back to figuring out who really did this?"

"I—"

"Audra!" the sheriff says, sticking his head into the pit, stopping me from finishing my sentence. "I thought I told you to go home. Hayden has work to do. This isn't social hour."

"I'm going," she says.

"Now," he insists.

"Fine." She turns her attention back to me. "Keep me posted," she whispers.

I nod, and I will—within reason. I don't think she took Cassie, but I do think she's hiding something for her father. Something big. Something Cassie wanted out in the open, that Audra's family didn't. And Audra may not have it in her to kidnap her best friend because of it, but would the sheriff? Did Audra say something to him, let something slip that put him on a crash course with Cassie? He definitely didn't rush to investigate when he heard she was missing. He *still* hasn't put out an Amber Alert.

Is he following protocol or trying to give himself more time to cover up something he's done?

I look from Audra to her dad.

What kind of man is he? And how much is she willing to lie for him?

What did he do that he's so ashamed of, and how far would he go to keep it a secret?

My mom flashes into my mind. Who has she gotten herself mixed up with? Would she sense if he's evil?

No, she doesn't read minds. Just emotions. And, uck, while I really don't want to think about it, if they're having an affair, what's on his mind when he comes to the cabin is probably her.

I really hope they're not together. I haven't noticed any signs of anyone else being in our home, but I don't know if it's because it hasn't happened or because Rafferty is a detective and good at covering his tracks.

I watch Audra go. I'm going to have to be careful around her. I can't risk her slipping and saying something she shouldn't around her dad. Or worse, actively covering for him if she knows he's guilty and that he did something to her best friend.

That's one less person who can help. I don't know how this happened, but somehow, the only one I know for sure is on Cassie's side is the guy I couldn't even look at without disgust days ago.

He has an airtight alibi, he was locked up in jail when she was taken, and he'll do anything to find her and bring her home.

Which means that, in some bizarre twist of fate, the only person I can trust is *Brody*.

25

HAYDEN

Brody is already there when I get to Cassie's mini-mansion. When I park Greta, he gives a slight nod in my direction, but he doesn't smile, wave, say hi, or give any sort of greeting as I walk over. Instead, he kicks his foot into the edging of the lawn. "Audra told me what you guys found. All that stuff that was bought on Warmack's card, it has to be linked to Cassie's disappearance," he says, and drives his foot into the ground again. There are clumps of grass and dirt on the road. He must have been at this for a while.

He lets out a harsh breath and shakes the mess off his shoe. "We can't freak him out," Brody says, and inhales sharply. I'm not sure if he's talking to himself or to me; his eyes are squarely on his feet.

"Okay?" he asks when I don't answer. "I don't want him to lose faith that Cassie will come home."

"Yeah," I answer. I don't want to upset Mr. Lee, either. "Maybe you can talk to him, see what he knows while I look around her room, see if I can find anything? If that's okay with him."

Brody nods. "Okay."

I'm glad he doesn't give me a hard time about it, or insist on searching with me. Audra already saw me have a vision today. I don't need an audience if I get another one.

I follow Brody up the walkway to the house and stand back while we wait for the door to open.

Mr. Lee greets Brody with a forced smile. I get the impression it's not because he doesn't like him, but because he's worried about his daughter. He doesn't seem to have gotten much sleep. His hair is disheveled, his shirt rumpled, and his eyes are tired and red. I wonder if the sheriff told him everything they found.

"Come in, come in," he says, patting Brody's shoulder. "Can I take your jackets?" he asks.

"It's okay," I say. "I'm good." I don't plan on being here too long; I can wear it.

"I know where to put mine," Brody tells him, and hangs it on a hook kitty-corner to the door. Cassie's dad nods and leads us to a table in the kitchen. The room looks like it's straight out of a magazine, but I try to keep my focus on Mr. Lee, not the marble countertops and massive fridge that I'm pretty sure actually sparkles.

"Peter," Brody says, introducing us, "this is Hayden, the one I was telling you about, the one who's really good at finding out things."

"Right, hello." He nods at me.

"Hi."

I don't know what else to say, but Mr. Lee—Peter—fills in the silence.

"Cassie's done this before," he says. "Taken off without telling me, but she always comes back. Adventurous spirit, that girl. Like her mother. She'll be all right." I get the feeling he's trying to reassure himself rather than convince us.

"Yeah, she will be. We're going to bring her home." Brody stands up. "Hey, have you eaten anything?"

Peter shakes his head.

"Let me get you something," Brody says.

"No, no, I should be the one offering, you're my guests."

Even I, someone who rarely passes up free food, would never take him up on that. Not now.

"Sit," Brody says. "Let me do this."

Then he goes and grabs a glass of orange juice, another one of water, and puts some fruit and a muffin on a plate. He definitely knows his way around here. He brings everything over to Peter. "Try to eat something. She'd want you to," Brody says. "I want you to."

Peter squeezes Brody's hand. "The sheriff's office told me not to worry when I called the other day. That it was too early to do anything or get worked up. But when I finally spoke to Phil . . . Did you know they found her car? Her phone?" he asks.

"It doesn't mean anything. She might have ditched it to take a train, didn't want to be tracked." I know Brody doesn't believe what he's saying, but it's what Cassie's father needs to hear.

"You don't think she's hurt, do you?" Peter asks. "In danger?"

"No," Brody tells him. "She's the strongest, smartest person I know. She'll be okay."

Peter nods and absently takes a bite of the muffin. Brody watches him, the concern in his eyes palpable.

I nudge Brody. I want to go upstairs, both because I can't take watching Cassie's father anymore, and because I really want to find something to help.

"Would it be okay if Hayden took a look around Cassie's room?" Brody asks. "Maybe there's something that will give a clue as to where she went."

"Yeah," he says. "That's fine."

Brody points me in the right direction. Up the stairs, second door on the left.

I get to her room and pause, my hand on the doorknob. I feel gross. The idea of snooping around Cassie's room feels wrong. It feels like an invasion.

Only I have no choice. If I want to help, this is how I have to do it.

I go inside and switch on the light. There is a *lot* of stuff in here. And a lot of pink. Walls, fluffy rug, bedspread, a giant stuffed bear sitting in a rocking chair in the corner by the door.

I pick up the bear's paw, just in case. No vision, but I do see a little gold bracelet wrapped around it. It's engraved with *Happy Valentine's Day. I love you beary much, Brody.*

Beary much? *Really?*

There's also a date etched in. Five years ago. Looks like sixth-grade Brody was a little bit of a dork. Possibly even semi-adorkable. What happened to *that* Brody? I don't like it, but I have to consider that maybe he's still there, and I just haven't had a chance to see it.

Whatever. He trashed a store for the fun of it, I remind myself. My instincts couldn't have been too off. I shake my head. Why does it matter? I need to focus. This is about Cassie. Finding her.

I don't know where to start. She has so many things. You can fit all my possessions in Greta's trunk and still have space left over. This is overwhelming, but I don't know how much time I have before Cassie's dad or Brody start wondering what's taking me so long, so I just have to get to it.

I start running my fingers over everything, hoping I strike lightning.

I open the closet and rummage through the clothes. I've had luck—if you can call it that—with clothing in the past. Several items I picked up at the thrift store sparked episodes. But despite Cassie's massive wardrobe, nothing hanging up in the closet or folded neatly in her drawers shows me anything other than that she has enough clothes to wear a different outfit every day of the year.

I move over to the floor-to-ceiling bookshelves. They take up most of a giant wall. Cassie could open up her own mini-store with her stock. She has more YA books than the whole library at my last school. I'd borrowed every one of them. Twice. I run my hands over the spines. No visions. A few pangs of jealousy, though.

Why can't my visions come on command? That would make life so much easier. I pick up the little collectible figures in front of the books. I can't make out who most of them are supposed to be, probably some TV show characters. But they don't trigger anything, either.

Neither do her other knickknacks, or the purses hanging behind her door, or the gazillion pillows on her bed, or her shoes, or her easel, or the tubes of paint and cups of brushes in front it, or the bedside drawer filled with pens, colored pencils, a typed English essay, a mock-up of the *Grease* program, a framed photo of Cassie and Brody with a giant cotton candy, and a couple of sketchbooks. I flip through the pages of those. The first is all renderings of the sets for the musical. The second has most of the pages ripped out. The remaining ones are filled with drawings. A cliff. A waterfall that looks like the one close to the cabin. The moon. Stars. Mostly outdoorsy stuff. Until the second-to-last page.

There are words there. Sentences. Fragments. It's chicken scratch written haphazardly on the page. But I'm able to decipher some of the lines. One in particular jumps out. It says: *Talk to Kristoff*, and it's circled. Okay. That's something. I guess I need to have another chat with Kristoff. My very first Lightsend High Robin Hood target. I'm sure he'll love hearing from me again.

But Kristoff's name isn't the only thing written on the page. Another line says: *Others like me?* A different one has: *What does he know?* Then there's a . . . name? A company? A something? *Scottley.* It's underlined. Twice.

Is that the he? Or is the *he* Cassie's dad? Is Peter keeping things hidden the way my mom is? I rip the page out and put it in my pocket. Maybe it can help me figure out my visions.

A wave of guilt washes over me. I'm here to help find Cassie, not solve my own issues.

I have to focus on getting a vision.

I pick up the wastebasket. It's not the first time I've looked through trash, but it's still not my favorite activity.

There's nothing of help. Just a bunch of tissues, a Sour Patch Kids wrapper, a tag from a sweater: $180. I toss it back in disgust.

Don't judge, don't judge, don't judge. She's missing. And maybe if I had the money, I wouldn't think twice about buying absurdly expensive things, either. Although probably not. It's such a waste. *Come on, Hayden, back to the task at hand.*

Where are these visions when I need one?

Did the one at the station zap me of my juice?

"Come on, give me something."

I'm so frustrated, I'm talking to myself as I go over to her desk. There are no drawers, nothing to go through. I open the laptop, no psychic episode, and no access to what's inside it, either. It asks for a password. One I don't have, and honestly, that's okay with me. The computer can be a Brody job. I'm already going through Cassie's belongings. He can go through her documents.

Nothing on her desk sets off a vision. I look at the vanity mirror. Cassie has twinkly lights hanging up over it with little pictures dangling off them. There's a bunch of her and Audra, her and Brody, one of her and her dad, and a slew of randos from school.

I touch them all and it's nothing. Nothing. Nothing. And more nothing.

Although something does seem off about the whole setup.

I take a step back. It's the spacing. The pictures are all evenly spread apart, but there's a gap over by the right. One's missing. I check the desk, the floor. I don't see anything. Then I pull back the chair, and there it is.

The edges are worn; it's clearly been held a lot. It shows a guy giving a woman a piggyback ride. Her arms are wrapped around his neck, and her frizzy blond curls are in his face, and she's caught in mid-laugh.

Part of the man's head is covered, but I recognize him. It's Cassie's dad. But not the Cassie's dad of today, with the short hair and creased forehead. This Peter is much younger. He has long black hair pulled into a bun. His biceps bulge out of his T-shirt.

But the biggest difference is the look on his face. It's light, it's joyful, it's happy. The woman must have been his wife, Cassie's mother. I pick it up for a closer look.

Finally, it happens.

I'm still in Cassie's room. Still in front of the vanity. Still holding the picture. But there are slight differences. I'm sitting in the chair instead of standing, and out of the corner of my eye, I can make out Peter in the mirror. He looks even more upset than when he opened the door for Brody and me this morning.

"I let you down," he says to the photo. "I let you both down. Kell—I should have been a better dad. I will be a better dad. Just let her be safe. Let her have run away and come home to me. I'll fix things. I will, I promise. It's my fault she takes off. It's my fault she doesn't have the answers she wants. It's just, when I look at her, I get so . . ."

He puts the picture on the desk and rubs his hands over his face. "You know," he continues, "it's not even the big things. I'm used to those now. It's the tiny similarities. The way her left eyebrow goes up when she's in deep concentration. The way her nose scrunches if she eats something that has cilantro. The six sneezes every single time. All of it makes me see you. Makes me miss you all over again. And I love you, Kell, but I am still so mad at you. You knew. You knew you were going to die if you had her. You saw it, but you didn't care. You wouldn't listen. You left me. You left us."

He closes his eyes and tilts his head back, a tear running diagonally down his face.

"But it's not her fault," he continues. "I know that. I've always known that. And I try to be strong, but I'll try harder." He opens

his eyes and picks up the picture again. "You were right, you know. She is special. She is amazing. She will do big things. As long as she is okay. Please be okay. Please just have run away. I spoke to Phil, and he said—" More tears slip down his face. "I can't lose her, too. I'll make it up to her. She wants to know about our families, her heritage? I'll tell her, I'll tell her whatever she wants. I'll make up with my parents. I'll let her get to know them. I know you wanted that. I'll be a better dad. I'll go back to therapy. I'll find someone to help. I know you told me I'd need it. It was just easier not to think about it, but I'll do it. As long as she comes back to me. As long as I have a chance."

He stands up, and the picture drops onto the seat.

Oh my god. Cassie's mom had visions, and Peter knows about them. Whoa. This is big and a lot to absorb. I didn't learn anything that will help me find Cassie, but it does help me understand her better—and her father.

I'm not sure there's anything more I can do in here. I take another look around the room just in case. I don't see anything that tells me who took her, and I'm not going to get another vision. I already had two, and it's not even five o'clock. The chances of a third are unlikely.

I look under Cassie's bed and any last nooks to be safe, but when I come up empty, I head back downstairs. Peter and Brody are still sitting at the table.

"Anything?" Peter asks as I take the chair next to Brody.

I shake my head. "But is it okay if I ask you a few questions?"

"Of course," he says.

I'm not quite sure how to bring up what I saw. "Can you tell me more about the rest of Cassie's—and your—family?"

"It's just me and her. Been that way forever."

I bite my lip. If he's not going to be forthcoming, I'll just have to dive in. "She's run off before. Was it to find some of your family?" Brody had said Cassie was looking for answers about her visions—that it's why she took off in the past. If I had any clues about who my relatives were, that's where I'd start.

Peter doesn't answer at first. He looks so tired. "I'm fairly estranged from my family, we rarely have any contact," he says, rubbing his temples. "Cassie was curious, of course. But she's never been to see them. Every time she's disappeared, I've reached out to my parents, despite the hostilities, to see if that's where she went. She didn't. She's not there."

"What about her mom's side. Did she ever go there?"

"No. Cassie's maternal grandparents died when she was young, and my wife was an only child."

"Can you tell us more about your family? Your wife's too?" I ask. I realize I'm pushing it, but his wife was a psychic and his daughter inherited her powers. Maybe he knows a lot more about the supernatural than he's letting on.

He hesitates again. "Not much to tell. They thought we were too young to get married, so we took off. If they'd supported us, maybe we'd still be in California . . . maybe everyone would be . . . ." His voice trails off.

"Is that where everyone's from?" I ask.

He nods. "Suburbs of LA."

"That's it? Not from anywhere more specific?"

He sits up stiffly. "They were all born there. But I'm Korean, and her mother was part German, part English, if that's what you're getting at."

Brody is staring at me like *what is wrong with you*, and I feel my cheeks burn. "No, that's not what I mean." I don't care if Cassie is one-fourth British or whatever. I want to know if she is one-fourth lost island of Atlantis, one-fourth mermaid, one-fourth genie. Something that will explain how she and her mom got their visions, how *I* got *mine*. Like maybe they were part of some mystic cult, or lived over the jaws of Hell, anything that can give me answers or a good lead.

Both Peter and Brody are still looking at me, so I spit it out. "I know Cassie sees things. And that her mom did, too, and that you know about it. She was looking for answers, and I guess I'm just curious if you have them."

Peter's eyes go wide. "She told you that?"

"Yeah," I lie.

He sucks in some more air. "I didn't know she knew. Yeah, her mom saw things, but it was just a part of her. I don't know how it came about, how she got it. It was just there. And I didn't talk about it with Cassie, because I was hoping she would ignore it. Think of it like a dream that meant nothing. Those visions just bring trouble."

Brody stands up. "Maybe we should get going," he says, sensing Peter's agitation.

"Just one last question," I say. "Do you know a Scottley?"

"Who?" Peter asks.

"Scottley."

"No." He shakes his head. "Lee is a very common last name. We don't all know each other."

"Right, sorry." He thinks I said Scott Lee. Not Scottley. I don't correct him, even though it makes me look like an ass. I don't want to explain what I found. "Just someone from my old town," I say so that Brody doesn't ask any questions, either. I'm not ready to tell him why I have an express interest in Cassie's quest to find out about her visions.

We say our goodbyes, and Brody gets his jacket and makes Peter promise to call him if he needs anything.

"I've never seen him like that," Brody says once we're out of earshot. "The sheriff told him everything we know. Please tell me you found something in her room."

"Possibly," I say. "There was a piece of paper that said 'Talk to Kristoff.'"

Brody runs his hand through his hair, pushing back the piece that's fallen into his eye. "Kristoff? What would she want with him?"

"No idea. Should we go find out?"

He shakes his head. "Better off catching him at school," he says. "Less threatening. We want him to talk to you, not clam up."

"Okay."

"Maybe we should just go back to Warmack," he says. "There's rehearsal today. See if the deputies missed anything or if she can think of something else."

"Yeah, you should probably do that one alone. She won't talk with me there. Never liked me, and now that she thinks I tried to steal her phone . . ." I let my voice trail off.

Brody nods. "Good point. Let's touch base later if we find anything?"

I nod.

We say goodbye, and I watch him as he heads home to get his car and go. What am I doing? I shake my head. Why am I staring after Brody?

Okay, I'm not thinking clearly. I go over to Greta, who is in a friendly mood today and lets me right in.

I need to go back to the cabin and regroup. I turn on the engine and listen to the low roar.

Kristoff, Scottley, Cassie's mother having visions . . . What does it all mean? And does it bring me any closer to finding Cassie?

26

HaYDen

My mom is in her bedroom when I get back to the cabin after my visit to the Lees'. When I peek inside, she is sleeping, or pretending to anyway. I do a quick sweep of the place. Nothing seems out of place, no signs of a guest, no lingering smell of the sheriff's cologne. If he was here, he did a good job hiding it.

I take the laptop from Mom's end table. I can't just sit here and do nothing while I wait to hear from Brody, not with Cassie still missing. Who knows what she's going through? Every minute could be the difference between finding her and losing her forever.

I plop down on my bed and start a Google search on the sheriff. I wind up down a rabbit hole on everything Phillip Rafferty. If he is dirty, no one is writing about it online, not that I can find. They're just praising the stunning couple of Phillip Rafferty and Delaney Lamont at random events and red carpets, talking about him being the husband of a rising star, and the many accolades he's received as sheriff. There has to be more. No one is this squeaky clean. Everyone has a skeleton somewhere, and I saw it with my own eyes. Sheriff Rafferty has a big one.

I need to talk to someone who knows this town. Someone who will speak with me. Someone who may have the gossip that's not at my fingertips. Audra is clearly out. I don't want to ask Brody—he could mention something to Audra.

I scroll through my list of contacts. It's surprisingly long for a girl with no friends. Not that any of them, other than my mother and Brody, gave their info to me willingly. People don't tend to give their numbers to their extortionist. They're funny like that.

I pause when I hit the *G*'s.

This could work. Fiona Gavini.

"Okay, Fiona," I say to the phone. "Time for you to pay up on that little IOU."

I dial her, and just when I think it's going to go to voice mail, she picks up.

"Hello?" Fiona's voice is filled with skepticism. It's like she forgot phones can actually be used to talk to people.

Well, if she's wary now, just wait until she finds out who's on the other end.

"Guess who?" I say in a singsong trill. "Bet you didn't expect this call. Or maybe you did. It was just a matter of time, right?"

I don't know why I'm toying with her. I need her help—but some habits are hard to break, and the Lightsend crowd just brings it out in me.

"Hayden," she says. Her voice is devoid of expression.

"Don't worry," I relent, my conscience getting to me. "I'm not calling to blackmail you. I'm just taking you up on your offer."

"Huh?"

How quickly they forget.

"You said you owe me one. I'm cashing in."

"Oh. Right." After a pause, Fiona asks, "What do you want?"

"It's easy. I just need info."

"What kind of info?" she asks.

"What do you know about the sheriff?"

"Audra's dad?"

"Yes," I say.

"I don't know. He'd buy the good candy when we had sleepovers at her house when we were little, didn't make us go to bed—well, when he was there anyway. He seemed to be out a lot."

"Where was he?" I ask.

Fiona tuts into the phone. "You think I paid attention to what Audra's father was up to? I was ten, Hayden."

"I need you to think harder then. Anything on him? Anything weird, unusual? Anything Audra said that sounded off? If you give me something useful, we're even. No more owing me one, no more worrying that I'll show up out of nowhere asking who knows what."

There's no reply, but I hear her breathing.

"Fiona?"

"What?" she asks, and I can't restrain the giant eye roll I give the phone.

"Anything?"

"I'm thinking," she says. "What do you want this for anyway? Are you trying to blackmail him, too?"

Of course that's what she thinks. Not that I can blame her. "I'm the one asking the questions here. Do you have anything or not?"

"Nothing too exciting."

"Tell me anyway."

"Fine. He used to be super close with Cassie's mom. They were best friends or something before she died. Cassie and Audra practically grew up like sisters because of it. I'm not sure how tight he and Mr. Lee are, but with Cassie's mom being gone, the sheriff always had a soft spot for Cassie."

This has my interest. "How soft?"

"I don't know. Always includes her in everything they do, watches out for her."

Yeah, watches out for her so well that she got kidnapped, and he didn't even go looking. "In what ways?" I ask.

"The first time she went missing, it was freshman year, the town practically went into lockdown. APBs, Amber Alerts, Delaney—and all the stations really—reporting it on the news, checkpoints, interrogating everyone at school. When Cassie showed up a few days later, hopping off a Greyhound bus like it was no big deal, people were pissed."

"Where'd she go?"

"She said she wanted to get away, that she bought the first ticket out of there."

"What did the sheriff say?" I ask.

"I don't know. It all blew over, but when Cassie took off the second time about six months later, things definitely weren't as hyped up. Still a search party, but the third time she did it, there wasn't even that. Although the sheriff did come by asking us a million questions, but I think it was more unofficial. After that, even he stopped doing it. Everyone knew Cassie would come back when she was ready."

"Him and Cassie's mom," I say, circling back. "They were just friends?"

"I guess. I don't know. I heard Cassie whispering something to

Audra last year at lunch about Audra's dad knowing more about Cassie's mom than he let on. That he was hiding things."

I lean forward on my bed. "Like what?"

"They stopped talking when they saw me listening," she says.

Could Mr. Lee have gotten it wrong? Was it childbirth that took his wife—or did it have something to do with the sheriff?

"What else?" I ask her.

"I don't have anything else. Are we done? Even?"

"Yeah," I say, "just one more question. Anything going on between Kristoff and Cassie?"

She laughs into the phone. "You're kidding, right? I mean, they were in classes together and cordial and everything, but they weren't friends, and she certainly wouldn't be with someone like that. King Douche. Or at least in the running."

"She went out with Brody," I say.

"Yeah, so?"

"So, it's not like she doesn't have a bad track record," I say extra slowly. I should not have to spell this out.

"Nah, Brody isn't like that. He's one of the good ones. Total catch."

"Okay," I say. It's not worth arguing.

"Are we done?" she asks again.

"Yeah."

"Good."

She doesn't say goodbye, she just hangs up. I toss my phone down on the bed. She's given me a lot to think about. What kind of tie does the sheriff have with Cassie's mother? Is it linked to what happened to Cassie now? Like mother, like daughter?

I'm jarred from my thoughts by my phone. It's blaring.

I pick it up, and my eyes bulge at the screen.

It's an Amber Alert. For Cassie. The sheriff's office is finally taking this seriously.

27

cassie

t's quiet. My breathing, the hiss of the furnace, the creaks of someone walking above are the only things I hear.

I rest my head back against the wall and close my eyes.

A hand is over my mouth. A gun in my face. A knife at my neck.

Not visions, memories. My whole body tenses. The images flash through my mind, and I jolt back up, my breathing fast.

I rock myself back and forth, trying to forget what I saw, to picture something nice, comforting.

Audra.

I try to concentrate on her face, on the little details. But all I can think about is her telling me to come to the recital. I should have gone.

The basement door slams open, and I jump.

My captor is back.

There's nowhere to move, but I find my whole body pushing back against the wall.

I watch and wait.

My heart thumps faster and faster as they come down the wooden steps and approach me.

It's a different person than before. So there are two of them. Two people holding me captive. At least.

This one is wearing a tiger mask—like something you'd see at a theme park or school rally or basketball game. We have a lion at Lightsend. Do any of the surrounding towns have a tiger mascot? I don't know. I don't go to that many games, and when I do, that's not something I pay attention to.

I move to get up.

"Sit," I'm told.

It's a man's voice. Low and rough, and it doesn't sound fake. Do I know it? Do I know him?

He's tall, broad, but I can't tell.

My focus goes to the huge box he's carrying. He drops it in front of me, letting out a groan as he does. The package lands with a thud.

"Please," I say, my voice trembling. "Let me go. I'm no good to you here. Is it money you want? I can get you money. Just let me go home. You can't keep me locked up forever."

He doesn't say anything.

He pulls out a knife and stabs it into the box, turning in my direction as he does it. He lets out a laugh as I gasp.

My blood goes cold. Is he enjoying this? How sick is this man? Who am I dealing with? What does this mean for me?

He pulls the knife back, slicing open the top of the box.

My eyes widen as I see what's inside.

A shovel, a bag of cement, chains, all sorts of binding items.

I can't look away. I can't move. I'm frozen, fear permeating my veins.

Maybe he *doesn't* plan to keep me here forever, but from the looks of that box, he doesn't plan to let me go, either.

28

HAYDEN

With the news of Cassie's disappearance out, the whole school is buzzing first thing in the morning.

"Okay, everyone straight to the auditorium," Mr. Thadwell calls out, but most people ignore him. I'm not sure they even hear him. There are so many conversations going on at once, the principal's voice mingles into the commotion.

I still haven't laid eyes on Kristoff, but I'm sure he's here somewhere.

"Can I get some help here?" Thadwell says, turning to a few of the faculty standing nearby.

His assistant, Ms. Quill, lifts her shoulders like, what is she supposed to do? But the two gym teachers step in. Coach Bates ushers a small cluster of girls in the right direction, while Coach Hill makes one of those loud whistles with two fingers in his mouth. "Auditorium, now," he growls.

It works. Everyone starts migrating there, myself included.

I barely step foot inside when Brody and Audra rush me. "What is with you ignoring texts?" Audra asks.

"I wrote back."

She glares at me. I guess she didn't like the I-want-to-know-what-Cassie-had-on-your-dad response.

"I wanted to talk about the Amber Alert," she says, "and you went dark."

"You don't answer my questions, I don't answer yours."

"What's this about?" Brody asks.

Audra shakes her head. "What I told you about. Hayden has some convoluted idea that me and my dad are involved in Cassie's disappearance."

Well, not so much her . . . but she's summed it up fairly well.

"Oh," Brody says.

"Oh?" I repeat. "That's it?"

He shrugs, like what do I want him to do about it? The same response Ms. Quill gave Thadwell. No wonder the principal is always so frustrated. When that's the type of support you get from the person who's supposed to be helping you, it's tiring. And I know I'm not going to get any assistance from Brody on the Audra front. He doesn't think the Raffertys are involved. Audra is his true partner in this whole search. He won't take any accusations that involve her seriously.

"Anyway," I say. "How'd you do with Warmack?"

He raises an eyebrow but doesn't question me on changing the subject. Probably prefers it.

"If you'd answered my texts, you'd know already," Audra says, clearly still as annoyed with me as I am with her. "Have you seen this?" She takes out her phone and plays a clip of her mother reporting on Cassie's disappearance. I find myself transfixed. Her mom is mesmerizing.

"Yeah, yeah," Audra says, shutting the video. "She's great. Dynamic. Perfect. You don't know the half of it. You should see her in person. But that's not the point. The point is, this is getting real attention. This is good."

"If it leads to anything," I say. The more help the better, but I'm not counting on some news piece to bring Cassie home.

"That's why we're not letting up," Brody says.

"Yeah," Audra agrees. "We're definitely keeping at it. Whatever it takes."

"You mean like telling me what the deal was with your fight with Cassie?" I shoot back at her.

"This again?" She squeezes her wrist and looks at Brody. "See?! Are you hearing this? She thinks I had something to do with my best friend going missing."

"You're not exactly clearing your name," I tell her.

"Come on," Brody says, rubbing the back of his neck. "The two of you fighting isn't going to help find Cassie." He shakes his head at me. "And really? Obviously Audra didn't take her. People get into arguments sometimes. Look what's happening right now."

I can't believe Brody is trying to be some sort of voice of reason. "Fine, whatever," I say. It's not like I can tell Brody it's not as clear-cut as it looks—that I had a vision proving Audra isn't as innocent as she's claiming. "Don't tell me your secret. Happy?" I say to Audra. "Now did Warmack help or not?" I'm assuming not. Brody said he'd be in touch if he learned anything, and I didn't get any texts from him last night—just Audra.

Brody takes this one. "No. Nothing we didn't already know. She was pretty upset about the whole thing. Doesn't look like she's involved."

"She runs the musical," I remind him. "Means she's into acting. I wouldn't write her off yet."

"No, we can't write *anyone* off, can we?" Audra says, irritation spiking her words. Clearly, I'm not the only one who hasn't dropped this.

I want to snap back that I wasn't the one caught threatening a missing girl over something my father did, but I bite my tongue.

Brody is right. While those words feel wrong, they're true. Making an enemy of Audra isn't going to help me *or* Cassie. If Audra and her dad are innocent, then great. But if either of them is guilty or involved in any way, keeping her close is smarter than alienating her.

Just then a piercing sound fills the room. Feedback from a microphone.

"Sorry about that," Mr. Thadwell says, tapping the mic in front of him. "Testing. Testing. Here we go. If everyone can get seated. We're about to start."

"Over here." I spot Kristoff near the back and head to the row behind him. This way I'll be able to hear if he says anything during the assembly, and I'll be in a good position to corner him afterward. Audra and Brody follow me, each taking a seat next to me, sandwiching me in.

Once everyone quiets down, Mr. Thadwell clears his throat. "As most of you've heard by now, Cassie Lee is missing. The sheriff's office believes she was taken. If you have any information pertaining to her disappearance, please come forward to the office and let us know at once. We all want her back safe. Now, I know how hard and scary this news is, but I want you to know we are here for you. Ms. Drake"—he pauses to look over to his right, where the guidance counselor is standing by the wall—"will be available for appointments all day. Please take this opportunity to see her and talk about whatever you need. Gretch—I mean, Ms. Quill—will have a sign-up sheet in the office. We've added security around the school. So don't worry if you see deputies roaming around. We want to make sure you are all safe. If you see anything out of the ordinary, please report it immediately. We've sent emails to your parents, so they're aware of the steps we are taking. And of course, if any of you have any questions or concerns, you can come talk to me at any time."

When he's done speaking, Ms. Drake gets up there and talks about the importance of sharing our feelings. I tune her out and instead take stock of the people around me. Some faces look worried, others are checked out, and still others are whispering, joking, laughing. Kristoff is silent, but Brooke and Ollie Easton aren't. Their heads are almost touching, and Brooke has a smile on her face. I'd call it an evil one, but it's how she always looks, so I have no basis for comparison.

I lean to my right and nudge Audra. "Are they dating now?" I jut my chin toward Brooke and Ollie.

"Who can keep track?" she whispers back. "I think so. She dumped Kristoff after the game." Audra doesn't need to explain. Everyone knows what "the game" is—the infamous one where someone put laxatives in Kristoff's shake, and he crapped in his pants on the field. "She was hanging out with Luka after that, but I don't know. Guess she's on to the next stooge. Again."

I've heard enough. I know way too much about Brooke's dating life already.

After the guidance counselor is done, Flemming takes the mic.

I hadn't noticed him; maybe he was circling, checking the area for anything off. He talks about the added security. At one point he catches my eye and gives me a slight nod. I'm so caught off guard that he's actually acknowledging me outside the office, I don't return it.

When he's done, Mr. Thadwell ends the assembly, and everyone gets up and begins to file out.

Kristoff slaps Luka on the back. "Yo, if I can get out of first period again, I hope more people go missing." Then he does his awful hyena laugh, all squealy and high-pitched.

"Right? Can I put a request in for next Thursday?" Luka asks. He talks like a low-key surfer dude, but it's an act. A good one, but an act. "I have that presentation in Kaplan's class I'd kill to get out of."

"Really?" I say, and they both turn to look at me. "Cassie is missing, and that's your reaction? Hooray, you get out of class? You'd kill, huh? Maybe I should find the deputy. Let him know. Would you kidnap someone, too?"

"Whoa, relax." Luka holds up his hands. "It's a joke, don't come blackmailing me over it."

"Let's get out of here," Kristoff says. "Nice company you're keeping," he adds to Brody as he tries to make his way to the exit.

"Not so fast," I say, following him. "What do you know about Cassie?"

He snarls at me. "Uhh, what everyone in the room knows. Were you not paying attention?"

"I'm not asking about everyone in the room, I'm asking about *you*."

"And you know what I think about that?" He holds up both

of his middle fingers and backs away from me while moving his raised fingers in all different directions like he's conducting a song.

I'm about to lunge at him, but Brody holds me back.

"We'll try him later. You're not going to get anything from him now."

Kristoff's irritating laugh permeates the hall. Brody's right. I let Kristoff go, but I'm not happy about it.

"Asshole," I say, and glare in the direction Kristoff walked off in.

I turn my annoyance on Brody. "I can't believe you are friends with them."

"I'm friends with everyone," he says.

"Yeah, I know. Brooke, Kristoff, all of them. Ever think maybe you shouldn't be? Do you know the kinds of things these 'friends' of yours do? How much hell they've inflicted on others? You're aware of that, right?"

Brody looks down and nods. "They're not always great." His voice is quiet, and he's now gripping his phone so tight, I think it's going to break.

"'Not always great'? They break the law, they bully people, they ran a girl out of school."

"That Leighton situation made us sick," Audra pipes up, but she's not innocent, either. It's not like she helped.

"But not sick enough to do anything," I remind her.

Audra gets quiet, too. "We tried," she finally says. "We always . . ." She stops herself. "You're right. We didn't, we don't, do enough."

"I know," I say.

They don't get it. They don't get what it's like to have everyone attack you, to be the butt of all the jokes. They wouldn't; they're the charmed ones in this town. I walk away. I don't want to hear their excuses. I just want to find Cassie.

I don't see Kristoff again until Donnelly's class. I'm waiting when he walks in beside Ollie Easton.

"Kristoff," I say, and hold my arms out like I'm welcoming him. "How nice of you to join us. I wasn't done talking to you, you know."

"You didn't get my message," he says, keeping his back to Donnelly and pointing his middle fingers at me again before sliding into his chair.

"Oh, I got it. I just have one in return, you poor little *puppy*," I say.

His eyes go wide. I don't have to say any more; he knows what I'm getting at.

"Okay," Ollie says, taking his seat next to Kristoff, "you get weirder every day. You understand that no one wants you here, right?" he asks me.

"Oh no, whatever will I do?" I say in a robotic monotone voice, before switching to my regular one. "And you get that no one was talking to you, right? This is between Kristoff and me. And he wants to talk."

Kristoff's fidgeting so much, his knees keep bumping into the bottom of the desk, making it rise off the ground. "Mr. Donnelly," he says, "can you tell Hayden to stop bothering me?"

He gives a quick hyena laugh.

Seriously? The jerk is tattling to the teacher? What is this? Second grade?

"Seat now," Donnelly tells me.

"Bell didn't ring," I say.

"I said, seat now," he repeats.

I have no choice. I move to my desk. Ollie and Kristoff elbow-bump, like getting rid of me was some huge accomplishment.

Kristoff looks my way and sneers, and I return it. God, I hate these people.

When class ends, I try to get to him, but he's faster than me. He's already booked it out and into the hall. I go and look, but I can't tell what direction he went, and there are too many people around to spot him. I don't know what's going on with him, but he's definitely acting like a person with something to hide.

29

HaYDen

I stop by the office before lunch, and Ms. Quill is going overboard on the niceties.

"Of course we can set you up with an appointment with Ms. Drake. I'm so glad you decided to come in. I wish more kids would. Let's get you signed up," she says as she shuffles through some papers on her desk before pulling out a sheet. "It's so upsetting what happened to Cassie. Were you two close?"

"Yeah." I'm not about to tell her my real motive. That I want to see if anyone has responded to Mr. Thadwell's request and reported anything about Cassie's disappearance, or if Ms. Drake has found out anything useful, or maybe touch something in her office that one of my classmates held that will give me an episode—give me something that can help.

"Good, good. Happy to hear you're making friends, staying out of trouble."

I raise my eyebrows at her.

She plays with the gold butterfly charm on her necklace, rubbing her finger over the diamond in the center. "Oh. I just mean after that whole Brooke fiasco. I hear things sitting out here," she says, leaning in, as if she's taking me into her confidence.

I bet she does. That's why I'm here. I wonder if it's anything I can use or if she'll even talk. I take her in. Looks to be in her twenties, dark circles under her eyes unsuccessfully covered by layers of caked-on concealer, bouncy blond curls pulled into a side pony. Blazer. Silk top. Pearl earrings. Dainty necklace. Full face of makeup. Tries hard. Probably eager to please—which could be useful. Put-together. Almost. One side of her collar is partially sticking up, and her mauve lipstick, the same color as her blouse, is smeared with a look I'm fairly sure is not intentional.

"Anything about Cassie?" I ask.

She shakes her head. "No, not yet. That poor girl. Such a sweetheart. Don't know why anyone would want to hurt her."

"You knew her? Did she come in here a lot?" Cassie does not seem like the type who would spend a lot of time in the office. Juniors only recently started their appointments with Ms. Drake to discuss college, and I cannot picture her getting called to the principal.

"Oh, no. It was just . . ." She leans forward again. "I shouldn't be telling you this, but Brody. Her ex. I dated his father for a bit."

Gretchen Quill and Grayson Brody II? This really is a small town. Brody never mentioned this. Not that he tells me stuff. "You dated his dad?"

"Yeah." She waves her hand like it's not a big deal, but there's something in her eyes that says it is one. "Long time ago already. Moved on. Much happier. You don't want someone born with a silver spoon. A go-getter—that's the way to go." She nods. It's like she's assuring me, but I'm pretty sure she's trying to remind herself. "Anyway," she goes on, "I would see Cassie around the house. Always so kind. Brody, on the other hand . . . If the sheriff wants to look somewhere, that's where I'd start. A temper on that one. Always watch out for the exes."

I nod to humor her suggestion. Better to have her assume I think she knows what she's talking about. Ms. Quill may not be any help today, but I may need her down the line. Access to the office is always valuable.

She looks down at her sheet. "Ms. Drake will be free the beginning of next period if you want to talk to her then."

"Spanish class I can't miss," I tell her. I don't want to go now. I need to give more people time to spill their guts. "Anything tomorrow?"

"Free most of the day. How about the start of second period?" she asks.

"Sure," I say. That should be enough time. Anyone who's going to talk to Ms. Drake is going to do it today. The ones I'm interested in, anyway. I read the guilty often like to check in on an investigation, see how people are reacting, find out whatever they can. It will be telling to see who takes Ms. Drake up on her offer.

"You got it," Ms. Quill says, and writes my name on her sheet. There are already a bunch of people signed up for appointments, including a few of the football guys. Luka, Hunter, and Chuck. But other than that, none of the names stick out or set off any bells. She then hands me two hall passes. One for now and one for my appointment.

"Nick," I hear Ms. Quill say as I step into the hall, "did Ms. Drake give you a hall pass?"

"No," he says.

Nick Kellog? He wasn't on the sign-up sheet. Was he there about Cassie? One way to find out.

He walks right past me as he exits the office, almost scurrying away.

"Nick," I call out.

He looks back in my direction, clearly seeing me, but continues down the hall without any acknowledgment.

"Hold up," I say, but he doesn't stop. He turns the corner instead.

Nice. Save a guy from imprisonment in a locker room, and he doesn't even slow down for you.

I run to catch up. "Nick!"

He jumps at the sound of my voice and finally stops moving. "What?" he asks, turning to face me.

"What were you doing in there?" I ask.

"Nothing." The way he says it, it doesn't sound like nothing. He looks around to make sure no one else is nearby. They're not. We're in a pretty empty part of the school.

"Were you there about Cassie?"

"Cassie? No. It was nothing to do with her." He shifts from side to side.

Okay, he's uncomfortable, almost squirrelly, but that's not exactly an uncommon reaction to my presence around this school. "Then what were you doing there?"

"Nothing. Just a misunderstanding. It's all cleared up, it's all fine." He's talking quickly now, waving his arm wildly to emphasize his point. "Nothing anyone needs to worry about. Especially *you*. Just reporting some bullies."

"Careful!" I reach out and stop his wrist as it comes dangerously close to my nose. My fingers wrap around his iWatch, and before I can let go, I'm somewhere else.

I'm back in the girls' locker room, but this time Nick isn't alone. Paisley Marcus, the captain of the volleyball team, is there, and so are a few others from the team.

"Here we go again," Paisley says. She has Nick cornered, her finger jabbed into his chest, and the other girls look ready to pounce on him.

The volleyball team was harassing Nick? That I didn't expect.

"You're dead," Paisley says.

"I didn't do anything."

"You didn't do anything?! I've caught you twice spying on us in here. You think getting shoved in a closet is bad, wait till you're in a jail cell."

"I wasn't spying. You can't prove it. My dad is a lawyer, you know. A good one. You'll be the ones in trouble for bullying me."

No. Nick is a perv? I saved a creep? I should have left him in the supply closet.

"Then we'll have to take care of this ourselves," Paisley says.

Nick doesn't wait around to find out what she means. He squeezes by Paisley and the others and darts out of there, ducking into the guys' locker room.

There's a sound, someone's coming. Nick stuffs himself into one of the lockers and shuts the door. It takes no time. He's clearly had practice at this. He's done this. A lot.

It's incredibly scrunched in here, but Nick's focus is on what's happening outside the locker. He's staring intently out the slits in the door. I expect Paisley to walk in, but it's not her.

It's Coach Hill. He looks around, and when he sees no one there, he takes a seat on the bench. "Yeah, I can talk. Practice is over. The team went home. We good?" he asks into his phone. "What? You're wearing what?"

Oh god, no. Am I going to have another gross teacher vision? I do not want to know about their sex lives. Donnelly was bad enough. I don't need to know this much about Coach Hill.

Nick's iWatch vibrates. He's getting a call.

He slaps the screen to silence it.

He sucks in a huge breath and holds it as the coach does another sweep of the room. He doesn't see anything, but he doesn't stick around, either.

"What was that?" Nick asks. "You just zoned out."

I don't owe him an explanation. I don't owe him anything. "You creep," I say. "Tell me, Nick, where were you in such a rush to get to? Planning on going into the locker room and spying again?"

"What? No! What are you talking about? You saw what happened. They put *me* in there."

This hall is empty. Everyone's in class; it's just him and me. I move in closer and push him back into the wall, jamming my finger into his chest like Paisley did. Nick's bigger than me, but my reputation is scarier. In some ways.

"I know what you did, Nick," I say, giving him my wildest eyes. "I know you're lying, and I don't approve."

"I didn't do anything."

"Tsk, tsk, tsk," I say, and push my finger deeper into his chest. "Lying only makes it worse. Haven't you heard about me?"

"What do you want?"

"For starters, I want you never to spy on anyone again. It's gross. An invasion of privacy. And enough to land you at the sheriff's. These people may be afraid of your dad. I'm not. I will make sure you're exposed. I'll make sure every college, every future employer, every person you have a glimmer of interest in, knows your story. If you even think about doing it again, I will make you regret it." I cock my head to the side and try to look as unhinged as possible. "And I will know."

"Okay, fine. I promise."

He scoots out from in front of me and tries to leave.

"Not so fast," I say, spinning around to face him again. "You don't get off that easy."

"All right, all right. How much do you want?" he says, reaching into his pocket and pulling out a wallet. His hand is shaking.

The wad of cash he's holding is huge, and I'm tempted. Very tempted, but—and this hurts—I swat his arm away.

"I don't want your money." Lie, lie, lie, lie, lie. "I want information."

He looks confused. I am, too. Maybe I can take the money *and* the info?

Sheriff Rafferty's warning flashes into my head before I can reach out for a few bills. I don't want to lose my job, so I force myself to look away from the cash.

"What were you doing in the office?"

"I told you, reporting some bullying."

I want to strangle him. "Who?"

He shrugs.

"Paisley?" I ask.

His eyes get wide.

"Yeah," I tell him. "I told you I know everything. You're going to go back to the office and clear her name."

"Fine," he says.

He tries to get away again, but I push him hard against the wall.

"You don't leave until I say you can go," I tell him. "What do you know about Cassie?" I ask.

"Umm. Really smart. Top of our class. Dated Brody forever. Pretty."

"No," I stop him as he rattles off random things about her. "I don't care about that. I mean about her disappearance. What do you know?"

Nick's eyes blink in rapid succession. "Friday night. Last seen at school. Any information, call the sheriff's office or Crime Stoppers."

He's obtuse. He's reciting the Amber Alert. "I mean," I say slowly, "what do *you* personally know?"

"Me? You think I had something to do with it? I wouldn't. I couldn't. I don't know anything. I never talk to Cassie, other than a hello in the hallway. We haven't had a class together since eighth grade."

"Meaning you were free to spy on her when she had gym or something."

"No." He shakes his head furiously. "I didn't. Not intentionally. I mean, she may have been there, I don't remember."

He is disgusting, but I don't think he took Cassie. Still, maybe he knows something.

"In your little extracurricular activities, did you hear anyone else talk about her?"

Nick doesn't know where to look. I've got him scared. *Good.* He deserves it.

"No, not really," he says. "Everyone likes her."

I throw my head back. Come on, this doesn't help.

"If it's intel you want," he says, his breathing forced and his speech picking up speed again, "I have so much dirt. Better than cash or turning me in. Other people have done so much worse than me. Luka was the one who put the laxatives in Kristoff's shake. Willow Snyder is cheating on Jamie Bungler. Tori Winger and Carol Dolli—"

"I know all of this, and I don't care. I want to know about Cassie."

"I don't know anything about her."

I believe him.

I take a step back.

"Does this mean I can go?" he asks.

"Go," I say, "but if you ever spy on any of the girls again, you'll wish you were still locked in that closet I found you in."

He doesn't wait to hear any more. He takes off so fast, he's out of sight before I fully comprehend all of what I just saw.

I feel my phone buzz, and I look down. I missed six messages from Brody, wondering where I am.

Stop smiling, Hayden. That is not something to smile about.

I look at the time. Still have part of the lunch period. I text him that I'm on the way to the cafeteria.

He is pacing the hall by the entrance and runs up as I approach. "Finally. There you are."

"Wow, look who's excited to see me."

"Look who's excited to find out if Kristoff said anything to you," he corrects me. "He's blown me off."

"Me too," I say, "but I'll get him to talk. He can only avoid me for so long."

"Believe me, I know. I've tried my best to steer clear of you and look what happened."

"Uh, hello," I say, "who was blowing up whose phone trying to find them?"

"You can thank Audra for that. She wants to know what happened, too, but doesn't think you'll reply to her, so she made me do it."

I take a step back. I don't know why, but I'm a little ticked that he didn't reach out to me of his own accord.

His phone buzzes. "That's Audra now."

"I don't want to deal with her. I can't take two of you at the moment." That, and I still don't trust her. I grab his phone and text Audra back from it.

Brody
Haven't found her yet.

His eyebrow skyrockets. "How do you know my passcode?"

"I'm very observant, and you are not very discreet," I explain, handing the phone back to him. I saw him jam the numbers in when we were in the car the other day.

"Good to know."

"Like you didn't already," I say.

"Hey," he says, raising his hands, "just because you seem to be taking in every little thing about me doesn't mean I'm doing the same for you, Grim."

"Please." I cross my arms. "You're watching. You have a whole frickin' notebook about me."

He laughs. "Someone's getting defensive. How about this: I pay attention," he says, his voice sounding amused. "Is that better, or did I strike some sort of nerve? An I-need-a-healthy-serving-of-Brody-in-my-life nerve?"

"Ha ha," I say, but oh my god, he did strike one. What is wrong with me? "I paid a little visit to the office," I say, changing the subject. "Had quite the conversation with Ms. Quill. She thinks you're suspect number one."

"Good thing I have an airtight alibi then." He winks at me and leans back on the wall, but the playful quality from before is gone. He sounds upset.

"Good thing," I repeat, and position myself next to him.

I don't say anything else. I wait for him.

"Let me guess," he says, "she told you she used to date my dad."

"Might have come up."

He shakes his head. "She tells everyone she can, like landing my dad was some big coup."

"She also said you had quite the temper."

"Well, when your mom is in the hospital and your father cheats on her with a woman closer to your age than his—who, by the way, he met at my teacher conference night—yeah, I'm not going to welcome her into my mother's home with open arms."

"Oh." I don't know what to say. "I'm sorry. Your mom . . . is she . . . ?"

He shakes his head. "No. She's hooked up to machines at a

long-term-care facility. Been that way for a few years now. He started with Gretchen"—he says her name with disgust—"*two* months after my mom was admitted."

I have so many questions, but none of them seem appropriate.

After a minute of neither of us saying anything, his mouth lifts into a sad, crooked smile. "Well, look at that," he says, "I figured out how to stop you cold." His eyes lighten. "Bet people in this school would pay big for that power."

"Shut up," I say.

"No, no, no, don't you see, Grim," he says, his dimple fully showing. "Not me. *You.* People don't care if I come around to say hi. I'm positively charming. You're the one that scares them."

"Positively charming?" I ask, but he takes it as an affirmation.

"I knew you'd agree," he says, and winks again.

I don't want to like the wink. It's so I'm-trying-to-be-cool-and-suave, and yet I like it anyway. And fine, it—and he—may be a little charming, but they're also really frustrating.

"Sometimes," I concede, since he did just open up to me about his parents, "on rare occasions, you can be charming. But"—because he still is Brody, and I'm not about to forget all that he's done—"that asshole quotient of yours runs pretty high."

"Me?" he laughs. "I am never an asshole."

"You tore up the market," I remind him, "threw things everywhere."

"I was an asshole *once*," he corrects himself, and damn it, he has me smiling again. "But for good reason."

I'm not sure it's "good," but he clearly has some issues with his dad that he's working out, so maybe he needed to do something like that.

213

"The rest of the time," he insists, "total sweetheart."

He cups his hands around his face and bats his eyelashes.

I snort. "I beg to differ. 'The book of Grim,' plus how many other obnoxious comments have you made to me since I got here? I've lost count. You don't fall under Mr. Nice Guy."

"Whoa, whoa, whoa," he says, shaking his head emphatically. "Let's remember who came to Lightsend, brushed off anyone who tried to welcome her, had snide comments for everyone, and then blackmailed half the school. People were afraid to even walk by you in the hallway."

"So I deserved you being an ass is what you're saying?"

"Kind of. How many times did Cassie go out of her way to be nice to you, and do you remember how you responded?"

I do. I wasn't exactly friendly. "But do you remember the death glares you'd shoot at me every time she did that? Audra, too. Maybe I would've taken Cassie up on some of her offers if you two weren't flanking her like bodyguards ready to pounce." I'm not sure that's true, but I'm not sure it's not. There was something about Cassie that was different, that made me almost want to reach out.

"I guess we—I—did do that."

"And I guess I came in guns blazing."

I lean back against the wall again, almost shoulder-to-shoulder with Brody, and take in the silence. It's not uncomfortable, it's just still.

I turn my head to him. "So we're both the asshole?" I ask.

Brody nods. "Both the asshole."

He puts out his hand. "Truce?"

I shake it. "Truce."

I guess he's not so bad. Sure, he's definitely pompous at times, but he's not malicious. I mean, he's no saint or anything, but neither am I.

"You okay there, Grim?" he asks.

I nod, but the truth is, I have no idea what to do with this cease-fire. I've hated Brody and everyone in this town for so long. I was so sure they deserved my wrath, but maybe I have been too harsh a judge on some of them, some of them like Brody.

He's still looking at me.

I don't mean to, but I look back and catch his eyes.

His gaze is so intense, I feel my cheeks get warm. Can he tell? I turn away, but that doesn't stop my whole body from buzzing.

"I'm going to go . . ." I point to the cafeteria, because I've somehow lost my ability to articulate.

I feel him watching me as I walk inside—and if I'm honest, I don't hate it.

30

HAYDEN

"Mom," I call out when I get home. "They"—I look around the cabin—"didn't need me at work. Flemming let me go early." I mumble that last part to myself after realizing she's not here, and I'm alone.

With the hunt for Cassie, the sheriff's office had too many people in and out. Apparently, I was more in the way than helpful, so they told me to go after an hour and a half.

"Where is my mother?" I say, still talking to myself, while I take off my jacket. It's not like she can go anywhere.

Maybe she took a walk down by the falls. She likes the woods and finds the sound of water soothing. She didn't leave a note, though. She always leaves a note.

I shake my head and open the fridge. She didn't expect me home for another few hours. Why would she? Not everything is a mystery, I remind myself. The contents of this fridge, for instance. Definitely no surprise there. I shut the door. Once I get my paycheck, I really need to do a grocery run. It should be a decent amount. The sheriff's office is even paying me for right now since I was scheduled, and they were the ones who asked me to leave.

At least Mom left the laptop here. She's not sitting by the waterfall in an attempt to write one of her articles.

I take a seat at the counter and power it up. Time to do a deep dive on some of my suspects. I pull the pad closer so I can take notes. When I pick up the pen, I'm no longer in my eyes, but my mom's.

"Thank you, Phillip. I can't tell you what this means to me," she says into her phone.

"It's working?" he asks.

"I think so." She twirls the pen between her fingers. "I understand. You're busy. There's a lot going on. It's okay, we don't have to meet today. I'll take a walk. Spend some time at our spot on my own."

My stomach lurches. She is having an affair with him. They have a spot. I shudder. I don't like this at all.

"Great," he says. "I'll call you when I get another minute."

"Sounds good," my mom says, and hangs up. She's sitting there doodling on the pad. Hearts, stars.

What the hell!?

She stands up and drops the pen onto the pad.

I look down at the pad. Those drawings are still there right on top. Was this today? The sheriff was slammed with the Cassie case but took the time to call my mother? Nice priorities. I feel sick.

I pull out my phone to text my mom.

Hayden
Where are you? What are you doing?

Mom
. . .

There's a long pause, and I can see her typing.

Mom
Getting air.

That long for two words?

Hayden
By yourself?!

Mom
Of course. Taking a nice long hike. Home in an hour or so.

Hayden
What spot?

Mom
Nowhere particular. See you soon.

She's never going to tell me what she's up to, even if I confront her with my vision. More denials. If I want to know, I'll have to find it out myself.

She should have taken her computer. I jump in. Nothing unusual on the desktop. I go to the calendar. With the exception of one article deadline date, it's empty. There are no new downloads or files. I check the internet search history. It's been cleared.

I try to open old tabs, but they're gone, too. My mom did her due diligence.

There has to be something.

I look on the finder tree. There's a folder I never noticed before. It's called AJ, and it's locked.

AJ?

My mom's initials.

I try to get in. I put in a few passwords. 1, 2, 3, 4. My name, my birthday, her birthday. None of them work.

What is she hiding?

The folder was last updated yesterday. How long has it been on here? What's with all the secrecy? She never locked anything before. It can't be bills or documents or taxes—I take the lead on dealing with all that. This is something else. Something different.

I call her.

It rings only once before she picks up. "Are you okay?" she asks.

"Yeah," I say.

"What's wrong? I told you I'm on a hike."

"Doesn't sound like it." No heavy breathing, no wind blowing or trees rustling, no spotty reception.

"Because I stopped to take your call. What's going on? Are you sure you're all right?"

"Yes. I'm just trying to do the bills. And the spreadsheet folder is locked. What's the password?"

"There's no password."

"Yeah," I say. "The AJ folder."

There's a long pause. "If you have a question, just ask it, Hayden. You know that's not where we keep the bills."

"Fine. What's in that folder?"

"This could have waited until I got home. It's where I'm keeping my articles. I don't want you to accidentally erase one. I work too hard on them for too little money."

Like I would ever.

"Who are you with?" I ask.

"Bambi and Thumper," she replies. "What is this?"

"I saw you, Mom. I had a vision of you talking to the sheriff. How often do you two get together? How often does he come here? You know he's married, right? And he might have something to do with Cassie's disappearance. You can't trust him."

"I think you're going overboard here. First, I am not having an affair with the sheriff, Hayden. Have I talked to him? Yes. He's a nice man, and he called to check on me after I collapsed at the school."

"I heard you tell him you were going to 'our spot.' 'Our' as in yours and his!"

"I don't know what to tell you. Maybe you saw one of my dreams? It gets lonely being locked away here. Maybe my subconscious locked onto a friendly face. We can talk about this later, okay? It's going to get dark soon, and I want to make sure I'm back on the trail."

"Okay."

We say our goodbyes, but I know she won't talk about this later. She didn't give me a straight answer now, and she never will. What I saw was not a part of a dream. It happened, but I'm never going to get her to admit it.

I try the folder a few more times. No luck.

So frustrating.

I need to do something else. I try another search of the sheriff. Nothing new.

I try one of Kristoff. Most everything, other than the social media that I already scoured, is about his football career. I check the school's athletic schedule and smile. That's it.

I shut the laptop.

I need to get out of here. I need to do something productive. I take out my phone again and punch up Brody's name.

Hayden

Want to go to a football practice?

31

CaSsie

'm curled up in a ball in the corner in my new chains. *Chains.* I squeeze my eyes shut. Captor 2, the tiger, set up some sort of contraption. He put me in handcuffs and attached them to a chain that he bolted to the wall. He then added a second chain around my waist for extra restraint. The two give me enough leeway to walk to the bathroom, but not enough to reach the window or the cabinets or anything else that might give me a chance of escape.

Will anyone ever find me down here? Is this my forever? I start to hyperventilate, feeling a wave of terror and a sense of foreboding crash through me. But panicking won't get me anywhere. It just makes things worse. I need to think. I need to come up with something, anything that can help me.

Why haven't I had any visions yet?

Because there's no future for me.

My stomach turns.

I said no panicking.

Okay. I got this. I can figure out something. Maybe I can *will* a vision. I've done it before. A couple of times. But how would it even help?

An inkling of an idea forms. Maybe I don't need to actually have one for it to serve me.

I stand up and wave at the cameras with both arms. "Hey, hello. I need to talk to you. I can help you. I know things. Things other people don't. If you promise to let me go, I'll show you."

I don't know if they heard me. I don't know if they're watching. I think they're home. At least one of them. I hear walking above me.

"Come on," I cry. "You must have picked me for a reason. Ransom? Money? Information? I can help you with all of it. Please. I just want to see my dad and my friends again."

A few minutes go by. Just when I think it's hopeless, the door creaks open.

Vader is back.

I perch myself on my knees.

"Well," they say, "you have my attention."

"Let me go, and I can get you whatever you want."

"And just how do you plan to do that?"

I swallow. "I'm good at finding things. Hacking. Tell me what you need, I'll get it." I don't admit that I have visions. I prefer them to think I can dig up intel or pay, lie, cheat, steal to get it. Not that I can see the future, that I one day may see their identities. "Want to know something about someone in Lightsend, just give me a few days, access to a computer, and it's yours. Money? I can find that, too. Tell me what you want. If you let me go, I can make it worth your while."

"Do you really think it's wise to lie to me?" Vader asks.

I shake my head. "I'm not."

They take a step closer to me. "So what did you hack exactly to know that someone wanted to give you a flat tire?"

They don't punch me, but it feels like they did.

They know about my vision.

Think, Cassie. Think. "I didn't. It was the nails on the ground by my house," I answer quietly. "I figured someone put them there for me, not my dad." They're not going to buy this. I feel numb, hollow.

"And someone with a knife looking for you in the halls at school?" they ask.

Another punch. This one harder. *They know.* "Doesn't everyone feel like they're being followed at school?"

"How about someone sneaking in through your always open garage door—or wait, what used to be an always open door, that all of a sudden is closed and locked?"

My throat tightens. None of these things were hackable. They weren't broadcasting their plans over the internet. They know I saw what happened. They know I changed my path because of it. I sink down lower on the ground. "I wanted to be safe after the nails," I try, although I'm not sure why I bother.

They know everything.

I don't need further proof, but they provide it anyway. Vader reaches into their cape and pulls out my journal. They must have gotten it from my backpack. I want to reach out and grab it. That is for my eyes only. I don't share what's in there with anyone. Not with Dr. Mukherjee, not with Brody, not with Audra. Sure, I may tell them some stuff, but not everything. I don't even leave my old journals lying around. I hide them in a box of my mom's old things in the attic, just in case my dad decides to snoop around my room.

"Just stories," I say, my voice a whisper.

My lie won't cut it. That was going to be my excuse if someone ever grabbed my journal at school. That I was writing a book. All fiction. But that won't fly here. They know that what I wrote about is real.

I have only one option left to save myself.

The truth.

"I have visions," I say. "Not of everything. But enough. Enough to know things that could help you."

"Fine," they say. "Winning lotto numbers. Go."

"It doesn't work like that."

"Really? Because it's pretty coincidental that a psychic's family won a five-million-dollar jackpot."

I didn't tell them that. They must know me or have googled me. Googled my family.

"That was before I was born."

"Then is it like *father*, like daughter or like *mother*, like daughter?"

I don't want to answer, but I also don't want them going after my father. "Mother," I say.

They nod. "Still waiting on those numbers."

I close my eyes. I try. Nothing comes. Do I lie? Do I make them up? It will buy me a little time, but what then? What happens when they find out the numbers are wrong? Do they take their wrath out on me? It's too big a risk.

"I don't know, but I know other things that are just as good. If you need money, leverage, I have info that you can use. You'll be set. And then you won't need me, you can let me go."

"Blackmail is your big idea? No. Too many moving parts. Too many people. Too much risk of getting caught."

"I can do it for you. I'll be the contact person. I'll do it if it means freedom."

"Good try," Vader says. "But you don't have it in you, and I don't trust you. You're no blackmailer. That friend of yours, though— she's another story. Takes the visions you tell her and runs with them." Vader laughs. "Her I might've given a chance. Wonder how much she scored before they busted her."

They're talking about *Hayden*?

They know her? Know what's she done? What she's like? What *I'm* like?

Are my kidnappers from school?

Do I know them?

Oh my god. It was Hayden. *I'm not the one with inside knowledge around here.* Those words of hers in the hall really did change everything. My captors think it's *me*, that I'm the one who was supplying Hayden with intel. Did she blackmail the wrong person? What did Hayden latch onto that she wasn't supposed to?

A new fear suffocates me.

I'm no use to these guys. Worse, I'm a liability.

If my captors don't think they can work with me, they'll never let me go. They can't. They know I can see things. They know one day I may be able to identify them.

My visions may have just sealed my fate.

32

HaYDen

get to the school about forty minutes before I tell Brody to show up. I want to do a little snooping first, and while a lookout might be nice, I'd prefer to have to come up with an excuse for a teacher about why I'm in an area I'm not supposed to be in rather than have a vision in front of Brody. I'm just not ready to have a whole conversation about it. Feels strange to even think about sharing. I was taught not to talk about them; I'm not sure I even know how. But if Audra was able to identify a vision, Brody will be able to as well, and I don't want to go there yet.

The school's extra security amounts to one deputy wandering around outside. They don't even bother to lock the side doors, not when practices are taking place. Sports before all else in Lightsend. I wait and watch. Eventually, Deputy Thomas circles around. After he takes a turn around the building, I go inside, using the entrance by the gym. The same one I ran out of the day Sheriff Rafferty busted me. I'm hoping for better luck today.

The gym is empty. I certainly hope the boys' locker room is

too. I don't want anyone thinking I'm like Nick. I do a quick look around. I don't see anyone, so I slip inside.

A couple of bags are lying around, but I don't see Kristoff's. His is a dark slate color, and that's what I want. It's either on the field with him, home, or in one of these lockers. But which one? I let my fingers run over the doors. I don't get anything. A few have locks on them. A few don't. I try those. No visions. Nothing good, either. Just smelly clothes.

Chances weren't high that Kristoff would just leave some diabolical evidence sitting around, but I had to check anyway. Not all criminals are smart. If he even is a criminal. If he'd just stop acting so cagey and talk to me and tell me why Cassie would have his name written in her room, this would be much easier.

There's not much left to investigate here, but there's a little room off to the side. If it's anything like the girls' locker room, it's an office for the coach that the team captains and star players usually take over. Kristoff is a star—or used to be anyway. I'm not sure how his standing is since the laxative game, but I'd guess it's still up there. The office door is open, which probably means there's nothing worth locking up, but I'm already here, so it can't hurt to look.

The place is small. It doesn't take long to go through everything. I probably touched every square inch, but it didn't strike a vision. All I found were schedule upon schedule upon schedule. I put a copy of the one from the night Cassie went missing into my bag. Wasn't a super-active night. Looks like most teams had practice after school and were home by dinnertime. Means Kristoff can't use the football team as an alibi, but that doesn't mean he doesn't have something else airtight for that evening. I take one last look around and then head back out. No deputy in sight.

Despite my little excursion, I make it to the parking lot before Brody. I wonder if he was surprised to hear from me. If so, he didn't let on, he just said, *Tell me when*. He didn't bring up our talk from this afternoon outside the cafeteria, either, which is a relief. I was worried things would be weird after our last conversation, but maybe we've turned over a new leaf in our friendship or whatever this is called.

I'm leaning on Greta when he pulls up alongside me.

"You know," he says, once he's out of the car. There's no hi, no how are you, he just jumps right in. "I thought you might ask me out one of these days, just didn't expect it to be for a football practice."

"This is not a date." I know he knows that, but I feel my ears burning anyway. So much for that new leaf.

He nods. He gets it. He knows what this is about. He wants to know what Kristoff has to say as much as I do.

But then that right side of his mouth curls up. "*And* you wanted to see me."

If I had something in my hands, I'd throw it at him. "No." I drag out the word. "I just thought you might be interested."

"In you?"

If I knew *truce* meant more free rein for him to mess with me, I might have reconsidered. I head to the field. I am not dignifying that with an answer. If I do, he'll just keep on going. He eats this stuff up. It's like he gets bonus points every time my ears turn red.

Brody jogs up next to me and swipes the hair out of his eyes.

"Nothing to be embarrassed about. Lots of girls like me. You're in excellent company. Lots of high-quality people."

I stop and turn to him. "Oh my god. I take it back. Everything I said earlier. *I* am not the ass here. It's all you. One hundred percent."

He gives me a full smile now, and I look away when I realize I'm staring at his lips. "Well, I wouldn't want to do anything *half-assed*."

I groan at his pun, and he laughs.

"Just come on," I say, and lead him to a spot on the bleachers. I scan the field. "They're all out there."

"That usually happens at a practice."

I side-eye him. "They take breaks. People sit out. At least here Kristoff can't run away from me like he does in school."

"Really? Because it looks like all he's doing is sprinting up and down a field." Brody points as Kristoff practices some sort of play. "I'm pretty sure he can outrun you, but I'd like to see you try."

I swear, this guy just likes to rile me up. Or is this his idea of flirting? The idea shuts me up. Any response I had flies right out of my mind.

"There you guys are," Audra says, climbing the bleachers and taking a seat next to me. "What did I miss?"

He invited Audra? I didn't tell him to do that. I only reached out to him. I shift my body toward Brody. "What happened to this being a date? You invited someone else?" I ask. I mean to say it in a joking, light manner, but somehow it comes out pretty pissed.

"Okay," Audra says, "I'm seriously missing something. Are you two . . ."

"So now it *is* a date?" Brody asks, ignoring her question and keeping his eyes on me.

"No, it's not a date," I say to answer both of them at once. "But wasn't that the whole bit?" I ask, turning back to Brody. "And yet you go and invite a third person."

"Well—" Brody starts, his eyebrow rising.

I put up my hand to cut him off. "I swear to god, if you make a three-way joke, your phone will find its way under Ollie and a whole mound of players during their next tackle."

"Fine," he says, "but missed opportunity. You set it up so beautifully for me to just lob it right over the net."

"Will someone please tell me what is going on here?" Audra says.

"It seems Grim wanted some one-on-one time with me," Brody says, and rubs his elbow against mine.

I swear, this guy.

"I was just surprised to see you," I tell Audra. "That's all."

"Yeah," she says, "because you keep leaving me out of the loop. Just because I don't want you to know everything about my personal life doesn't mean I have anything to hide. It's just none of your business. We *all* have things we like to keep to ourselves, don't we?"

"I know," I say, and ignore the fact that she's alluding to my visions. She knows the two are not the same. "We're fine. Okay?"

"Then next time don't make me harass Brody to find out what is going on," she says.

Harass Brody? So maybe he didn't go out of his way to invite her.

Ugh. It doesn't matter.

"So what are we doing here?" she asks, snapping me back to attention.

"Trying to talk to Kristoff," I say. "And some of the other guys."
I fill them in on seeing a few of the players on the list to talk to the
guidance counselor about Cassie.

"None of them are that close with her," Audra says.

"I guess we can't rule anyone out. They all have their secrets.
Trust me. This town is full of a lot of crappy people. And there's
a good chance they think Cassie knows what they're hiding," I
say, and squeeze my eyes shut. That image of me walking to
the office in front of the whole school, yelling at Cassie that she
should have warned me, hits me hard. This is my fault. If I hadn't
blackmailed anyone, none of this would have happened. It has to
be someone with a secret. Either one they're afraid of having come
out, or one that I already uncovered.

I watch the football team. So many secrets. So many lies. So
many things they want kept hidden.

A few minutes later Coach Hill calls a break.

"Finally," I say. I grab my bag and climb down the bleachers. I
get to the bottom and realize I have two shadows. "What are you
guys doing?" I ask.

"You tell us," Audra says.

"*I'm* going to go talk to Kristoff."

"Okay," Brody says, but as I take another step, so do they.

"Alone," I clarify. "He's not even going to want to talk to me.
Three of us walking up to him is definitely going to scare him off.
Just wait here. I'll fill you in on what he says. I promise."

To my surprise, neither of them argue. They take a seat on the
bottom bleacher. Kristoff is talking with the coach, so I bide my
time and head over to target number two, who is standing by the
water cooler.

"Luka," I call out, and walk in his direction. The four guys he's with scatter immediately. Good to know I haven't lost my touch, despite Brooke's best efforts to take me down.

He sighs as I approach. "No way, dude," he says. "I am done with you."

"I know that's what you were hoping, huh?"

When I get closer, he takes my elbow and pulls me farther away from his teammates. "I paid you," he whispers. "We're square."

"That's the funny thing about extortion," I tell him. "You can just never trust your blackmailer to keep their word. What's to stop them from coming back for more?"

"Hayden . . . ," he says. "You promised."

I laugh. "Honor among thieves?"

Only he's not smiling.

"Look," I say, "I'm not here for more money. I just have a few questions. Since when are you and your teammates so concerned about Cassie that you all needed appointments to talk about her disappearance?"

"We all love Cassie. Her kidnapping hurts me here." He points to his heart.

I stare him down. "Really? And that worked with Ms. Drake?"

He gets a sheepish look. "Sort of. She likes us."

When I don't say anything, he keeps talking. "Fine. Hunter heard that in college if your roommate dies, you get automatic straight As."

"That's not true."

"You don't know that," he says. "So we figured if we all act extra upset about Cassie's disappearance, at the very least we'll get some pop quizzes and exams canceled."

"Meantime, Cassie is missing and going through who knows what."

He shakes his head. "You know she does this all the time, right?"

"This is different. She was taken."

"Maybe."

I study his face. "What do you know?"

He backs away from me.

"Luka . . ." I step in closer.

"Nothing. I promise," he says.

"You didn't do anything to her?"

"No, why would I?"

"I don't know," I say, getting up so close that we're almost touching. "Why would you spike your best friend's drink and ruin his chances with that scout?"

Luka looks away from me. "That was different."

"How?"

"It doesn't matter," he says, and drills his toe into the dirt.

"I think it would matter to Kristoff. Messed up his game. Screwed things up with Brooke. Embarrassed him in front of everyone. Should I call him over and see what he thinks?"

"You promised," he reminds me, burrowing his shoe deeper into the ground.

"And I'd like to keep that promise," I tell him. "Now tell me why I should."

He grunts. "You're the one with all the intel. Don't you already know?"

"Clearly not. Do we have to do this the hard way?" I ask. "Kristoff is in shouting distance. Want me to show you?"

"Stop. If I tell you, then we're done, right? For real this time?" His eyes bore into mine. "I don't want to worry about you popping up again."

"Yes," I assure him. "Tell me what I want, and I'm out of your hair for good."

"Fine," he concedes. "But this stays between us."

When I nod, he continues.

"I was so sick of him getting everything. Brooke. Most valuable player. Coach's star. On his way to a full ride to college."

"So you were jealous?"

"No. I mean, yes, but that's not why. If he earned it, that would have been one thing, but he was cheating. Taking crap to up his game. It was making him the breakout star when he didn't deserve it. I did. I was just leveling the playing field. Giving the scout a chance to notice me."

Wow. Not what I expected.

"What was he taking?"

"I don't know. Whatever he could get. Steroids, Adderall, coke, ephedrine, you name it. If he thought it could give him an edge, he took it."

"And you?"

He looks at me in disgust. "Have you seen this body? I'm not risking it. Besides, you get caught, your career is over before it starts."

"Kristoff wasn't worried about that?" I ask.

"Apparently not."

"Who else knew that he was using?" I ask.

"I don't know. It's not like he even told me at first. Only after I called him on it. Found a stash in his drawer when I was looking for some money to pay the pizza guy. He was drunk and forgot the drugs were in there when he sent me up to his room."

"Fine. Who else do you *think* knows?"

"His dealer. And before you ask, I don't know who it is. He wouldn't say."

"Who else?"

"I told you I don't know. Brooke, probably. Are we done?" he asks. "People are looking, and I really don't need to be seen with you."

"Aww, that just warms my heart," I say. "Luka, will you be my valentine?"

He glares at me.

"Just one more thing, and then you can go," I say. "Was Kristoff involved with Cassie at all? Anything going on there?"

"Not that I know."

My head is spinning. Does what he told me have anything to do with Cassie, or is it just another thing that goes on in Lights-end?

It could be either. There's no way to know.

This could be really bad. What if Cassie got in over her head? Did she stumble onto something big? Did she say something to the wrong person?

Did I?

33

HaYDen

"Kristoff!" I say, waving my hands over my head and pointing at him. "Your turn." The coach is not in sight, and I take my opportunity to pounce.

"Lightsend's leech trying to suck another of us dry," I hear one of the guys on the team say. There's a general murmur of agreement and disgust. I ignore it; I'm not here for them today.

Kristoff turns away from me and goes back to his conversation with Ollie and Hunter.

No. No, no, no, no, no. Not this time. That is not going to fly. I need to know what he's mixed up in and if it has anything to do with Cassie.

"Fine, if you prefer to do this in front of everyone . . ." I'm not even thinking, I just start barreling toward him. "Woof, woof."

That did it. He jogs over to me. "What the hell, Hayden?"

He moves us farther away from everyone. Funny how no one wants to talk about their indiscretions in front of a crowd.

"I paid you to keep quiet about that."

His face scrunches up, and he gets a faraway look. I wonder if he's remembering exactly what he did.

When I don't say anything, he keeps talking. "You know I feel shitty about it, but I can't change it. I donated to the animal shelter like you told me to, even started volunteering there. What else do you want from me? More money? Fine. I probably deserve it. Nothing you can do will make me feel worse than I already do."

I get a surge of doubt. He does sound really guilty. Would this guy have it in him to hurt Cassie? He feels bad about killing the dog. I know that. He always has. Yet not enough to own up to it. When his freedom is on the line, how far would he go to protect his own skin? Or someone else's?

"This isn't about the dog," I tell him. Then a thought occurs to me. It might be connected after all. "Were you high when you hit him?"

He wipes his forehead with his arm. "What are you talking about?"

"Kristoff, answer me."

"No. I wasn't."

He won't look me straight in the eyes. Close, but he's keeping his gaze just off to the side, and he's biting his cheek. This is exactly how he acted when I blackmailed him the last time. He's so lying.

"Kristoff . . . ," I warn.

"I said no."

"Let's find out," I say, and study his pupils, the ones that still won't focus on me. "You're using now, I'd bet money on it, and you better be sure I only put money on things I know I'm right about. Maybe I should call a tip into the sheriff's office—you know I work there now—about conducting some random drug tests on the football team. What do you think?"

"Screw off, Hayden," he says, and turns around.

"So is that a yes, I should call it in?"

He faces me again. "What difference does it make?"

"I want to know."

He's chewing both cheeks now. "All right, yeah, it's why I took off and didn't report it. I didn't want them to make me do a drug test. What does that change?"

"Maybe a lot. Brooke using, too?"

Kristoff's lip curls. "What?"

"You heard me. Were you two wrapped up in something together?"

He laughs. "Is that what this is about? Brooke takes you down, burns your little blackmail gig, and you want revenge? You're obsessed with her, aren't you?"

Now it's my turn to look away. "Just answer my question."

Kristoff shakes his head. "Sorry to disappoint, you got the wrong girl. Brooke doesn't use. Can't even swallow an Advil, afraid of needles, and would never shove anything up her nose. You'll have to find something else."

He waves and starts to walk away again.

"I'm not done," I tell him. "Did Cassie come and talk to you?"

"She's not talking to anyone. She's missing, remember?" He does one of his annoying laughs.

"Yeah, I do," I say, "and did you have anything to do with that?"

"No!"

"She had your name written down in her room. Circled. Why would she do that?"

"I don't know," he says. "Secret crush?"

I glare at him, and he shrugs. "You'll have to ask her."

I wish I could.

It is like pulling teeth with this guy. "When was the last time you spoke with Cassie?"

"Like really spoke to her?" He rolls his eyes but answers. "I guess a little before homecoming. She was being real odd. 'Don't drive home after the game,' she kept saying. 'Promise me. Don't do it.'"

"Did you?"

"No," he says. "She freaked me out. Made feel like I was going to die or something."

He probably would have. "Let me guess, you used before that game, too, huh?"

"Whatever," he says.

"Where do you get the drugs?"

"I am not telling you that."

"So you want your secret out then?" I ask.

He snorts. "Try it. There's no proof that I hit that dog. Just the word of a liar versus me."

"I meant your other secret," I say. "That you're only the star of the team thanks to a little help."

"It's not a big deal," he says. "I only do it sometimes. Big games, important practices. A lot of the guys use."

"Not a big deal? I'm sure the sheriff, your coach, the local paper, and Channel 6 local news will see it the same way."

"Sorry, Hayden. Can't do it. I think you're bluffing. You're not going to tell. Taking me down takes you down. You were warned about blackmailing."

"I'm not asking for money."

He shrugs. "You are if I say you are. Like I said. Who are they going to believe, you or me?"

He's actually threatening me.

"Kristoff," I warn him. "I just want a name."

"No."

"Tell me." What if this is the key to finding Cassie? What if they thought she was onto them?

"If I have to risk their wrath or yours—I'm taking yours," he says. "No way I want this circling back to me."

I can't believe I'm about to do this, but I want answers. I reach into my bag and pull out my bear spray. "Afraid of what they might do?" I ask, and hold the can out right at him, the nozzle pointed in his direction. "Maybe you should be afraid of what I'll do. Don't make me put you down. This can knock out a bear. What do you think it will do to you?"

"Hey, hey, hey," Coach Hill says, and runs over. "What is going on here?"

"Oh, this?" I say, and give him my biggest smile. "I was just showing Kristoff my spray." I lower the can. "He was telling me about a bear he saw in the woods the other day, and I said I had something that could help if it got too close to him or his *dog*. Right, Kristoff?"

I turn to him and telepathically warn him with my eyes that he'd better go along with my story.

"Yeah," he says without much enthusiasm.

"I don't care why you have it," Coach Hill says. "It's not allowed on school property."

"But what if I need to protect myself here?" I say, and eye Kristoff.

The coach crosses his arms and glowers at me. "Then you'll have to find another way. I hear you have it again, you're expelled."

"Okay, I'll leave it at home."

"Get out of my practice," Coach Hill says, and points toward the parking lot.

"Just leaving anyway." As I walk past the bleachers, Audra and Brody jump up and join me.

"What was that?" Audra asks.

"Keep walking," I say. "Tell you guys after."

I feel every set of eyes on us as we head for our cars.

"Well?" Brody asks when we get to the parking lot.

I glance at Audra, and I see her stiffen at my look.

I'm not in the mood for another fight. I don't have it in me. "You won't tell your father?" I ask her. "Any of it?"

"I promise," she says.

I let out a sigh and start spilling everything that went down on the field with Luka, Kristoff, and Coach Hill.

"This is so good," Audra says after I finish my story. "This is what we need."

"Did you not just hear the story I told you?" I ask, leaning back on Greta. "I got nothing."

"Yeah," Brody agrees. "It doesn't put us any closer to finding Cassie. She never mentioned drugs or any of the guys on the team. At least not to me. This sounds like it might be totally unrelated."

It might be, but I'm not so sure.

"It doesn't matter," Audra says. "This is our big break in the case."

Okay, she's losing it. "I know you want to find her," I tell her, "but we're no closer than we were an hour ago."

"You're wrong," she says, her eyes wide. "Don't you see? Cassie's vision. This is it. Finally. You're supposed to break in to a class and find some phones. Kristoff's has to be the one you want."

Brody stands up straighter.

"Huh?" I ask.

"Think about it," she says, her voice practically squealing. "Cassie saw the two of you finding some phones. Doesn't it make sense that one of them would have information you're looking for, information like who's dealing at Lightsend. Kristoff wouldn't tell you, but chances are it's all right there in his texts and call log."

"You're right," Brody says, and his expression is lighting up, too. "We can set it up. A sting. Is Kristoff in Donnelly's class? That would be the easiest. He's always taking away phones."

They're so excited that I'm hesitant to point out the obvious— that this isn't us stumbling onto something that can help, this is us just re-creating a vision. A vision that, paradoxically, could have happened because we were trying to come up with a way to find Cassie. Not because we actually knew anything real. The concept is making my brain hurt.

"Do you know?" Brody asks.

"What?" I ask.

"Does Kristoff have Donnelly for anything?"

"Yeah," I say. "Trig. We have it together. Right before lunch."

"Perfect," Audra says. "I have art that period. Ms. Portnoy won't notice if I pull out my phone. I'll block my number and keep calling Kristoff. After enough times, he'll get curious. He'll look. And when he does, you," she says to me, "do something to make sure Donnelly is looking. Drop a book, fling a pencil, I don't care."

Before I can jump in with my concerns, Brody adds to the plan. "You should have him lock up your phone, too. Just in case we can't get into the desk, when it's time to pick it up at the end of the day, you get there first and grab Kristoff's instead of yours."

Audra nods. "Smart, but you'll get in. We've seen it. Well, Cassie did."

"Guys," I finally say, "stop. Cassie's vision didn't show us finding her. It shows us finding phones. Don't get your hopes up. This might not be anything."

"No," Audra says, "you're wrong. This is something. I can feel it."

I look to Brody to see if he gets it.

The sides of his mouth rise into a sad smile, and he shrugs. "Hope is all we have."

He needs this. They both do. "Okay," I say. "I'm in. But if we get his phone—"

"When," Audra corrects me.

"*When* we get his phone," I say, "how do we get in? I don't know Kristoff's password. Some people aren't as obvious as others." I direct that last part to Brody.

His smile turns sheepish. "I changed mine already."

"Don't worry about that. Leave it to me," Audra says. "You guys, we're going to find Cassie!"

34

HayDen

First period Tuesday was a blur, and by the time of my guidance appointment, I'm extra antsy. My mind is on the setup in a couple of hours, on everything Kristoff and Luka said, on Cassie, and for some ludicrous reason, on Brody. My thoughts keep wandering back there, no matter how much I try to stop them. I try and shake it off, but all of a sudden there he is again, like a fruit fly on a rotting banana. It's become the Brody network in my brain. It's our conversations playing on repeat. It's that way he raises an eyebrow, the dimple that pops up when he smiles, and that smile—the way it starts with the right side quirking before the other side catches up, then there's his quick comebacks, the cut of his jaw, the—

I'm doing it again. I need to smack myself.

Cassie. Cassie. Cassie. She is the focus. I've been drawing blanks there, though. In the past twenty-four hours, I've only raised more questions about her disappearance and gotten no answers. Nothing solid from football practice or work. The latter is thanks to Flemming. Despite acknowledging my existence at school, it was back to anti-Hayden rhetoric in the office, with him shooing me away when I tried to listen in on a briefing about the case. I'm pretty sure that's why he sent me home yesterday. Don't get me wrong, I'm glad the office is working on finding Cassie, but the hours are ticking, and if they know something, they certainly haven't acted on it. Whatever the deputies are doing, it's not enough. Unless they're hitting roadblocks because the sheriff wants them to.

Ughhh . . . more questions.

That's why I'm hoping I can get a vision that will help. Something clear and concrete. Something to end this case and bring Cassie home. I want her back. Not just because, yes, a missing girl should be found, but because I'm invested. I feel like Cassie and I are connected.

"Hayden," Ms. Quill says when I walk in. "You're a little early. Ms. Drake should be with you soon, though."

"No problem." I stand by her desk. "Did a lot of people sign up to speak with her?" I ask.

"Quite a few," she says, tapping a piece of paper on her blotter. That's what I want to see. Looks like a lot more than yesterday. I catch a few names. More football players, which after what Luka told me doesn't really surprise me.

"I didn't realize Cassie was so close with the football team," I say, pointing to the list, hoping it will get her to open up and let me see the rest of the names.

"Oh, you shouldn't be looking at this," she says, picking it up.

"It's just . . ." I sniffle and take a tissue from the box on the desk and blow my nose. "This is so hard. Ms. Drake is great and all, I was just hoping to talk to other people my age who might understand." I throw out the tissue and rub my eyes with the back of my hand.

"You poor thing," she says, and offers me another tissue. "I'm sure your friendship means a lot to Cassie."

"I hope so," I say, and blow my nose again. "What if they don't find her? What if I never see her again?"

"Okay," she says, and hands me the list. "Here, if you think it will help, take a look. But I have to warn you, most of them didn't come to talk about Cassie. They came to get out of class."

I'm surprised she figured that out.

I memorize the names on the list. Other than class-dodgers, none seem particularly unusual or send off any flares, but I'm hoping Ms. Drake—or her office—will clue me in if anything is amiss.

A shadow crosses over me. I look up to see Coach Hill standing there. "Here to see Thadwell," he tells Ms. Quill.

"Go right in," she says.

He scowls at me as he passes.

"Don't worry, no bear spray," I call after him.

While I'm in Ms. Quill's good graces, I decide to take it a little further. "What's your read on him?"

Her eyes widen for a split second as she turns to see if the coach is out of earshot. "What? Oh, good guy."

"Really?"

"Yeah," she says, but I'm not buying it. Her voice doesn't match her words. "Don't know him that well but seems nice enough."

Just then, Hunter Toyerbro, one of the football guys, walks out of Ms. Drake's office. "Oh, look here," she says. "That means you're up. You can go on in." She gives me what she must think is a reassuring smile, but it's not. Her sympathy look needs a lot of work.

"Hayden," Ms. Drake says when I walk in, "have a seat."

I sit in the chair, put my hands on the armrests, and slide them up and down. No vision. I get up and move to the next chair. Nothing there, either, so I scoot the seat up as close to Ms. Drake's desk as humanly possible.

"Thanks," I say, ignoring the look she's giving me. For once, I don't care if I have an episode in front of someone. It's for a good cause, and I'll just blame any spacing out on being upset about Cassie.

"How are you feeling?" she asks.

"Not well," I say, and flick around the pens in the jar on the desk. "It's been hard." I pick up her name tag and put it back down. "All I can think about is, who did this to Cassie?" I run my hands over her picture frames. "Why did they want her?" I lift the bud vase and pluck out the rose, before returning them both to their proper places. "Do we all have to worry?"

"Hayden, please," Ms. Drake says as I shuffle through the papers in her in-box. "Boundaries. Please leave my things alone."

"Sorry, when I get nervous, I'm all touch, touch, touch, touch, touch." With each "touch," I tap my hands on a different part of her desk.

"Hayden!"

"Sorry," I say, and lift my hands and sit on them to appease her. All of that and not even a glimmer of a vision. "Nervous tendencies."

"I understand you're anxious. But there's a lot of security

around the school, and the sheriff's department is working around the clock to find her."

"But who would do this?"

"I don't know," she says.

"No idea?" I press. "You're a guidance counselor. You know people. What's your hunch?"

"I wish I had one. I wish I knew."

I lean forward. "Any teachers, students, giving you some sort of bad vibe? What about—"

She cuts me off. "Hayden, are you here to talk about your feelings or to find more dirt on your classmates?"

I feign outrage. "What are you accusing me of?"

She cocks her head at me. "Do you think that's going to work? I was at the meeting where you got in trouble, Hayden. I read the reports. You've been accused of blackmailing quite a few people. Are you telling me you're not here to try and get some fresh material?"

I take my hands out from under me and slap my heart. "I am shocked, Ms. Drake. I work at the sheriff's department now. I've turned over a new leaf."

"I hope so, but you have to understand why I question it. Here you are coming in to talk about a girl you weren't even friends with."

Anger rises in me. Yeah, fine, maybe I had ulterior motives for coming in here, but she doesn't know what I'm feeling. I'm so sick of being the bad guy in this school. "And maybe a good guidance counselor," I say, standing up, "would realize that someone getting kidnapped from their school is traumatic whether you are friends with them or not."

"Hayden—" she starts.

"Save it," I say, and pat my hands on the walls, paintings, and light switch as I leave.

That was a waste of time. I got nothing.

The principal opens his door. Coach Hill is still in there. "Is everything okay out here? A lot of commotion."

I didn't realize I was so loud that he could hear me through a closed door.

"Just peachy," I say.

He's watching me. They both are. I head out.

"You all right?" Ms. Quill asks as I pass her desk.

"Yeah," I say. "I'm just upset about Cassie. She was kidnapped, and no one here seems to care."

I don't wait for her to respond. I just leave.

"Cassie," I say out into the ether, "help me. How do I find you?"

I wait, hoping for some sort of psychic connection. It doesn't come.

35

HaYDen

Ollie and Kristoff stop talking when I walk into trig class. They watch me as I head to my desk. It's at the end of the last row, diagonally to the left behind Kristoff.

I wave as I take my seat. "What? Did you guys miss me? Sad I couldn't stay at practice and chat a bit more? Feeling left out, Ollie?"

"You know me so well," he says.

"Just stay away from our games," Kristoff says.

"No problem," I tell him. "I'll just pretend I'm a scout. You won't have to worry about me showing up at all anymore."

That gets him to shut up. For a second, anyway. They start saying some more crap, but I've tuned them out. It's a skill that has proven handy more times than I can count.

The bell rings, and within minutes, Kristoff's phone goes off. It's in his bag, and it's on silent, but it comes to life when he gets a call, and I can see the light shine through. The question is will he notice.

It goes off a few more times, but he's absorbed in figuring out some problem Donnelly wrote on the board.

Why couldn't he make this simple?

"Kristoff," I whisper.

I see his eyes turn to slits. He hears me, but he's ignoring me. "Kristoff," I repeat.

He doesn't turn around, but a couple of other people do. Great. I don't want to get Donnelly's attention. Not yet. But I do want Kristoff's.

I fold up a piece of paper and flick it at his head. Perfect aim.

He turns and glowers at me.

"What is with your phone?" I mouth.

He gives me an eye roll and ignores what I said at first, but a minute later, he's checking his bag. Probably to make sure I didn't steal his phone. It lights up again.

His eyes widen. He must notice the kajillion missed calls. He picks it up and starts scrolling.

Donnelly isn't paying attention, so I go with Audra's idea. I slam my book to the floor. When he looks up, my focus is on Kristoff and his phone, as if I'm trying to see what his texts say.

I don't know if that's what does it, or if he notices it himself, but Donnelly calls out, "Kristoff, phone, now."

He takes it up, but the look he gives me as he returns to his seat is one of murder. If Kristoff had anything to do with Cassie's disappearance, I am definitely next.

When I am no longer the focus of his death glare, I sneak Audra a quick text, letting her know it worked so that she can stop calling. I then shut off my phone and put it out in full display on my desk. If Donnelly is going to confiscate it, there is no way I'm

leaving it unlocked and powered on. The man hates me. If he has a chance to set me up, there's a good chance he'll take it.

Donnelly is not on his game today. My phone is literally out as clear as can be, and he's not even glancing in my direction. I become more obvious with my fake texting. I pretend I'm typing up a storm. I even throw in a giggle. If any of these people knew me at all, that would be a red flag that I'm up to something. A giggler I am not.

It works, though. In my peripheral vision, I can see Donnelly get up. Before I know it, he's standing over me, grabbing the phone right out of my hands. I swear he looks like a kid at Christmas. Even more excited than when he got a message from Vera. Nabbing me has pretty much made his day. Maybe his month. "I'll take that," he says.

I want to say something to wipe that satisfied look off his face, but I bite my tongue. Kristoff is pretty pleased, too. They actually think I care about being without my phone for a few hours. The only reason I did the last time was that my mom was blowing it up, but that was a fluke. The electricity guys showed up at the cabin unannounced and unplanned, and she was spiraling. It hasn't happened since.

The whole period, Donnelly looks at me with that awful grin on his face, like he really got one over on me. *Let him have this*, I remind myself. It's all part of the plan, but still, making him this happy really irks me.

I watch the clock, only a few minutes to go.

Finally, the bell rings.

"Phones can be picked up at the end of the day," Donnelly says, turning his attention to me even though Kristoff had his phone taken, too. "You should have known better. Catch you again, maybe I'll just have to keep it." He looks so smug, like he won.

It takes everything I have not to tell him that Vera is really an eighty-three-year-old from Boise who is catfishing him. I remind myself I just need to tune him out like I did Ollie and Kristoff. I need him to leave for lunch, not send me to the principal's office.

Still, my mouth is incapable of completely staying shut. "You could," I find myself saying instead, "but keeping it would be stealing, and I bet you don't get tenure for that, do you? Would be such a shame if you don't make it to that three-year mark."

I leave before he can respond, but I can hear him muttering something. Good, no more ecstasy look for him. One mission accomplished. I elbow past Ollie and Kristoff, who intentionally try to block me, and head for my locker.

Audra and Brody are waiting for me when I get there. I hold back a laugh when I catch sight of them. It's the first time I'm seeing them in person all day, and they're both in all black. "You guys came to school dressed like this? Did you plan it?" I ask. "You know we're not breaking into the national bank, right?"

"Shhh," Audra says. "We know, and no, we did not plan this. Besides, I look super cute."

She does, I'll give her that. Ribbed black formfitting sweater, black denim skirt, opaque black tights with black combat boots that look more like something I'd wear than she would.

"I think it's more just the brilliant minds thinking alike thing," Brody adds.

I shake my head. "Sure it is." Yeah, I'm working with real criminal masterminds here. "Every single light is on in this building. If you wanted to blend in, you should have worn dirty pastel yellow to match the walls."

"Like I own that?" Audra says, and I'm not sure if she's playing with me. I think so. "Okay," she continues. "I'm up. I'll text you, Brody, when Donnelly is gone and the area is clear."

Then she takes off as if she's some character in a heist book, slinking along the wall and looking in all directions. That one's definitely for my benefit; she looks back at me and laughs, throwing her head back.

All right, maybe she isn't so bad, and even if it turns out her father did kidnap her best friend, I suppose I can't really hold that against her. She cares about Cassie, that much is clear, I concede.

"You doing okay?" Brody asks.

"Uh, yeah," I say. "What's with the formalities?"

"What do you mean?"

"Never mind." I'm just not used to him being all *how are you?* What's next? *Nice weather we're having for fall?*

"I know you didn't want to do this," Brody continues. "But thank you. Really."

"No big deal."

"Yeah, it is. You didn't know Cassie. Not well. You didn't have to do all this for her, for us, but you are. I won't forget this."

I'm taken aback. I was expecting snarky, exasperating, pulls-you-in-even-when-you-don't-want-to-be-pulled, and yes, enticing Brody, but it looks like I got the soulful, kind, self-reflecting, still-pulls-you-in-when-you-don't-want-to-be-pulled version instead.

Say something, Hayden. Since when am I at a loss for words? "Well," I laugh. "The sheriff killed my side business, had to find something to keep me busy."

"No," he says, "that's not why you're doing this."

His eyes are boring into mine, and I feel my breathing quicken.

"Then why am I doing this? *You?*"

He shakes his head. "No, not that, either. You're doing this because you care about people more than you like to let on."

For some reason, I feel tears welling up. "Whatever," I say.

He leans in closer to me. "I see you, Hayden Jefferies."

No Grim.

No more words at all. He's just watching me.

His phone buzzes, and we both break away.

"Ready?" he asks, reading the text. "It's time."

"Ready or not . . . ," I tell him.

Audra is pacing outside Donnelly's classroom when we get to her. She jumps right into it. "He left a minute ago, shut the door and lights. I don't think he's coming back, but I'll stand watch and signal to you if he does. The hall has been pretty empty in general. A late straggler to lunch, but so far no teachers or anything." She reaches into her bag. And pulls out a baggie with a piece of melted wax in it. "Here you go. My little arts and crafts project. This should get you into his phone. Good thing he has a finger reader. Making a face would have been a challenge."

She googled this little phone hack in five minutes. A candle, Elmer's glue, and a lighter. Plus the print she lifted from Kristoff's homeroom desk this morning. That's all it took. Being a sheriff's kid teaches you a few things.

"Go, go, go," she says.

"Yes, boss," Brody says, and salutes.

"Be careful," Audra warns, but Brody doesn't look nervous. He looks excited.

Me, on the other hand, not so much. I know Audra's on guard, but if we get caught, I'm the one who is going to pay.

We go inside and shut the door behind us. I head straight for the desk, and Brody stands by the entrance, looking out the window in the door watching for a warning from Audra.

"Locked," I say, crouched down by the drawer where Donnelly keeps the phones. "No surprise there." I pull out a paper clip, straighten it, and get to work.

"And no surprise that you know how to break into it," Brody says.

"Lucky for you, I am resourceful."

He nods. But I know he's thinking lucky for *Cassie*. The unspoken words hang in the air.

"Almost got it," I tell him. I can feel the metal in the prongs. I just need to twist it the right way and pull.

"We're good. No sign of Donnelly," he says.

Come on, work for me, just pop open, I will the drawer. *A little more. Do it. Open.*

"Yes," I yell when I hear a soft click, and the drawer pops open. "That is how you do it!"

Brody rushes over.

"One, two, three," I say, pointing to the phones.

"You did it," he says, taking two of the phones in one hand and squeezing my palm with the other. "Thank you. This may be the key. We're going to find her."

I shrug. I'm having one of those mind freezes again. I suck in my lip and try to get my mouth working, but it's not happening. Brody is still holding my hand, and he's still watching me. All I can do is watch back.

He lets go of my hand.

Oh. Okay.

I start to look away, but then he wipes a piece of hair off my face, and that hand, the one that was just on mine, is grazing my cheek. He lets it stay there.

My eyes are locked on his, and he's so close I can feel his breath, and I'm no longer sucking on my lip. Instead, my lips are slightly parted, and I find myself leaning closer to Brody.

It almost feels like a magnetic force drawing us closer together, and yet keeping us just far enough apart that we're not touching. A force that could snap any second, making us collide.

He's going to kiss me. I *want* him to kiss me.

The door squeaks open, and I jump. We both do. It's just Audra. I'm relieved and disappointed.

"We do not have time for all this," she says, waving her hands in the direction of Brody and me, "although we will be discussing it later. Now, did you check the phones?"

The one still in the desk is mine.

"That's Kristoff's cell. The bigger one," Audra says, pointing to one of the phones in Brody's hand.

He gives it to me, and I take out the fake fingerprint Audra made. I put it on the phone's sensor, and it works! The phone unlocks.

"Ha! Look at that. Who's a genius?" she asks, and does a little happy dance.

"Maybe not the person leaving the door unguarded?" I say.

"Oh yeah, should probably get on that," she says, and heads over to peer out.

I check Kristoff's call log. Virtually empty other than all the missed calls Audra made, a few dozen from his mom, and one call to "Uncle Riley." I open his texts. Now this section is crowded. So many names and so many messages in each one.

I start from the top, reading as fast as I can. Exchanges with Luka, Brooke, Hunter, random classmates. Nothing that screams drugs. There's not even anything worth blackmailing over. It's just texts to his friends. Some are obnoxious, but none that give me pause. Until I get to his interactions with Ollie.

"Look at this. Both of you," I say. "It's from last month. Kristoff and Ollie."

Audra comes back over, and I hold out the phone so that she and Brody can see.

Kristoff
Where are you? I need what you've got.

Ollie
XXX

Kristoff
Come on.

Ollie
Told you already. Not here.

Kristoff
Dude. I'm not saying anything for you to worry about. Chill out.

There's nothing else written. Nothing suspicious, anyway.

"This could be it," Brody says. "I wouldn't have thought of Ollie, but I also wouldn't be shocked to learn he was into some crap. What's XXX?"

"I bet it's a burner," Audra says. "Doesn't want anything

incriminating on his real phone. Bet Kristoff erased those texts or calls."

I don't know how to check, but I do have an idea. I punch up his contact list. "And look here. XXX and a phone number."

"Call it," Brody says.

"Not from his number," Audra warns. "They eat lunch together. If it's Ollie, he'll know something's up if it's from Kristoff."

I hit *67 so he can't tell where it's coming from and dial the mystery number. I put it on speaker.

It rings a few times. I'm not sure anyone's going to answer. Another ring. Then another. Just when I think it's going to go to some generic voice mail, someone picks up.

"Hello."

We're all silent.

"Hello? Anyone there?"

Brody pushes the button to hang up the call.

None of us need to hear any more.

We all know the voice.

It's Ollie.

cassie

My captors are going to kill me. That sentence has been living on a loop in my brain. I sit in a daze, thinking about everything. My dad, how he's going to think I took off again, that I left him. My mom, and all that I still don't know about her and her abilities. My visions. Audra. Brody. What I've done, what I want to do. I pick at the sandwich they left for me. It's not fair. I'm supposed to be getting ready for the musical, visiting colleges, hanging out with my friends. I'm not done living. I take the paper plate and fling it across the room.

They are going to kill me. It's all out of my control.

The metal chains drag as I pull my knees up against my chest, bury my head in them, and cry.

When I look up, I'm not in the basement anymore.

I'm on the football field, wearing a long white gown. Hayden runs up to me. She's in a blue one. "We did it," she says, tossing her graduation cap into the air and catching it when it comes back down. *"Good speech there, Ms. Valedictorian."*

Wait, what? Graduation? That's more than a year away. And I'm there.

"I did have some help," I say, bursting with happiness.

Hayden takes a bow. No. No way she'd help me. No way she'd be this . . . nice. She shot me death glares when I invited her to sit with us at lunch when she moved to town. But in this vision, I can feel that we're friends and that I care about her.

None of this makes sense.

"My favorite part," Hayden says, *"is that Brooke isn't here, and Leighton is."* She juts her head in Leighton's direction. *She's by the podium, taking pictures with her parents and a few of our classmates.*

Leighton?

"The town owes us for that one," future me says, linking arms with Hayden. *"Guess two psychics can take down an evil entity."*

Two psychics? Wait, what? Hayden gets visions, too?

"Oh!" Hayden says.

"What?" I ask.

"Someone's coming this way with what looks like a pretty big gift for you," she says, and lets go of my arm with a wink. *"I'll take that as my cue to leave. Really don't think I can take any more of your PDA."*

Who was she talking about? Or even more importantly, does this mean I'm going to live, that I get out of here? Is that really a possibility? Or is it a future I would have had if none of this happened?

I don't know what to make of any of it. My head is spinning.

What did I just witness?

Hayden, my friend and a psychic . . .

Graduation . . .

A new love . . .

A future . . . One with me in it.

Yeah, visions don't always come true, but they can. For the first time since I've been trapped down here, my chest fills with something other than fear. There's hope.

I still have a chance to make it out of here alive.

37

HaYDen

"Hurry up," Audra instructs me, looking out the door window in Donnelly's class. "Lunch is almost over. We need to get out of here."

"I'm trying," I say. The drawer didn't automatically lock when I closed it, so I'm attempting to use the paper clip again.

"It's good enough," Brody tells me, taking my arm. "Let's go. If it's open, he'll think he just forgot to lock it. Even if he suspects someone tried to break in, he can't prove it. You're leaving the phones there. He'll assume you would have taken yours, at the very least, it if it was you."

I nod and let him lead me out of the room. We don't speak until we're at my locker—far away from Donnelly's classroom.

"What now?" Audra asks.

"Call Ollie out. I can grab him right after lunch," Brody says.

"Not without me, you're not," I tell him.

"Okay, *Lethal Weapon*, will you two hold it?" Audra says. "I think we should get my dad involved."

"No!" I say, at the same time Brody shakes his head and tells her, "Ollie will just deny everything."

"Besides, your dad has to go the legal route," I point out. "We have a little more leeway." That, and for all I know, her father is still playing a role in all of this.

"Hayden . . . ," she says.

"What? Didn't you want someone who'd break the rules? It's why you wanted me. That's my thing." Well, it's one of my things.

"Yeah, but I don't want you to get hurt," she says. "This feels different. Ollie's using burners and is wrapped up with dealing. Who knows what else he's involved with? This isn't risking your job, or playing junior detective on the football field. This could really be dangerous. If he had anything to do with Cassie's disappearance, who knows what he'll do next? We might be getting in over our heads. It may be time to loop my dad in."

She doesn't get it. I need to see this through. Besides, Ollie doesn't scare me. "We'll be fine. I blackmailed him before and he didn't do anything."

"Maybe he just didn't have the chance. Or didn't feel threatened. Or who knows what?"

"How about this," Brody suggests. "You see if you can get anything out of your dad, maybe plant seeds about Ollie and the drugs, so his office can look into it, too. And I'll—" He sees my look and fixes his sentence. "*We'll* meet with Ollie. I'll text him now, that I need to talk to him ASAP, to meet by his car before last period. Main parking lot, cameras are there, school's in session, a deputy is wandering around. We'll be safe."

"She doesn't have to go to her dad," I say.

"It could help," Brody answers. "What's the harm?"

Oh, I don't know, that I still haven't ruled the sheriff out as a suspect yet? Ollie isn't working alone . . . and maybe Audra's father is the one supplying the drugs. Although, if it is him, Audra tipping him off that we're closing in could take some of the focus off Cassie and onto us.

"Fine, whatever," I say. I need to concentrate on Ollie. "Do you really think he'll agree to meet you?" I ask.

"Yeah," Brody assures me. "He cuts out of school early all the time. He'll think I just want to grab food or something."

"Great friends you keep," I tell him.

"Same circles. Not friends, friendly."

Like there's a difference. I don't say it, but my look does.

"We used to play lacrosse together," he explains. "He—"

"Who cares?" Audra interrupts. "If you think it will work, just do it. But I'm getting out of here. I can't sit through another class. I'm going to find my dad *now.*"

"Okay," Brody says, and turns to me. I agree too.

A couple of periods later, we're walking up to Ollie in the lot.

"Seriously, man," Ollie says, jumping off the hood of his car when he sees us. "What is this about? Why are you with her?"

"*Her,*" I tell him, "can answer that. We have a few questions for you."

"What?" he asks.

"You're dealing drugs?" Brody asks him.

Ollie turns his focus to me. "You tell him that? I thought the whole idea of paying you off was that you keep your mouth shut."

Oh crap. Is that what Ollie was hiding?

It didn't even occur to me. When I approached him several weeks ago, he practically pushed money in my face before I even opened my mouth. I didn't have anything solid on him—no vision, no evidence that I unearthed in one of my own little searches— just my gut. It was right after Hunter had stolen a copy of the Spanish exam. I figured Ollie was in on it. Or had cheated on Erin, the girl he was dating at the time. I knew he had something worth hiding, I just never realized how big of a something.

"Well?" Ollie asks again.

I'm still in disbelief. He thought I was blackmailing him over his drug dealing. Maybe I really did get Cassie in serious trouble.

I move closer to him. "Where's Cassie?"

"How the hell should I know?"

"Did you do something to her?" I'm right in his face now. I don't care if he's dangerous. If he's responsible for Cassie going missing, and it was because of me, I need to know. I need to find her.

He takes a step back. "What is your problem?"

Brody steps in between us. "Where were you the night Cassie went missing?"

"You two are unbelievable. Maybe check the obvious before coming out here all attack-dog style? Then you'd know I was hanging out with the Waxler twins and Davidson that night. It's all over Instagram."

Brody pulls it up on his phone. It's true. They posted pictures. Nancy Waxler even went live from the movie theater, and there's Ollie throwing popcorn at some other guys from the team seated a few rows in front of him. Ollie has an alibi. The time stamp matches up with when Cassie was taken.

"Let me see your phone," I tell him.

He holds it up.

"You know what I mean. Unlock it. Give it to me."

"Okay, psycho," he says, "you want to see it so bad, be my guest. You're not going to find anything on me."

Ollie hands it over, and I take it. I half expect a vision, but I'm not that lucky. Instead, I go through the device manually. He's right. There's nothing on this. He wouldn't have given it to me that easily if there were something incriminating. I hand it back, and he puts it in his coat pocket.

"How about the other one?" I ask. "The one you do your business on?"

"How about you screw off?" he says.

"Ol," Brody says, his voice calm, kind, "we're just looking for Cassie. Help us out."

"And how is my phone going to do that?" Both of Ollie's hands are grasping the back of his head.

"It could have something," Brody explains. "What does it hurt to show us?"

"Hmm," he says, pacing now. "What could it hurt to give the school blackmailer the phone that I do my deals on? Yeah, that's a tough one."

"How about this," I say. "The school blackmailer can tell what she knows to her coworkers at the sheriff's office. I can think of a few hungry junior deputies who would love to bust a school drug dealer, get a commendation, maybe a promotion."

"Screw you."

"Be nice," I warn him. "I'm the one who brings the food to people in their holding cell. I'd hate for you to get food poisoning while holed up like that. Not the greatest accommodations."

"You know what, Hayden," he says, then goes into his car and searches the glove compartment. "You should have known I didn't take Cassie. It's easy. If I had to get rid of anyone, it would have been you."

He's a charmer.

"Watch it, Ollie," Brody says, and I give him a side-eye.

I don't need him coming to my rescue. I can hold my own. "I got this," I tell him. "Stand down."

Ollie emerges from the car, and he has something in his hand. If that's a gun, I'm going to have to eat my words. I will need Brody's help to talk him down. Then I see what he's holding. It's not a weapon. It's his other phone. "Go to town," Ollie says, and tosses it to me.

I'm holding the phone, but it's not me.

The hands are bigger, hairier, and the nails much more manicured.
They must be Ollie's.

The phone vibrates. A message from X.
I read it.

X
**She played you. She's not the one getting the
info. Someone else is feeding it to her.**

"Shit," Ollie says, and puts the phone in his pocket.

I'm back.

Both guys are staring at me.

"You get weirder and weirder," Ollie says.

No. No. No. This is tied to Cassie and me. I ignore him and look at the phone. It's empty. No messages. No numbers. No contacts. Everything's erased. Damn it, Kristoff must have tipped him off that I'd be coming. Or maybe someone else did.

"Who is your supplier?" I yell.

"Keep it down," he says.

"Answer me, Ollie. Who's involved? They took Cassie, I'm sure of it."

"What?" he asks.

"You heard me."

He shakes his head. "I don't know what you're talking about. I told you I had nothing to do with Cassie. I like her. Wouldn't hurt her. I'm just making some cash."

"Okay," I say, "if you like her so much, then help me help her. What do you know?"

He throws his hands up. "Nothing. Every week the product I request is left in my locker. I use burners. My suppliers do, too."

"Text them," I command. "Tell them you need something now." I hold the phone out.

"Won't do any good. That's a paperweight now, thanks to you. And I'm not due for a supply for a few days."

Days may be too late.

"If you hear from them, let me know," I tell him.

"Yeah, okay," Ollie says.

"I'm serious. Please," I plead. "They may know about Cassie. They may have her. They think she was the one onto you, onto them, but it wasn't her. It was me. Tell them that."

He starts walking back to the school, and I run up after him and grab his arm, stopping him.

"Ollie, you have to do this."

"No, I don't. I think you're messed in the head. They keep their identity hidden. They're not going to risk themselves to kidnap some girl. But if, for whatever reason, you're right, and they did, I'm not going to make myself the next victim."

He shakes me off and continues toward the school.

When I turn back, Brody is still staring at me, frozen in place.

"You were real chatty there," I say. "Thanks for jumping in to help."

"You told me to stand down, that you could handle it."

I hate when people use my words against me.

"Fine," I say, but he doesn't move. He's still a statue, his eyes glued on me. Only this is not like when we were in the hall or in the classroom. This is different, and not in a good way. "Why are you looking at me like that? You're weirding me out."

"You didn't tell me," he says, his eyebrows furrowing.

"Tell you what?" I ask.

"That you're like her. That you have visions."

38

HaYDen

With everything that happened with Ollie, I completely spaced on the fact that Brody was there witnessing me having a vision firsthand.

He's still watching me. "Why didn't you say anything?" he asks.

I can't make out his expression, his voice. Confusion, anger, surprise, wonder? A little of them all?

"Didn't seem worth mentioning."

"Hayden," is all he says, and he steps closer to me.

Yeah, yeah, I know. Obviously, it was relevant when we were searching for a person who herself has visions. I refuse to look at him. "I don't know. It's not something I bring up. Not something I talk about."

He's close now. I can feel his body near mine.

"You could have told me," he says.

"I didn't want to."

Brody nods. I catch it from the corner of my eye. "Okay."

"Audra knows," I say. He might as well hear it all. "I didn't tell her. She figured it out like you did. I asked her not to say anything."

He doesn't respond. We're just standing there. Him looking at me, me looking at my dirt-covered sneakers. The silence seems to last forever. I want to say something, but I don't know what, so I just stay there motionless. So does he.

He doesn't push, he's letting me take my time, but I don't have the right words. Finally, when I think I'm going to explode from the pressure, I say, "It's not like hers. It's not like Cassie's. I don't see the future. I get glimpses of the past."

I look up at him just for a moment.

I can almost see his mind drinking it all in, but he's not judging me. He's just listening.

"And the visions don't just come to me like hers do. I have to touch something first."

"That's still pretty amazing."

I shrug. I'm not so sure.

"Hey." He taps the tip of his shoe against mine, and while it's only the slightest of touches, my whole body goes warm. "A vision's a vision," he says.

"More like a curse is a curse," I answer so softly I don't know if he'll hear me, but he does.

"I don't know," Brody says. "I wouldn't mind it. Instead, I just—"

He stops himself.

I look up at him, allowing my eyes to catch onto his. "Just what?"

Brody does one of those silent chuckles, where you see someone's chest and throat moving but don't hear the actual sound. "Nothing." Then he smiles. "Guess I have a type." He says that part low, but loud enough for me to hear, and his eyes on mine.

Did he want me to hear that? He's still looking at me, so that's probably a yes. It has to be a yes, right?

He gives me that half smile of his, and I can't look away, but I can't keep looking at him, either. My whole chest feels heavy.

Oh god, why is my breathing so loud? I try to relax, to slow everything down, but my body won't cooperate.

"A type?" I finally say.

"A type," Brody repeats. He steps in closer, but he doesn't say anything, he doesn't lean down to kiss me. He's just watching me, waiting.

Okay, there's no misunderstanding. I know what he's saying. He likes me.

And I . . .

I . . . don't know . . . I don't know what to say, what to do, what to feel. And not just because it's Brody. This is new. All of it. I swore off people ages ago. Between the different schools, the unwelcomed judgments on my clothes and where and how we lived, and my horrific first-and-also-last kiss, it seemed better that way.

I still cringe thinking of that seventh-grade misery. Corey Crenshaw in the back of the bus on the way home from school. I had a vision right as his lips touched mine. His ChapStick triggered it. As if that wasn't horrifying enough, there was what I had to watch. Corey catching the lip balm, and Frank McConnell offering him five bucks if he could get the "freak" to kiss him. He put it on his lips and said something that gross was going to cost Frank ten. When I came out of the vision, everyone was laughing, calling me a zombie, and I had to sit there for another fifteen minutes until we got to my stop. I swore I would not let any of those people see that they'd gotten to me. I sat there stone-faced the whole rest of the ride. When I got home, I held back my tears, but my mom couldn't. She felt everything I was trying to hide. We moved three weeks later, and I started practicing how to better keep my emotions from my mother.

Brody nudges his shoulder against mine, and when he moves it away, it's like I can still feel the warmth of him there.

He isn't Corey. This is different, but still . . .

I look away.

"Hayden?" he says. He's never said my name like that before. Soft, kind, something more.

If I say yes, what will he say? Will he tell me he cares, or that I'm beautiful? Will he ask to kiss me? Will he want to know how I feel?

I can't take it.

"I saw something when I touched Ollie's phone," I spit out, changing the subject. Part of me regrets it, the other part is relieved. The tension is gone. Well, some of it.

"What did you see?" he asks.

His voice is still tender, he's still watching me, but it's not as intense as before, not as heart-stopping. This I can handle. I explain my vision to him, focusing on business, on Cassie, not on what's going on in my head.

"And there was no name on the text?" he asks.

"Just an X. But don't you get it? This means it's my fault. They thought she was giving me information." I lean against a car. I don't know who it belongs to, and I don't care.

"We don't know that," Brody says, taking the spot next to me. "We don't even know this is connected."

"Yeah, we do. Cassie knew. She told me. I changed things. I caused this. It was after I yelled at her in the hall that she should have warned me. Ollie was there. *Everyone* was there. If I hadn't done that, they would have thought it was me, she would have been safe. I took suspicion off me and put it on her."

"No," he says. "You're wrong."

I put up my hand. "Don't."

"Listen to me," he insists. "You didn't change this. It was in motion. Cassie had the vision of us looking through the desk—looking for her—*before* the incident in the hall. It played out the way she saw it. She just didn't realize it."

"Really?" I want to believe that.

"Really," he says.

I let the silence engulf us once more.

He bumps my shoulder again. "So what do we do next?"

I'm not sure if he's referring to "us" or the case, but I'm only ready to deal with one of those things right now. "I don't know," I say. "See if we can pull anything off Ollie's phone, if there's a way to get the deleted texts?"

"Okay," Brody says, "let's take it to the sheriff's office. We can give it to Rafferty."

"The tech crew," I correct him. I'm not putting something this important in the sheriff's hands.

He nods.

"We're getting there. We're going to find her. They can set up cameras to capture Ollie's locker, and they'll see who drops off the drugs."

"Except he's not expecting a drop-off for days, and that's too long. And we—*I* haven't been exactly subtle with the snooping.

They're all going to be more careful now, avoid their normal routines. I should have been smarter."

I don't mean to be such a downer, he's being so great. It just all feels like a lot.

"This isn't on you," he says. He sounds convincing. I want to believe him, but I'm not so sure.

"Trust me. We're going to find her. I can feel it. We're close," Brody says, and he squeezes my hand.

I don't let go.

39

cassie

can't stop thinking about that vision, about a possible future with me in it.

After days of no glimpses of what's to come—which is practically unheard-of for me—*this?*

It's a relief but also scary. I know that not all visions come true, that they can be changed, but I *need* this one to become reality.

I can't stop wondering why I haven't seen any other visions up until this point, not even in my sleep. Trauma? Panic? Or because there's a scenario where I don't have a future . . .

Did something happen to change it?

I squeeze my hands into fists and release them. It doesn't matter. This new vision means there's also a scenario where I survive. I have to make sure that's the one that comes true. If I only knew how. I take a deep breath and let it go.

I'm in a café. I see Audra's dad. He's with some woman. Okay, Sheriff, who is she? Does Delaney know?

Her hands cradle a mug. She closes her eyes and inhales. "I can't believe I'm here."

"I can," he says.

She opens her eyes. "That's one of us, then. Less than six months ago I needed to be at least a quarter mile from groups or my brain fried, and now look at me." She turns to take in the tables. "All these people practically next to me."

"And what are they feeling?"

She laughs. "I don't know, and I don't want to."

"It's official." Audra's dad raises his mug to her. "I declare you a graduate."

"I would never have been able to do this without your help."

"I didn't do anything. It was all you."

"No." She shakes her head and leans in, her voice a whisper. "You helped me learn to control my ability. To turn it off, to pinpoint it, use it with purpose." She gets a faraway look. "Feeling everyone's emotions all at once, it was killing me." She squeezes his forearm. "I couldn't have done this without you. Thank you. I owe you."

No way. Phil Rafferty actually found another person with powers and got them to come to Lightsend.

"I know how you can pay me back," he says.

"Name it."

"Get your daughter to keep her nose out of my cases."

"Ooh." She shakes her head. "I meant something doable. You know, you were the one who suggested that Hayden work there in the first place. You saw her record. You kind of brought this on yourself."

Hayden?

Despite all the visions I've had of her, I've never seen her mother.

And she's an empath.

I don't know what to make of it all. Did I see it for a reason? Not all my visions have a purpose, but usually they're so I can help someone, or they show me something that I need to know.

Where does this one fall?

And why is Hayden at the center of everything today?

A memory hits and answers my last question. My vision from weeks ago. With her and Brody alone in a classroom. It all comes rushing back. They were searching for something, for someone. They were searching for *me*. Did they make the vision a reality? Is that what changed?

Would Brody really have worked with Hayden, though? He's been logging overtime to make sure none of my visions happened. He wouldn't partner with her.

Unless he thought it could help me.

Oh my god.

All this time I thought Hayden caused my attack, that her words changed everything. But I had this vision before she yelled at me in the hall. There was always a chance it would play out this way. I mean, her blackmailing probably didn't help, but maybe she wouldn't have done that if circumstances were different, if Brody fell for her when he was supposed to, if I hadn't told him what I saw. It's enough to make my head spin.

It doesn't matter now.

What does is that someone is looking for me.

My friends. And it's not just them. It's someone with visions.

40

HaYDen

"Any luck at Ollie's locker?" Audra asks when Brody and I get to the sheriff's office. She's waiting at her father's desk in the pit. Brody had called her. Told her we were going to see if I could get a vision from the locker. He also filled her in on everything that went down. Well, not everything. Our hands are no longer intertwined. In fact, I'm standing a good six feet away from him, pretending we didn't have a moment.

"No," I tell her, and sneak a glance at Brody. When the locker proved to be a bust, I couldn't just go to last period. So Brody and I left for the station instead.

Audra's expression falls, and I regret how hard I've been on her. She's obviously beyond worried about Cassie and would do anything to get her back.

"You have the phone, though, right?" she asks.

"Yeah." I pat my jacket pocket.

"Good." She looks relieved. "My dad's still out. Hopefully he'll be here soon. Can I see—"

Deputy Flemming comes into the room, and Audra stops

talking mid-sentence, I stiffen, and Brody looks up at the clock. It's reflex. Don't need Flemming knowing we're playing amateur sleuths.

"You don't all look as guilty as sin," he says as he pours himself a cup of coffee. "Not at all . . . And isn't this a school day? Why aren't you all still in class? Wait, you know what? Don't tell me. I'm not on the clock yet, and your dad's due back soon," he says to Audra. "You can be his problem."

Flemming pours some sugar into his cup and then turns back to me. "Don't think you're getting paid overtime for this," he says.

"Don't worry," I tell him, "I just needed an extra dose of Flemming to carry on with my day."

"You—" He stops himself. "Not on the clock. Not my aggravation." He puts a cruller in his mouth and leaves us alone.

"Should we just fill him in?" I ask. "He can get started." Despite my early misgivings about Flemming and our numerous clashes, he cares about his job, and I trust him.

"No," Audra says. "Let's wait for my dad."

I don't love the idea, but I decide not to argue. I'll just make sure Flemming is in the room when we talk to Rafferty. An extra set of eyes and ears to make sure the sheriff doesn't do anything shady.

It looks like we're in for a wait. I head over to the desk that's pushed up against the one Audra's sitting at, and toss my bag on it as I take a seat.

That was a mistake.

My bag knocks into the pencil holder on the corner. Pens, paper clips, and the keys to the cells and filing cabinets spill onto the ground.

Crap. I lean down to scoop them back up. I pick up the keys, and everything changes.

My back is pressed up to the sheriff's desk. I'm watching the entrance-ways, while I reach behind me into the pencil holder and feel around until I find the keys. I grip them in my fist, and after doing another check of the entrances, I make a beeline for the cell.

Brody is in there. He's standing, his face almost squeezed between the bars.

I know whose eyes I'm seeing through. The perfect French-manicured golden nails holding on to the keys are enough to tell me, but then I hear the voice. "Here." It's Audra.

Brody takes the keys from her and pockets them.

No. This can't be right.

Brody doesn't say anything, just nods at her. My stomach is churning. I feel sick.

"Audra!" It's the sheriff. "You shouldn't be in here right now."

She jumps and turns at the sound of his voice.

"Hi. Sorry, Dad. I was actually looking for you—to see if you wanted to go to the recital together?"

He looks from Brody to his daughter. "I have to finish up a few things here. You should get going. You know your mother hates being kept waiting."

"You had another one," Audra says.

I'm back in the present.

"Hayden?" Brody says.

I back away from them.

"You lied. Both of you." I toss the keys down on the desk. "You don't have an alibi. You had an escape plan. The two of you, I don't know . . ."

I grab my bag.

"Hayden, wait," Brody says. "It's not what you—"

I don't stick around for the excuses. I run out of the office and into my car. Greta opens on the first try. "Thank you, baby," I whisper. At least I can count on someone.

I pull out of there as fast as I can.

I can't believe I thought I could trust Brody. How naive could I be?

Everything was a lie. They were using me. I wonder if they came up with it together. Were they hoping I could help them find an alibi? Or someone to take the fall? Someone to frame? Someone like me?

Whatever it was, I fell for it. I let Brody in, and I got played again.

I reach up and wipe my cheeks. They're wet.

For the first time since seventh grade, I'm crying.

41

HaYDen

"Hayden!"

My mom throws open the door right as I get out of the car. "What's wrong? Are you okay?"

I nod, but the tears are streaming down my face.

She doesn't wait. She runs over to me and wraps me in a hug. "Come inside, baby. You're all right."

I let her lead me into the cabin. She takes off my jacket and guides me to the couch.

She pulls my head onto her lap and smooths down my hair with her fingers. "Tell me what happened. Why are you home so early? What's got you so upset?"

"It's—" I jolt upright. This is wrong. She's wrong. I study my mother's face. "You're not crying. Why aren't you crying?" I stub my toe and she practically has a meltdown, yet now she's calm? What is going on?

She lifts one of my hands and kisses it. "I'm working on control."

"How?"

The doorbell rings. I don't need to look. It's either Brody or Audra.

"Want me to get that?" she asks.

I shake my head.

"Are you sure? I can tell they're *very* anxious to see you," she says.

Well, at least they're not here to kidnap or kill me. Not at the moment anyway. My mother would be able to sense that.

The bell rings again.

"You should talk to them," she says. "You want to."

I glare at her. Empath or not, I don't need her telling me how I feel. Yet I find myself going to the door anyway. I glance at the bear spray on the counter. I took it out of my bag after Coach Hill threatened me with expulsion for carrying it around, but I consider taking it with me now.

I turn back to my mom. "No feelings of murderous rage?" I ask.

"No, baby," she says. "Concern."

Yeah. Concern that I'm going to turn them in, and they'll wind up in jail forever. I don't tell her that, I just nod and open the door.

It's both of them—Brody and Audra.

"Hi," Brody says. "Can we talk?"

I grab my jacket, step outside, shut the door, and move about twenty feet from the cabin. It's bad enough that my mom can sense everything that's going on; I don't need her to hear it all, too. They follow me.

"We would have gotten here even sooner," he says, "but we got turned around. Didn't realize how close you are to the falls. This cabin is hard to find."

He's babbling.

"Yep," I say, "nice out-of-the-way spot. Perfect to get murdered in. Tell me, is that what you two came for? Want to get victim number two?"

I know it's not why they're here, but I'm so angry, I want them to feel it. Especially him.

"What? No," Brody says.

"It's not like that at all," Audra says. "We were just trying to help Cassie. That's it."

"Sure," I say.

"It's true." Audra squeezes her wrist. "I kick myself about it every day. Brody getting arrested, me helping him sneak out, it was all before Cassie got kidnapped. If we had any idea she was going to be taken that night, we wouldn't have done it. We would have been with her."

"Oh. Okay. So glad you cleared that up." I reach up and snap a twig off the giant maple tree I'm standing under and squeeze it in my fist. I keep talking before they can go on with their excuses. "That doesn't explain anything."

Brody reaches for me, but I step away. "So many lies," I spit at him. "*You* weren't really locked up the night Cassie disappeared."

"I swear, I never left that building. You have to believe me," he says.

I throw the twig on the ground and crush it with my foot. "Why should I believe anything you say? I trusted you, and you . . . you . . . lied to me." I can't stand that that hurts so much.

"Only because you already hated me," he says. "I didn't want you to get the wrong idea. I didn't want you to suspect me. And—"

"Too late now." I break off another branch. A long one. "It's always the boyfriend," I mumble.

"It wasn't me. You know that. Let me finish. Please."

He's right. I don't really think he took Cassie, but I also really don't know what's going on, and I don't like it. When I don't say anything, he takes it as an invitation to continue. "This whole thing is complicated. I got locked up on purpose. I trashed the market so they'd put me in there."

"For an alibi? Smart," I say. I'm not ready to let him off the hook.

"No." He turns to Audra. They share a look, and she nods. It's like she's giving him some sort of permission, because he starts talking again. "It was to look at the files in the pit. The sheriff has one on Cassie. We wanted to see it. She was getting all those visions of being taken. We thought maybe something in there could help or lead to who was after her."

I swipe the branch against the dirt. "And you didn't think that you should tell me that? That maybe it could've helped us?"

"Was going to, but after Cassie was taken, her file, all the files in that drawer, were gone."

"We didn't think it mattered anymore. They were moved," Audra says. "I checked. The drawer was empty, wasn't even locked."

"Convenient," I say.

Audra's face is so somber. "It's the truth."

I believe her, but I don't get why they didn't just tell me about the file. No, *files*. With an *s*. What else was in there? What aren't they telling me?

"What did all these mystery files say?"

"I just saw a bunch of names on folders." Brody pauses. "Yours was in there."

"Mine?" I freeze and look at him. How could he not have told me this? "What did it say?"

"I don't know. I only got a chance to go into Cassie's before I heard one of the deputies coming and had to get back in the cell."

I study the design I've made on the ground with the branch. "What did hers say then?"

"It was just a list of her tips, her visions the police checked out, and how most of them were a bust. On the top, someone wrote, 'Trying to be like her mother, but doesn't appear to have the same skill set.'"

"So let me get this straight. In these missing files there was information not just on *Cassie*, the person we're looking for, but about her mother having visions, and who knows what other kinds of intel, but you didn't feel the need to tell me?" I ask.

"I didn't think it was important."

"Everything's important," I yell.

"You didn't tell me about your visions."

"That's different." I throw the branch on the ground. "Mine was about me. While you . . . it doesn't make sense. You just happened to know where a bunch of secret files were kept in the office and how to get into them?"

He shakes his head again. "It wasn't me."

"Then who was it?"

"Cassie," Audra says.

Cassie? What?

"She had a vision about the files," Audra continues. "*She* was the one who wanted to know what was in there—what was written about her. Cassie and I came up with the plan. She told us where everything was hidden and how to get in. Brody was supposed to grab her file, hide it in one of the empty desks, and I'd pick it up the next day. We were all going to regroup once he got out and go over it."

"If I thought she was going to be taken that night," Brody says, "I never would have gone through with it. I thought I was helping, but instead I was locked away while she was getting kidnapped."

I don't even want to look at him. "Unless you're lying again," I say.

"Come on," he says. "The Lightsend sheriffs may not be Robo-Cops, but don't you think they'd notice if I went missing around seven, eight o'clock? I didn't risk checking the cabinet until around three a.m., and I still almost got caught. I would have been seen."

"You understand, right?" Audra asks.

Is she serious?

I cross my arms over my chest. "No. You want me to really understand? Then how about this? No more lies. No more secrets. I've had it. I want to know it all. *Everything.* Like why were you and Cassie fighting? What did it have to do with your father?"

"Okay, I'll tell you," she says, "but you have to promise it stays here."

"That depends on what you have to say," I tell her. I'm not making that type of promise, not until I know what she's hiding.

Audra lets out a deep breath. "All right."

She moves to lean against the trunk of the maple tree and looks up at the sky, like she's figuring out how best to explain.

"Well," I ask, "are you going to spit it out or not?"

"Yes. I just don't know where to start."

"Try the beginning," I say.

"Fine. It goes back to my dad. I'm not supposed to know this, but he tracks down people with abilities."

My eyes widen. "He *what*?"

"Yeah," she says. "He doesn't have one himself, it's not like he can sense them. He does it through regular old investigative work."

"Why?"

"I don't know. I've been trying to figure it out. I think it started with Cassie's mom. They were really close. She'd help him with cases and things. I don't know all of it. He doesn't talk to me about this kind of thing. Most of what I know is from Cassie— her visions and her own little investigation. If it wasn't for her, I wouldn't know special abilities were a thing."

I look at Brody. He doesn't seem stunned about all this the way I do. He's heard it before.

"Go on," I tell Audra.

"I tried digging up some stuff on my own, too, but there are still so many holes. But from what Cassie and I have been able to suss out, her mom and my dad wanted to find others like her."

"Did they?" I ask.

She nods. "Apparently. You're here."

This is a lot to take in. I'm trying to keep my thoughts straight. "Did he find others besides my mom and me? What about all those files? Were they people with abilities your dad or Cassie's mom tracked down?"

"Yeah," Audra says. "And they're also why Cassie and I were fighting."

"I don't get it," I say. "What's to fight over?"

Audra squeezes her eyes shut. When she reopens them she

begins talking. "She had a vision about one of the guys my dad found. Greg Scottley." She says it with disgust.

Scottley. The name comes back to me. I know it. It was the one in Cassie's sketch pad. "What about him?" I urge her on.

"He can make people in a two-foot radius tell the truth," she says.

That could be useful. "Nice."

"No," Audra says, "it's not, and neither was he. When he found out there were others like him, he decided to use it to his advantage." Her eyes harden on me. "*Blackmail.* Said if my dad didn't pay up, he'd do an exposé. Make my dad confess all he's found to the world. All Scottley needed was to be close enough to my dad, and he would have to answer truthfully. Any question he wanted. About anything. It would have ruined my dad. Made him a laughingstock. Put him in danger. Or worse."

"So what did he do?"

"From the bank statements I found," she says, "he paid Scottley. Often."

Blackmail. No wonder Audra couldn't stand me. I probably reminded her of this guy.

"It gets worse," she says. "One day he showed up at the house. I was home. My dad sent me to my room, but I heard everything. Scottley wanted more. Wanted the names of the other people my dad found, and he was going to make my dad tell him. Hard to lie to a man who can make you tell the truth. My dad tried to fight it. He answered honestly but evasively. But Scottley kept pressing. He wanted those names, he wanted to blackmail them, too, or I don't know. My dad wasn't going to let that happen. He wasn't going to put them in danger. That's when he threatened Scottley back. And Scottley knew my dad was telling the truth, so he took off."

"I still don't get the Cassie connection," I say.

"I'm getting there. Just like my dad and her mom, she wanted to find more people with abilities. She was always looking for answers."

That I understood. Had I known there were others, I would have, too.

"And since neither of our dads were offering any," Audra continues, "she thought she could get them from Scottley. A guy who always gets the truth, she figured he could help. She wanted to talk to him, to reach out. But he'd threatened my father. I didn't want to bring him back into our lives. Just because he could make others tell the truth didn't mean he was trustworthy, or that he'd help her. More likely, he'd try to use her."

"Did she ever reach out to him?" I ask.

"No."

"How do you know? Maybe she did. Maybe he's involved in her disappearance."

Audra grips her wrist again. "She told me she wouldn't. I trust her."

"Maybe we—" I start.

"No," Audra cuts me off. "She didn't. She knew what that would do to me. And I know what you're thinking, but no, we're not calling him. If I thought he could help find Cassie, I'd risk it, but he's more trouble than he's worth. He's not going to come play detective for us. He's afraid of my dad now, and this guy doesn't do anything for nothing."

I step away from her, from Brody, who's just been watching and listening this whole time.

"So see," she says, following me, "the fight had nothing to do with her going missing."

I'm out in the woods, but I need air.

"Hayden?" Audra says.

"Yeah, I see," I tell her, but my thoughts aren't on her fight or Scottley. They're on her dad. He didn't take Cassie. And he's probably not having an affair with my mom, either. He probably just sought her out because of what she can do, what I can do. He knew all along, even back when he busted me for the Brooke stuff.

There's a hand on my shoulder. I don't need to turn to know who it belongs to. The shiver the touch sends through my body tells me it's Brody.

"You okay?"

I don't know how to answer that. My head is swimming.

"Grim?" He says it endearingly, but it makes that mix of anger, hurt, frustration, longing, and confusion muddle further.

I whip around. "You lied."

"I explained. It was like you and your visions."

"And I explained that's different." I back up from him. "Oh my god." I study his face. "Were you lying about that, too? Did you know I had an ability the whole time?"

"What? No!"

I don't know what to believe from him anymore. "You just saw my file in the sheriff's supernatural drawer and didn't think anything of it."

"I thought it was there by mistake. It was thrown on top haphazardly. Figured the sheriff just tossed it there because he'd been reading up on you after your run-in with Brooke. I don't know, I didn't really think about it."

"I trusted you," I say quietly.

"I know." His voice is just as soft. He puts his fingertips on mine. I let them linger together for a few seconds before letting my hand fall away.

We just stare at each other. Everything is still. I don't know what to make of him, but I can't look away, either.

"Umm," Audra says, "I think I'm just going to go wait over there for a minute."

Neither Brody nor I turn to watch her go.

"I don't want any more secrets," I say.

"Okay."

"Why did Cassie break up with you?"

Brody doesn't say anything.

"Brody . . ."

"It doesn't matter."

"Nice. So much for no secrets."

He reaches out to me again. "Please, come on. It's not important."

I twist away from him. "It's important to me. What's the big deal? Why won't you tell me? Is it bad? Did you do something to her? Was she afraid of you?"

"What? No!"

"Then why?" I demand.

"You," he shouts back.

He's making no sense. "What?"

"You," he repeats. "Cassie broke up with me because of you."

"Whatever, Brody. I'm sick of this. You don't want to tell me, then don't tell me. You can keep up your charade. I'm done."

I move toward the cabin, but Brody blocks my path.

"Wait," he says. "It's true. She ended things because she had a vision. A lot of them."

I stop and look him right in the eyes. "Of what?"

He stares back at me. "Of me. Of you. She saw us together. It's why I was such a jerk to you when you moved here. I wanted to show Cassie that visions don't always come true, that I wasn't going to be with you, that I didn't even like you."

"Wait, what?" Cassie saw Brody and me? Why was she so nice to me then? This can't be right.

His voice gets quiet again. "She was convinced we were going to couple up. Kept seeing it. I thought she was being irrational, but she didn't want to hear it. So I set out to prove it. At first you made it easy. You certainly dished back whatever I threw your way."

I feel my heart thumping in my head. "At first . . ."

"Yeah, you annoyed the hell out of me, and blackmailing half my friends? Not cool. But then you were also funny and sharp, and kept me on my toes. I found myself looking to spar with you. I told myself it wasn't because I liked you, that it was just entertaining."

"Glad I could amuse you."

"It wasn't like that. I thought it was, but I was lying. Not to *you*. To myself. The more time I spent with you, the more I knew Cassie was right. Her visions were coming true. She told me this would happen, that I wouldn't be able to help it."

What is he saying? "Help what?"

Brody pauses before he speaks again.

"Falling in love with you."

42

HaYDeN

Crap. Did he really just say he's in love with me, or falling in love with me, or about to fall in love with me? My mouth is open, and I'm standing here staring at him. I'm fully aware of it, but it's out of my control. I'm too stunned to move, let alone respond to him.

There is no clear-cut way to answer when a guy tells you he has feelings and that his psychic ex-girlfriend predicted that the two of you would be together. Especially when that girlfriend is currently in danger. Not exactly something they teach you in school.

But I need to say something.

The first thing that pops into my head is that Cassie's visions aren't always right, but I don't speak the words. I'm not sure whether I'm more worried that Brody will agree with me or that he'll say this one is on the money.

I turn away. I can't take the eye contact anymore. Not now. Not after that confession.

Yet I somehow make things even more awkward, because when

I look away from him, I catch Audra's eyes. She's been watching us. I guess I can't blame her. If the situation was reversed, I suppose I would have been listening in, too.

"You okay?" she mouths.

My expression must be pretty bad, because she has a look of concern mixed with amusement on her face.

I'm about to call her back over here. At the very least she can serve as a distraction from me dealing with what Brody just said, but then he starts talking again.

"Hayden," he says.

I don't want to turn back. I'm still absorbing all of this.

"Hayden," he says again.

Stop talking to me. "What?" I ask.

"Your phone's buzzing."

Huh? "My phone is in Donnelly's desk."

But then I hear a buzz, too, and I reach into my jacket pocket. It's the burner.

X
Back off, Ms. Jefferies.

"Oh my god," I say, and almost drop the phone. "Look at this. Both of you."

Audra rushes over, and they both huddle around me.

"You have to write back," Audra says.

XXX
Who is this?

X

Someone that you don't want to mess with. Not
if you care about your friend.

"Ask about Cassie," Brody says. "How she is."

XXX

Is Cassie okay?

X

That will depend on you, Ms. Jefferies.

XXX

Who are you? What do you want?

X

For you to drop this.

XXX

Can I talk to Cassie? Can you send a picture?
Let me know she's all right?

Nothing else comes.

XXX

Hello? Please. Just let Cassie go. I'll do
whatever you want.

We wait, but the phone remains still.
"I think that's it," I say.
Audra takes the phone. "We need to get this to my dad.
Now."

"No," I say. And it's no longer because I don't trust him. "We can't."

"What are you talking about? That was the whole plan before you took off from the station. They may be able to trace the texts."

"That was before *this*. Didn't you see what they said? They said for us to stand down. Going to the sheriff could get her hurt. What if they find out?"

I look to Brody. The tension from before is gone. This is about Cassie. Saving her. The other stuff can wait. Still, I need him to be on my side, only he looks skeptical, too. "They might hurt her anyway," he says. "What if the phone leads to her?"

"No way they still have it, not after what they just sent."

"But it still could be incriminating," he says. "It could be what gets Ollie to crack. He must have talked to someone. They knew you had his phone."

"More reason for us not to report this. Ollie's not going to admit anything to the sheriff. He doesn't want to get in trouble. We stand a better chance of getting something out of him."

They still look uneasy. "And you know what else will happen if we go to the sheriff?" I say. "We'll be off this case so fast. No way he'll let us continue digging, even though we've gotten so much further than he has."

"I don't know," Audra says.

"We're getting close. We're going to find her. The kidnappers wouldn't have reached out if we weren't on the right track. Just give me one more day. So we can talk to Ollie and figure out who else is involved. Please," I say. I need to do this. I need to set it right.

"Fine, you have *one* day," she says, holding up a finger.

I pull out my car keys. "I'll head to the school now."

"Slow down there," Brody says. "Have you looked at the time? By the time you get back there, everyone will be gone."

Crap. And I have to get to work, too.

"Tomorrow then. We're going to solve this. We'll get people to talk." I know it.

Don't worry, Cassie. I'm going to find you.

43

cassie

"So this is what it looks like when you have one of your little visions," Vader says, nudging my leg with their foot, as if trying to make me come to.

I look around the room. Still in chains. Still a prisoner. One of my captors standing before me.

A sob escapes and then another one.

"What did you just see?" they ask.

I shake my head. "Nothing." It's not convincing.

"Is it about your little friends? The ones playing Sherlock?"

I don't answer.

"Tell me." This time Vader kicks me.

I flinch, in both surprise and pain. They've threatened to hurt me but have never gotten physical before. They're spooked, too. Things are closing in. "I told you. Nothing."

My expression, my breathing, gives me away.

They bend down so that they're hovering over me. "Don't make me ask again."

I cry, but not because of any physical pain. "Please," I plead.

"Last warning." They reach into their cape.

"Fine," I say, swallowing a sob. I'm about to seal my fate. "I saw *you*."

"Me?"

"Yes."

"And just what was I doing?"

I shake my head again, and they clutch my arm and squeeze. "I said, what was I doing?"

"You were by the falls. Opposite side of the main lot. Marker W-3. Away from everyone. Near the end of the little dirt road that veers off past the welcome center. My friends were there, too. You said they were in the way."

"And . . . do I take care of the problem?"

"Yes . . . you . . . you . . ."

"I . . . I . . . what?"

The sobs burst out of me uncontrollably. "You kill them."

They let go of my arm and take off the mask. No need for secrecy anymore. I've already seen their face.

"Go on." They grab a folding chair by the filing cabinets and take a seat in front of me. "I want all the details."

How can they do this? How can they be so evil?

"No," I say, refusing to make eye contact. "Don't make me."

The gun comes out. It's pointed at me. "You don't have a choice. Talk."

44

HAYDEN

Brody, Audra, and I are the first students at school Wednesday morning. I've never gotten here this early, but we want to catch Ollie as soon as he gets in. Brody tried stopping by his house yesterday, thought he'd have better luck by himself, but Ollie wasn't home.

So now Ollie can answer to all of us. Someone knew I had his phone, and I want to know how. Who did he speak to? Ollie's the key to finding Cassie. I have to get him to talk to me, or pray a vision kicks in when I try.

The parking lot fills up, but still no sign of him.

"Think he's calling in sick?" Audra asks. She's perched up on the wall near the main entrance, her feet dangling over the side.

I'm pacing in front of her, and Brody is leaning against the wall. "If he does," he says, "I'm going back to his house."

Finally, a blue Bentley pulls into the lot. The cars people have at this school are obscene. Ollie isn't even the only one with that model, but he is the only one with a vanity license plate that includes his name.

Audra jumps off the wall, and the three of us make our way to where he's pulling in.

Ollie sees us coming and doesn't open his door. He just leans his head back on the headrest and rubs his hand over his temples.

I knock on the window. "Open up."

I know he can hear me.

He fills his cheeks with air and blows it out slowly. "Go away."

He sits up and puts his hand on the ignition. Is he going to drive away? Brody must have the same idea, because he moves and stands in front of the car.

"Don't think you're going anywhere," I tell Ollie. I'm still talking through the window, but I don't care. "Who did you tell about the phone? Do you know how much danger you put Cassie in?"

He wipes his whole face with his hands.

I beat on the window. "Are you listening?"

Ollie opens the window partway and turns to me. "I don't need this right now."

From his appearance, he really doesn't. Now that I'm getting a full-on look, I can tell he's a mess. This is not typical Ollie. He is always put-together, hair styled, clothes crisp. Today, he looks like he rolled out of bed, and his eyes look exhausted.

"Looking good, Ollie," I say. "Conscience getting to you, I hope?"

Then I get a sick thought. What if he looks this way because he did something to Cassie? What if I was wrong, and he isn't some henchman or pawn, but the mastermind of all this? And all my prying made him act. Oh god. Did I make a mistake?

"Did you hurt her? What did you do?"

"Ruined my life," he mutters.

"What?"

Audra comes closer. "Did you do something to her?"

"No, I did something to *me*."

"Ollie, what are you talking about?" I demand. "You get that Cassie is missing, right? Somebody you're working with did this."

"I know."

What the hell?

I look to Brody and call out, "He knows something."

Brody races back over to the driver's side of the car, and from the look on his face, I think he's going to pummel Ollie if he doesn't talk.

Although he may have some competition. Audra has already reached inside the window and is grasping Ollie's coat. "What exactly is it that you know?" she says slowly. "I'm not letting her die, not because of you."

"Enough," he says. "I already talked to your dad."

She lets go of him. "You what?"

He slumps in his seat. "I went to your dad."

I reach in, unlock the door, and open it. "Talk."

"You got what you wanted. Leave me alone," Ollie says. He pulls himself up and gets out of the car.

"Ollie," Brody says, "Cassie's still missing. Help us."

"I did. Why do you think I went to the sheriff?"

"Please, just tell us what you know," Brody pleads.

Ollie shakes his head. He looks so tired. "They told me to keep quiet. Not to say anything, act normal. Bad enough I'm in this mess, I'm not risking my plea deal over you guys."

"It's not for us," I say. "It's for Cassie."

"And you think you can do a better job than the sheriff?" Ollie asks, then snorts. "What am I saying, of course you do."

"Come on," I say. "And what if we can? Do you want to be the reason Cassie is still out there? We won't tell anyone we got the info from you."

He sighs, his fight gone. "Fine. After our run-in yesterday, I spoke to Coach."

"Coach Hill?" Audra says.

"Yeah." Ollie leans back on his car. "He's my hookup and the reason the team doesn't worry about any drug tests. I just told him not to use the phone, and that you were going off the deep end, thinking we had something to do with Cassie. He laughed it off, but the look he got? I don't know. I got spooked. I didn't want to get in trouble, but the Cassie thing kept eating at me. What if he did take her? I called my dad's lawyer. They worked out a deal. A teacher—a coach—dealing at a school is a way bigger priority than me."

"So what happened?" Audra asked.

"I was at the station all night. They brought Coach in, but he didn't see me, they kept him separate. They didn't tell him I was the one who narced, either. Not with Cassie still missing and his accomplice still out there. Which is why I'm here now. I'm trying not to draw more attention to myself."

"Any idea who his accomplice is?" I ask.

"No. I only dealt with Coach, and even our in-person conversations about it were few and far between."

"What about at the station? Did they say anything?"

He shakes his head. "My attorney says they're holding him,

haven't officially charged him yet, but he lawyered up. Not saying anything."

The bell rings. "Remember," he says, "you didn't get any of this from me. They're not making his arrest public yet."

We all nod.

"Whoa," Brody says once Ollie's gone.

"Yeah," Audra agrees.

Coach Hill. An accomplice. I grasp Audra's arm. "Oh my God. I know who has Cassie."

"What? Who?" she asks.

"Thadwell."

"You think the principal is in on this?" Brody asks.

"Yes. Those texts we got on the burner. They referred to me as Ms. Jefferies. *Ms.* He's the only one who calls me that here."

"That is pretty common, though," Audra says. "It could be a coincidence."

"No, I'm sure. It's not just the texts. When I had my guidance appointment, I saw Coach Hill and Mr. Thadwell together." I close my eyes and try to remember the details. "They both looked so intense. Coach was not there for a friendly chat. It was the day after the assembly. And come on, when one of your students is missing, football schedules are not going to be the principal's top priority. Why would he have the coach in his office then? The only reason he'd need a closed-door meeting with the coach is if it was about Cassie."

"It makes sense," Audra says. "He has access to all the locker combinations. He could easily send messages, phones, slip drugs into lockers whenever he wants."

I look to Brody, and he's nodding. He sees it, too.

"Think about it," I add. "Thadwell never lets anything bad come out about the school. He covers up everything. What if it's not because he's so worried about Lightsend High's reputation, but because he's worried that an investigation will uncover what he's up to? It's him. I'm sure of it."

Audra pulls out her phone. "I'll call my dad."

"It won't do any good. There's not enough evidence for the sheriff's department to question him. We need more proof for that. I need to talk to Thadwell myself. Get him to slip up, or maybe I'll get lucky and have a vision. I have to try. It's our best shot."

They don't need any convincing. We all go into the building, but I'm the only one to walk into the office. Quill likes me. I'm hoping it will get me an actual face-to-face with Thadwell.

"Hayden," she says when I walk in. "You don't have an appointment today."

"I know, but I need to talk to Mr. Thadwell. It's important."

She shuffles some papers on her desk. "I'm sorry, he has back-to-back meetings and calls all day."

"I'll catch him in between. He must have a few minutes."

Ms. Quill looks back at his office. "He doesn't like to be disturbed when the door is closed."

"Please," I say. "I really need to talk to him. In the assembly, he said if we had any questions or concerns, we could come talk to him at *any* time. I'm here now."

Ms. Quill shakes her head. "I wish I could help you, but I can't interrupt. He specifically said not to bother him, that he has a lot to deal with today." Yeah, like figuring out what to do now that his accomplice/staff member is sitting in the sheriff's office. "He's free tomorrow," she continues.

Tomorrow is too late. Cassie's already been gone five nights. I don't want to make it six, not when Thadwell knows the walls are closing in on his drug ring. Who knows how he'll react?

I debate pushing my way into his office, but I won't get any answers if he's in the middle of something. Instead, I thank Ms. Quill and head back to Audra and Brody.

"Well?" Audra asks.

"Booked solid. Couldn't get in."

"All right," she says. "It's okay. We'll catch him before he leaves for the day."

"And what if he takes off before then? What if having Coach Hill in custody scares him into taking care of his 'Cassie problem'?" I ask.

"We watch him," Brody says. "Make sure he doesn't leave. If he's here, Cassie's safe. We'll take shifts. I can miss a few classes. If he takes off, we follow him and call Audra's dad."

"I'll watch him first," I say.

"No," Audra says. "Brody and I will handle this. Teachers hate you. If they see you lurking, you'll get slapped with detention, and you need to talk to Thadwell after school. Brody and I will be able to talk our way out of it. We've got this. You're already risking it by being out here right now."

"I'm good for a few more minutes." I hold up a hall pass. "Didn't even have to ask for it. Told you Quill likes me."

Brody sneers at the mention of her name but doesn't say anything about her. Instead, he gets down to business. "I'll take this shift. I'll text if he leaves. We all meet up here after last period?"

We nod in agreement. The rest of my day drags by. I find myself bolting as soon as each bell rings, but it only brings me to my next class faster, and then it's more hurry up and wait.

"Ahh, look at you, here early. Let me guess, you want your phone," Donnelly says as I walk in.

"What?"

"Your phone. The one I confiscated yesterday . . ."

"Right."

He shakes his head and pulls it out of his desk. "Never know what to expect with you, do we, Miss Jefferies?" He holds it toward me. "Didn't know people could live without this. Most students are lined up for these things at the end of the day or begging for them back early. Never had someone forget about it."

That's because they all live on their phones, checking what their friends are up to, and texting them nonstop. I don't have that problem. I only have two . . . I don't even know what to call them—and they both know I don't have my phone and often don't respond even when I do. "Guess I'm not most students."

"And aren't we all grateful for that," Kristoff snarks, coming in with Ollie beside him. "Right?!" He starts his hyena laugh, but Ollie doesn't join in.

"What's wrong with you, man?"

"Nothing," Ollie says.

I take my phone and go to my desk. I turn it on. Shutting it off yesterday saved some power, but the battery is still pretty low. As suspected, no calls, no texts. I start to write to Brody.

"Don't make me take it from you again," Donnelly says.

"Bell hasn't rung."

"Just a matter of minutes," Donnelly says.

He's right, and I don't want to deal with him again, so I put the phone away. I'm anxious the whole period. I've been anxious all day, but this is worse. The class takes an eternity. I keep running everything through my head again. I wish I could talk to Thadwell now. Fish everything out of him.

Somehow I make it through the class, through lunch, through the end of the day. I take a deep breath as I head to the office. It's time to talk to Mr. Thadwell, and hopefully bring Cassie home.

45

HaYDen

"What do we have here?" Ms. Quill says, when Brody, Audra, and I walk into the office. "Brody, it's been a while." She twirls a piece of hair around her finger and tugs at it. Not in a flirty way, but a nervous one. "How is your dad?"

He refuses to look at her, and he definitely doesn't answer. He just stares off, jaw clenched, in the direction of the principal's office.

"Well, then . . . ," she says, getting extra fidgety. One hand is still playing with her hair, the other with the charm around her neck. "It's not like I want him back. I moved on. You can tell him that. Doing better than ever."

"Thought I'd try again to see Mr. Thadwell," I say, before things get even more awkward. I'm pretty sure Brody is about to lose it. His nostrils are flared now, and his lips are pressed so tight that I can't even see them.

Ms. Quill wags her finger at me. "Got to respect your willing-ness to go after what you want. You're always up to something, aren't you? But I'm sorry, I can't let you in there. He's finishing up for the day, and trust me, he is ready to go home. Tomorrow is your best bet."

I'm not letting her stop me. Not this time. "It's okay," I say. "Don't worry about it, Mr. Thadwell will want to see me. I'll just let myself in," I say. I don't wait for her to respond. I just head for his office.

I'm doing this ambush alone, but the others are sticking close by in case I need backup. Better chance of getting Thadwell talking if it's just me. I'm the one he's afraid of, after all. I'm the one getting the texts. I just hope Brody doesn't strangle Ms. Quill before I get back.

"Guess who?" I say, swinging open Mr. Thadwell's office door and marching inside. I pull the handle closed behind me.

"What are you doing, Ms. Jefferies?" Mr. Thadwell stands up, his arms pressed down against the desk, the slab of wood supporting all his weight.

"Thought we could have a little conversation."

"You'll have to make an appointment with Ms. Quill. Now please see yourself out. I've had quite the day. I just want to finish up here and go home," he says.

"Yeah, about that . . ." I shrug and point to myself. "Finishing up here isn't going to happen until you talk to me. I'm not going anywhere."

He sits back down in his chair and rubs the back of his head. "What did I do to deserve this?" he mumbles to himself. "I need a new job."

"What did you do to deserve this?" He wants to get right to the punch, it works for me. "How about kidnapping and selling drugs to students? And don't worry, I'm sure prison will have lots of new jobs for you to do."

"What are you going on about?" he asks.

I lean on his desk, striking the pose he used earlier. "I'm talking about you taking Cassie."

"Ms. Jefferies, I've had it up to here with you." He reaches for the phone on his desk and brings the receiver to his ear. "We don't need any more of your false accusations. I'm going to call the sheriff. He took you on as his little pet project. Let him handle you. I have important things to deal with. I'm not going to be talked to like this in my office."

"Please call him," I say. "Want me to dial? You can tell him where you're stashing Cassie, since your partner isn't talking."

"What?!"

"Maybe you can work out a deal if you spill on Coach Hill first," I continue, "help you get a better sentencing. Right now, Coach hasn't said anything. He's just sitting there biding his time."

"What? Coach Hill called in sick for the day," he says, hanging up the phone. He's twitchy. He knows what's happening.

Always trying to defend the reputation of the school, down to the bitter end. Or maybe trying to save himself. "Too late for that," I say. "I know where he is. You know I know."

"Then you know he hasn't been charged. He agreed to go down to the station of his own free will as long as there was no fuss, and I'm not talking about this any further with a student." I didn't know all that, but he certainly seems to be up on the case.

"Then talk about it with the sheriff. Where were you when Cassie went missing?"

"I've had enough," he says. "I had nothing to do with Ms. Lee's disappearance. I would never. Now leave, Ms. Jefferies."

"First tell me where you were when she disappeared," I insist. "It's all I want to know."

He sighs in annoyance. "Then will you go?"

"Yes," I say, even though the answer is probably not.

"I was home with my wife, Ms. Jefferies."

"Convenient," I say.

"It's where I am every weeknight." He rubs the back of his head again. "I go home, have dinner, watch *Jeopardy!*, try to forget about my day, and go to sleep."

"*Jeopardy!*?" I ask, and slink down into the chair in front of his desk. "You were watching *Jeopardy!*?"

"Yes. Seven o'clock. Same time every night. If you must know, it was the last night of teachers' week when Cassie went missing."

I forgot about my vision. His wife saying he never misses the show. If that's the case, he may have an alibi.

I look at him.

He doesn't give off a guilty vibe, just an agitated one, but that's geared toward me. Is it possible he's telling the truth? I think so.

I take out my phone. It's in desperate need of a charge, but it should be okay for the moment.

"You were supposed to go, Ms. Jefferies," Mr. Thadwell says.

"Hold on."

I text Brody to check out Mr. Thadwell's story. To pay a pop-in to his wife. Find out the last time he missed the show. Just to be positive. But that gut feeling I had that the principal was in on this is fading fast.

"Why was Coach Hill in here yesterday?" I ask Mr. Thadwell.

"What?"

"Why was he in here? What were you talking about?"

"Not that it's any of your business, but cuts to next year's football budget," he says as the last thread in my theory about Mr. Thadwell's guilt unravels. How could I have been so wrong?

"Look," he says, "I've been patient here. I know you've had your issues at this school. You're obviously worried about Ms. Lee, and this job at the sheriff's office is evidently not a good fit for you, seems to have you running in circles. I've been giving you some leeway, but you need to let the deputies do their jobs. Trust that they'll find her."

That's the problem. I don't.

He sees the look on my face. "You have to stop this. What if I had been the person who took Cassie? You would have put yourself in danger. Let the sheriff's office handle this."

I hear what he's saying, but I can't let this drop. Any of it.

"You want me to trust they'll do their jobs, but you didn't do yours." He's in a talkative mood; let's hear it all. "Why do you let everyone get away with everything? People are afraid to come to you. They know the Nicks and the Brookes of the world will just walk free."

"Are you including yourself in that list? Some might think you got off pretty light."

"Light? I'm stuck working at the sheriff's office!"

"Is that what this is about?" he asks. "Well, let me inform you, Ms. Jefferies. You getting punished for taking advantage of students and faculty is not the equivalent of letting Brooke or anyone else get away with things."

"This isn't about me. Do you know how many people have

been tormented at this school? Brooke alone has targeted Fiona, Cassie, Leighton—and those are just the first names that came to me off the top of my head. If you want Lightsend High to have such a shining reputation, don't you think that's an issue?"

"I assure you we take bullying very seriously," he says. "All matters are investigated thoroughly."

"Well, investigate this." I hold up my phone. "I have a recording of Brooke that may shed some light on things." When I have more battery, I'll send him the file.

"I should have known if you got a job in the sheriff's office, you'd try to become a little Veronica Mars," he mumbles to himself.

"Now it's time for you to go," he says, loosening his tie, "so I can finish up here and go home."

I stand up to leave, and oh god . . . No. I grip the arm of the chair. If Mr. Thadwell isn't Coach Hill's partner, that means the real accomplice is still out there. Cassie is still in danger, and I've been wasting time.

"Ms. Jefferies?" Mr. Thadwell asks.

"I'm going. I'm sorry," I say as I exit.

He grunts in response.

Who could have Cassie? Who's working with Coach Hill?

"Audra?" I call when I get to the main office area. Everyone's gone. Brody went to Mr. Thadwell's house. I guess Ms. Quill went home. But I have no idea where Audra went. She wouldn't have left without telling me.

I pop my head out into the hallway. It's empty, too. I check the closest bathroom. No sign of her.

I triple-check my phone. Three percent battery, enough to get a message. There's still none there, though.

I try calling her as I head back to the office. She doesn't pick up. I text Brody instead.

Hayden
Any word from Audra?

Brody
No. Why? Just got to Thadwell's. Wife confirmed his alibi.

I sit down on the bench to answer him, when I spot it.

What the . . . ?

Next to me, on the side of the bench, is Audra's bag. I pick it up and look inside. No vision. No phone, either. But there are her wallet and car keys. I may have thought something was off before, but now I know it.

Something is definitely wrong.

No more junior detective. I'm calling the sheriff. I go to Ms. Quill's desk. Her phone won't die on me.

The picture there makes me freeze.

It's of Ms. Quill. There's a muscled arm around her, but the rest of him is out of frame. But that's not the part I can't stop looking at. It's the way the sun is reflecting off the diamond in her necklace. The way it's causing a flash of light.

A sparkle, a flash. Like in the vision I had. The one I got when I picked up Cassie's journal in the bathroom the day she was a wreck and told me I changed everything.

I have a sinking feeling. I grab the frame.

For once, a vision comes when I need it.

I'm in a living room. Coach Hill is there. His arms are around me—around Ms. Quill.

"I don't want to keep us a secret," she whines.

"We have to, hon. With what we're doing, it's better not to be linked. We've been over this," he says.

"I know. It's just, how nice would it be to go into work together, share lunch, steal a kiss. Quill and Hill. We even rhyme. You know all the kids will be talking about us."

"And that's what we're trying to avoid. Just touch the butterfly," he says, pointing to her chain, "when you're thinking of me."

"It's not the same as seeing you."

He takes the picture frame and hands it to her. "Then just look at the picture."

"You're not in it."

"Yeah, I am," he says.

"Your arm doesn't count." She juts out her lip.

"Oh, yeah," he says, sweeping her up in it and walking to a bedroom. "Want to see what my arm can do?"

I do not. Please let this vision end. Please let this vision end. Please let this vision end.

My prayer somehow works. I'm in the office again. It's Ms. Quill. She's the coach's partner. She must have Cassie. She must have Audra. I reach for the phone.

"Ms. Jefferies!" Mr. Thadwell says, coming out of his office, coat on, briefcase in hand. "You're not supposed to be here. Time to go home."

"I just have to make a call." I pick up the receiver.

Mr. Thadwell reaches over and hangs it up. "And you can do that from the comfort of your home."

"No, you don't understand. It's Ms. Quill. She's the one working with Coach. They're together. She's behind all this. My friends are in danger." And I realize that, even though I haven't known them that long, and barely know Cassie at all, they do feel like my friends, and I need to help them.

He lets out a long exhale. "I took Cassie. She took Cassie. Who's next? Ms. Drake? Do the lunch ladies have some sort of criminal ring going on?"

"I'm serious," I say. "It's her."

"And you were serious and sure before. We talked about this. Let the sheriff's department do its job. Come on, I'm going to walk you out."

I grab Audra's bag. "But I have—"

"Nope," he cuts me off. "I don't want to hear another word." He turns off the lights and ushers me out.

"You have to listen."

"Hayden," he says. "Stop. It was too much before. But this is above and beyond. You are out of control."

He's not going to believe me. I'm the boy who cried wolf.

If he won't listen, Audra's dad will. I pull out my phone.

No.

It's dead.

I don't try explaining to Mr. Thadwell anymore. I take off

running for my car. I need to charge it. I need to get Audra help. Now.

I hook my phone up into the charger. *Come on, Greta, work for me. Don't be wonky. Not today.* I angle it in the cup holder forty-five degrees and pinch the cord.

Just a tiny bit of power. Come on. Enough to call 911. What I should have done all along.

Nothing.

Okay, don't panic. I'll just drive to the police station.

Where are you, Audra? Where would she take you?

My phone rings, making me jump. It's back on. It's getting juice. *Thank you, Greta.*

I answer.

"Hayden?" It's Brody.

"Brody." It's cutting out. "Audra's in—"

"Hayden?" he says. "Are you there?"

"Yes. But Audra's in—"

Crap. The thing died again. I don't know if he heard any of that.

I smack the lighter. "Work, damn it." I hold on to the cord as I drive, hoping it will give the phone some power.

"Okay. I should be at the station soon. Think, Hayden. Where would she go?"

I don't know. But my phone may. Find My Friends. Brody hooked us all up. It will show me where Audra is. At the red light, I try the phone again. It comes to life. I click her name in the app.

What? She's by my house. Why?

I switch over to the phone and dial 911.

Someone picks up immediately. "Emergency, how—"

Damn it, damn it, damn it. Why can't I keep a charge?

I'm still about ten minutes away from the sheriff's office.

The light turns green.

What if that's ten minutes too long? I'm not sure what to do.

Someone beeps their horn behind me.

"Okay, okay." I hit the gas, but instead of turning right toward the station, I go straight.

I'm going to Audra.

46

HaYDeN

My phone is useless. The car charger isn't cutting it. I can't bring the thing back to life.

So much for 911.

What was I thinking? What am I supposed to do if I find them? Maybe Audra and I can take Ms. Quill down together. Two of us. One of her. She's not that big. But what if she has a weapon?

What do I have? A couple of hangers in the back. Spare tire. Jack. What am I supposed to do with that? Throw it at her?

I do have Greta. I can just run her down. And then get charged for vehicular manslaughter. Perfect. Okay, not if it's self-defense, not if it's defending Audra. But hopefully it won't come to that.

I turn onto the winding road to my place. Where did I see that blue dot on Find My Friends? It was close to the cabin. Maybe a little south, a little east, near the falls.

I follow the road, and I don't have to guess anymore. A car is parked off to the side about a half mile from my driveway. The parking lot for the falls is much farther down. This has to be Ms. Quill.

Where are they?

I scan the area. I think I see movement by one of the wooden posts—marker W-3.

I can't fit Greta through the trees. So much for my weapon. I'm going to have to leave her here. Should I take the car jack? I check the trunk. The thing is not exactly the right shape to wield. It will be more of a burden, and it's not like I can sneak up on her carrying that thing.

I search the ground and grab a branch. Something is better than nothing. Barely.

This was a mistake. I shouldn't have come straight here. I should have thought this through.

I hear a scream, and a wave of panic runs through me.

No more time for second-guessing: It's now or never.

I run toward the sound but stop when I see that Ms. Quill has a gun pointed at Audra.

"Look who's joined the party," Ms. Quill says. "Guess she was right." She juts her chin toward my branch. "What are you going to do with that? Try and give me a splinter?"

I take a step toward her.

"One move and I shoot," she warns me. She laughs a little. "I always wanted to say that. 'Go ahead, make my day.'"

She's enjoying this. She's twisted, but I have to try to reason with her anyway. "Just let her go," I say. "You don't want to hurt her."

"Want, no," she says, gun still pointed. "Need to, yes. You're all liabilities now."

"You're already too late," I tell her. "The sheriff has the coach. They'll tie the two of you together," I warn her. "Better to turn yourself in now, before it gets worse."

"He won't turn me in, and we were careful. They won't tie us together. No one will. They'll have no reason to look into me."

"Except that I told them to," I say.

"You're funny. Like you have any credibility after all your lies. Brooke saw to that, and then you just helped her along. Mr. Thadwell, really? The man finds a penny on the ground and tries to find the owner. You think he could have taken Cassie? Come on. And I thought you were supposed to be the clever one."

"Where is she? Where's Cassie?" I ask.

"Like I told your friend here." Ms. Quill waves the gun. "It doesn't matter anymore."

"Did you kill her?" I ask.

"Instead of worrying about Cassie, I'd worry about yourself," she answers.

"If you shoot us, they'll pin it on you. They'll find you," I say.

Ms. Quill shakes her head. "I really don't think so. A couple of kids getting into a fight. Over a blackmail threat, maybe?" She laughs again. "You made this so easy, Hayden. Who wouldn't buy that during a fight at a clandestine meeting near your house, there's a fight, and you both fall into the ravine, tumbling to your deaths? Or if you make this difficult, I can shoot her and make it look like you did it before falling yourself. Either way is fine, really."

"It won't work," I tell her.

"Actually, it will." Then her eyes focus on something behind me. "Stop!" she yells.

I turn to look. It's Brody. He must have tracked us here.

I hope he had the foresight to call for backup.

"The whole trifecta is here. Even better," she says.

"Gretchen . . . ," he says.

"Oh, we're on a first-name basis now? How sweet. Don't worry, little Grayson Junior. I wasn't going to leave you out. I knew you'd be here. And if not, I had another plan for you. You know, you should really change the locks after you kick someone out. But this is preferable. Look at you guys helping me out."

"Gretchen," Brody says again. "Come on. This isn't you."

"No? Because you had a few choice names for me when I was with your father."

"I was wrong," he says, trying to calm her down.

She's fixated on him.

"I could have had something real with him. I would never have had to work a day in my life. You ruined it for me."

"Is that what you want?" Brody asks. "Money? We can still make that happen."

"Do you think I'm that gullible?" Ms. Quill asks.

While her focus is still on him, mine is on Audra. *Don't do it. Don't do it. Don't do it, Audra.*

The gun is still pointing at her, but she's going to try something. I can see it in her eyes, her stance. The way she's looking from Brody to Ms. Quill. She's waiting for her opening.

Don't, Audra.

"No," Brody says. "I think you were dealt a bad hand. And I was—"

Audra lunges. She tackles Ms. Quill to the ground. I expect to hear a shot ring out, but it doesn't come. The gun didn't fire. At least Audra's not hurt. Not yet. She fell on top of Ms. Quill. The gun is on the ground, about a foot from them. Both have their arms outstretched, fighting for the weapon. Ms. Quill almost gets it, but Audra knocks it away from her grasp. They each move in for it again. Brody and I race over, but we're not fast enough.

Ms. Quill overpowers Audra. She has the gun. She's in control.

She stands, aiming the weapon wildly at all three of us. "Get up," Ms. Quill tells Audra. When she does, Ms. Quill puts the gun to her temple.

"I've had enough," Ms. Quill says. "Junior. Over there. Now." She kicks her foot in the direction of the falls. "New story line. A little love triangle gone wrong. Murder-suicide. You first. Jump," she commands him.

"No!" I yell.

Audra is shaking. "You don't have to do this. Please let us go."

"I said jump."

Brody looks down the falls and back at me.

I shake my head, tears flowing down my cheeks. "No." The word is drowned out by my sobs.

"No? Then we can start with this one." Ms. Quill pretends to pull the trigger at Audra's head. "Would you like a close look at your friend's brain?"

"I'll do it," Brody says, "just leave them alone."

"Don't," Audra yells. "She's going to kill us anyway. Don't make it easy for her."

"Bang, bang," Ms. Quill says. "Time's almost up."

"I'm going," he says, and takes another step toward the ledge.

"No, Brody." My stomach is lurching.

He looks at me, the right side of his mouth lifting into a semi-smile. Tears blur my vision, but I see him give me a slight nod, and then the next second he's gone.

I fall to the ground, hunched over, and wail.

"Cut it out. We do not need the theatrics," Ms. Quill says. "Now who's next?"

How is this happening? It's all my fault. I should have gone to the sheriff's. I never should have come here. I look up.

Oh my god.

There's something moving in the trees behind Ms. Quill. Some*one*.

It's *my mom*.

She puts her finger to her lips to tell me to be quiet. I want to scream. To tell her to save herself. There are too many emotions going on around here. She can't do this. It's too risky.

She nods at me. She wants me to trust her.

I take a breath and try as she creeps closer to Ms. Quill.

I need to buy Mom time. I need to get Audra out of the way.

"I said, who's next?" Ms. Quill calls out.

"Me," I say. "I can't watch that again."

"You know what to do," she responds. "And leave that branch of yours on the ground. Don't want you getting any ideas."

"Run," Audra screams at me through tears. "You can still get away."

"I can't leave you."

"Isn't this sweet," Ms. Quill says.

Come on, Audra. I need you to move. I need you to clear space for my mom. Audra is still dangerously close to Ms. Quill. I have to try something else. "We're going to do it together," I say. "We'll jump together."

I put my hand out for Audra. I nod for her to take it.

"I will shoot if you try anything," Ms. Quill warns.

"We know."

Audra steps forward. Once. Twice.

And bear spray fills Ms. Quill's face.

"Mom," I yell, as Audra and I grab each other.

"I got this, baby," she says. "You're okay."

I rush toward her, but she's doesn't need my help. She swipes Ms. Quill's legs, making her fall to the ground, and then grabs the gun, training it on our attacker. Where was this mom my whole life? She's kind of a badass.

"Stay down," my mom warns Ms. Quill. "I'll know if you get any ideas." But I don't think she's going anywhere. Not without help. Ms. Quill is a heap on the ground, her arm pressed against her eyes. The spray got her good.

I take the gun from my mom. She's been holding it together, but I don't know how or if it will last much longer.

"Whoa," Audra says, stretching her hand out. "That's not how you hold a loaded gun. Give it to me." I guess I didn't pick up enough tricks at the sheriff's office. I pass it over. She empties the bullets, and then takes off her belt and uses it to tie Ms. Quill's wrists together. Talk about resourceful.

I turn back to my mom, as Audra makes sure Ms. Quill is secure. "H-how?" I stammer, wrapping my arms around her. "How is this possible?"

My mom holds me tight. "I felt you nearby. I felt your fear. Your panic. I felt my baby. I knew I had to come. I got you. The sheriff is on his way, too. I called him."

The momentary seconds of relief fade away as the memory of Brody jumping off the cliff returns. My mom saved Audra and me, but she didn't get here in time for Brody.

He's gone.

"It's okay," my mom says, but now she's crying, too.

"No, it's not. He's gone. Brody's gone."

It will never be okay. Brody followed me to his death.

Audra comes over and hugs me. I squeeze her tight, both of us sobbing into the other's shoulder.

"Umm, I appreciate the sentiment, but maybe a little help over here?"

Brody's head is peeking out from the cliff.

"Brody!" Audra yells.

He's alive.

The shock gives way, and we run over and help pull him up.

Brody is standing in front of me. I look him over. He's really here. He's got dirt everywhere, including a giant smudge on his cheek, and there's a small scrape on his forehead above his right eye, but he's in one piece. He's okay.

"You're alive," I say.

He smiles at me. "I'm alive."

I know he's safe, but my body shakes and my legs buckle. I fall to the ground. I cover my face with my hands, but I can't control my tears. I don't get it. He's fine, so why am I still crying?

He kneels in front of me. "It's all right. We're okay."

I hear sirens, and they're getting close.

I turn to look, taking in the scene as I do. Audra, with her hand on Brody's shoulder, as surprised and relieved as I am that he's all right. Brody, directly in front of me, back from near death after almost plummeting down the falls. My eyes catch on my mom next. She's standing by Ms. Quill, trying to pull her to her feet, but she doesn't seem steady. All these emotions have to be getting to her. "Mom!" I want to go to her, but I don't want to leave Brody. I look from one to the other.

"I got her," Audra says, before I have to choose. "And Quill. I'll bring them to the road. You stay here," she says, and leans her head toward Brody. "Watch over this one."

"Thank you," I mouth.

She squeezes my arm.

I turn back to Brody. I still can't believe he's here. "How?" I ask.

He takes my hand. "There's a giant ledge under there. I made sure to land on it."

I look over. And there it is, about six feet down, a large slab of rock.

"Thank god Ms. Quill picked this spot. Talk about luck."

Brody pauses. "Maybe it wasn't luck."

"What do you mean?"

"I think it was Cassie. I don't know how, but it's the only thing that makes sense. We'd come to the falls a lot. It's one of my favorite places, but she hates heights. So we found marker W-3. It was out of the way, but it was the only place she felt safe enough to sit and dangle her legs over. It's too much of a coincidence that Quill would pick this exact spot."

"It had to be Cassie," I say. "Maybe that means she's okay, too."

"I hope so."

The tears start falling again. It's like I'm making up for years of holding them in.

Brody brushes the pad of his thumb against my cheek. "We're gonna bring her home," he says. "And Ms. Quill and Coach will be going away for a long time."

I nod. "But you almost died. I thought you did." More tears come.

"I know. I'm sorry."

"Don't ever do that to me again," I tell him.

"I don't know," he says, and gives me one of those winks of his. "Look how much you missed me. How often does someone get this kind of concern from you?"

I whack his arm. "You are such an ass. Why do I even like you?"

"Ahh, so you like me after all?"

I shake my head. I do not know what to do with this guy.

He pulls me closer, until my head is resting against his shoulder, and whispers, "I promise, I won't do it again."

I let myself cry into his jacket.

"You okay?" he asks me, one arm holding me tight, the other stroking my hair.

Sitting here like this, wrapped up in him, I think I will be.

47

cassie

They have to be okay, they have to.

I'm so tired, but I can't sleep. Not since I had that last vision.

All I can do is think about Audra, Brody, and Hayden.

Did I help them? Did I hurt them? Did I mess things up? I couldn't have made it worse than what I saw, unless that was my fault, too. Unless I caused it.

The memory of Audra on the ground, blood pooling around her, Brody crashing into the falls, and Hayden going in after him runs rampant in my mind, haunting me.

Did my vision come true? Was I able to change it? Did I get Ms. Quill closer to the cabin, closer to Hayden's mom? Did she arrive in time, or was she still too late?

I rock myself back and forth. I haven't seen anyone since last night. Not in person, not even in a vision. I haven't eaten anything since I don't remember when, either. My stomach whines in pain, but it's nothing compared to what the images in my head are doing to me.

All that blood. The way Audra's eyes went cold.

I don't have tears left, my cries are dry, they shake my core and leave me spent.

My head aches. I rest it on my knees.

I can't help it, my eyes drift shut. I try to force them back open—the memories are more vivid in the dark—but I'm so tired.

There's a sound upstairs.

I sit up at attention. They're back. Does this mean it didn't work? That my friends are gone?

I smash the chains against the floor. Why wasn't I smarter? Why didn't I do more?

The door crashes open.

I blink as flashlights, several of them, shine in my direction.

It's not Ms. Quill. It's not the coach. It's the sheriff!

A laugh, cry, I-don't-know-what sound escapes.

I've been found.

"Cassie!" He runs over to me. "Are you okay?"

My voice comes out as a tremble. "Yes."

"Get the medic," he says, crouching down beside me on the mattress. "She's weak." There's a lot of activity. So many people.

"Audra?" I manage to croak out.

"She's fine, they all are," he says, pulling me toward him and cradling me. "You will be, too. We're going to get you out of here."

I nod. Relief washes over me.

I'm just going to close my eyes for a bit . . .

When I open them, I'm no longer in a dank basement. I'm in a very bright room. My mind is foggy. What is going on? Am I in a vision?

I'm on a bed, in a hospital gown, and my father is sitting next to me, holding my hand.

"Cassie, Cassie," he says, as I come to. He stands, never letting go of me. "I'm here."

Then it all comes back to me. The sheriff and the deputies. The rescue. I'm free. I'm in the hospital.

"Dad?" My throat is dry.

"Here," he says, lifting a cup with a straw in it for me to take a sip.

When he puts it down, I adjust myself so that I'm sitting up.

"How do you feel?" he asks.

I don't have an answer for that. Numb? Relieved? Terrified? Unsure? I just squeeze his palm instead.

He kisses the top of my head. "I was so worried about you. I love you, Cassie." His voice cracks. "I'm so sorry. I'm going to make things better with us. They will be better."

I believe him. "I love you, too."

"Can we say hi?"

"Audra!"

She, Brody, and Hayden are on the other side of the room. I didn't even notice them.

"I'll go get a cup of coffee and give you a few minutes with your friends," my dad says. "But I'm not going far. I'll be here if you need me."

I nod. "Thanks, Dad."

Before he's made it out the door, Audra comes over and gives me a giant hug. I start crying. She backs up. "Oh no, did I hurt you?"

"No." I pull her back in. "I'm just so relieved you're here. That you're okay."

"Me?" she says. "You were the one we were worried about."

I try to replace the image of her on the ground with the one of her smiling before me. "I should have listened to you."

"No," she says. "Do not do that. None of this is your fault. It's all Ms. Quill and the coach. You do not get any blame, do you understand me?"

I nod.

"I mean it," she says.

"Do I get a turn?" Brody asks.

"Brody," I say, and reach my arms out. He holds me tight.

Over his shoulder I see Hayden.

She raises her hand in a wave.

"Thank you," I say. I know I owe her a lot more than that, but for now it will have to do.

"No," Hayden says, "don't thank me. I got you messed up in this. I'm sorry. If I hadn't blackmailed Ollie—"

I stop her. "You didn't do this. This is not on you. You helped find me. We're good, okay?"

"Yeah." She smiles at me, and I smile back.

"We okay, too?" Brody asks me.

I reach out and squeeze his arm. "You have to ask?"

He turns to Audra and Hayden. "Can Cassie and I have a minute?"

"I'll see you in a few," Audra tells me, and she and Hayden leave the room.

Brody props himself on the edge of the bed and faces me. "How are you doing? Really?"

I shrug.

"You were right about Ms. Quill," I say.

"I'm right about most things," he says, and winks.

A tear slips down my cheek, at the sound of Brody being Brody. I almost lost him.

"I saw you die," I whisper. "I saw you all die."

"But you changed it," he says, wiping away the tear. "You saved us."

"I don't know what I did."

"Hey, hey," he says. "We're here, I'm here, because of you. Marker W-3. I knew that had to be your doing. It's an out-of-the-way spot. No parking, no nice color-coded trail leading there. She would never have found it on her own. You're the hero of the story."

I shake my head. "No, I'm not. I was trapped in a basement the whole time. Some hero."

"So what you're saying is that you're the princess who was locked in the dungeon and still managed to save the day?"

I swat his arm, and he smiles at me. "You're going to be okay." He reaches into a bag he's holding and hands me a new journal. "In case you want to write about it. I know it helps."

"It was so bad, Brody." The tears are flowing freely now.

"Talk to me. What happened?"

"It was . . . I was . . ." I'm not ready to describe what it felt like to be down there, what I went through, so instead, I explain my visions. "I wasn't seeing anything at first, but then all of a sudden the visions started coming. I saw Hayden's mom. What she can do. I saw a great future. And I saw a horrible one."

He puts his hands over mine, and I let it all spill out. "I saw Ms. Quill taking Audra to the falls. You and Hayden showed up. And she killed you all. Hayden's mom got there, but she was too late. Ms. Quill was already long gone."

"How did you get Gretchen to change things?" he asks.

"In the vision you guys were on the other side of the falls. Not too far from parking lot A. No ledge to fall on. No way for Hayden's mom to sense you or get there in time. You had no chance. So when Ms. Quill came down to the basement, I pretended I was having a vision. I knew she'd want to know what I saw. So I made sure to mention marker W-3 a couple of times and describe exactly where it was located. Made her think it was her idea. In the vision I described to her, she succeeds. I figured she'd want it to come true, so she would stick to what I said."

He squeezes my palm.

"At marker W-3 you were closer to Hayden's mom. I hoped she'd sense you all and call for help, that she'd be able to get there in time. I knew where the cabin was because . . ." I look down.

"Because you saw Hayden and me there in your visions."

I nod. "Are you two . . . ?"

"Cass . . ."

"No." I stop him. This time I squeeze his hand. "It's okay. I want you to be happy. And we weren't."

"We were," he objects.

"Yeah," I agree, "but not in the way we were supposed to be happy. I had a lot of time to think." I give him a half smile. "*Too* much time to think. And the visions of you and Hayden definitely came up."

"I—"

"Let me finish," I say. "Those aren't what broke us up. We could have changed the outcome if that's all it was. It was the feeling. Not just what I felt between you two, although that was definitely part of it. But if I'm honest, it was also the one that nipped at me, the one that I tried to ignore, the one that said we weren't right for each other anymore. That we were forcing it. I love you, Brody. I always have, I always will. But we're not . . ."

"In love," he finishes for me.

"You're like my family," I say. "And with my dad being the way my dad is, and your dad being the way your dad is, I think we stuck it out longer than we should have. I didn't want to lose you in my life."

"You're never going to lose me," he says, wrapping me in a hug. "Not even if you want to. You're my family, too."

48

HaYDen

The sheriff takes Audra and me to a parking lot in the boon-docks of the hospital. There are hardly any cars here, and the place is devoid of people, except for my mom standing in one of the spots.

"Still learning to control the emotions," she says. "Can't go in there just yet." I'm just amazed she can even be near the place at all. This is unheard-of for her.

"Okay," Sheriff Rafferty says. "We wanted to talk to you both. Together. It's been a long day, so we don't need to do this all tonight, but we have a lot to discuss. For starters, the two of you getting involved in an investigation I explicitly told you to stay out of."

Audra looks like she's going to erupt. "But if it wasn't for us—"

His look silences her. "And you could have gotten yourselves killed."

"How about we go back to the not needing to get into all this tonight," she says.

"This will definitely be discussed at another time," my mother says, taking a deep breath, and I can't stop looking at her. First she came through at the falls, and now she's at a hospital. A *hospital*. Where emotions are through the roof, and she's standing here acting like an almost typical parent.

"I get it," she tells me. "It's new to me, too, and I'm still working on it. Places like this are still a challenge." She takes another breath and closes her eyes.

"Hey," I object. "If you can control yourself all of a sudden, I want to be off-limits, too."

"If you were off-limits, today would have ended very differently," the sheriff says, and I don't have a good comeback for that. He's right.

"What the two of you did," he continues, looking from me to Audra, "was reckless. There will be consequences." Does he mean grounding? The thought almost makes me laugh. Would my mom even know how to punish me? "You should have trusted us," he says, "and not put your lives in danger."

"Trusted you?" I ask. "The two of you have done nothing but keep secrets and lie this whole time. Are you ever going to tell us how you know each other?"

Sheriff Rafferty twists his ring around his finger. "You do deserve some answers. I've been helping your mother control her gift."

"What? You were *helping* her?" This is so bizarre. "How did you two meet?"

"I found her on a chat room."

I turn to my mom and snort. "A *chat* room? You just started up a conversation with a random stranger and moved us to a new state? What did you google, 'help me control my empath skills'?"

They might as well have just said they met on Supernatural Tinder. That's almost as bad.

"He found me," she explains, her eyes still closed and her breathing slightly labored. "I vetted him, and I wanted the help." She counts to ten, each digit coming out a whisper, and continues, "I wanted to be a mother to you. I wanted you to have a home where you didn't have to pick up and move every few months."

Like I said, bizarre. I turn to the sheriff. "So you're the reason my mom and I are in Lightsend?"

"To a degree, yes. I hooked your mother up with the cabin rental."

"Now I want some answers," Audra says. "What is it with you looking for people with abilities, and why didn't you ever say anything? Does Mom know?"

He takes a deep breath and nods. "Yes, of course your mother knows. We don't keep secrets from each other."

"Just from me," Audra says.

"You are not my wife, you are my child," he tells her. "And I didn't want you wrapped up in it."

"Too late," she says.

"I can see that now. I didn't know Cassie's visions were real. I made a mistake. A big one. At first, I thought it was possible she inherited Kelly's gift. It's why I listened to Cassie's leads, her hunches, in the first place." He lowers his head. "But they led us on so many wild-goose chases. I figured she was making them up. I can't tell you how sorry I am for that. I just thought she was pretending to be like her mom, trying to have some sort of connection."

"I told you," she says.

Sheriff Rafferty nods. "I should have listened. I'm sorry. I owed that to you, to Cassie, to Kelly. She's why I started all this in the first place."

"Cassie's mom?" Audra asks.

He nods again. "She wanted answers. I tried to help, and after she died, I felt like, I can't explain it really, like I wanted to carry on her search for her."

Cassie's mom wanted answers, too? Like mother, like daughter, like random girl dragged to Lightsend.

When it doesn't seem like anyone is going to say anything else, I ask, "What's happening with Coach Hill and Ms. Quill?"

"They've been moved to more secure holding facilities. I suspect they will not be getting out for a long time. Between the kidnapping, selling drugs to students, and attempted murder, we won't be seeing them."

"Good," I say.

Audra grips her wrist. "Agreed. Cassie doesn't need to worry about running into either of those two."

The sheriff puts his arm around her. "I think we've all had a long day," he says. "Just want to do one last check on the Lees, and then I'll give everyone a ride home. Okay?"

"Yes, thank you," my mom says, and Audra and I nod.

He heads off, and Audra goes with him.

My mother pulls me in for a hug. "I don't know what I would have done if I'd lost you."

"Same," I tell her. "Thank you for saving me."

"I owe you for all the times you've rescued me over the years. I'm trying to be better. I really am."

"You're perfect," I say.

She kisses the top of my head.

"Look," she says, and points in the direction the Raffertys went off in. "Is that Brody?"

It is, and he's walking toward us. I crouch down behind one of the cars.

My mom laughs. "You're the one hiding from people? I thought that was my job."

"Shhhh," I tell her. "He'll hear you."

"Oh, sweetie," she laughs again, "you've got it bad for that boy."

"Stop it." I do not need her telling me how I feel. *I* don't even know how I feel. "Get out of my head."

She laughs again.

"This is not funny."

"Maybe not for you . . ." I am not finding her nearly as entertaining as she's finding herself.

"Why don't you talk to him?" she asks.

With her by my side? Not happening.

"No." I can't deal with this. Not now. I wonder how bad it would be to hot-wire one of these cars and make a getaway.

I stay crouched for a few minutes. "Is he still there?" I ask.

"Coast is clear."

I stand up. I didn't want to see him, it was my choice, but why am I disappointed that he's gone?

My mom puts her arm around me and gives me a squeeze.

She doesn't say anything this time. She doesn't have to. I know she understands.

49

HaYDen

walk over to the other side of the falls, out of range of my mother. Brody texted me yesterday after I got home from the hospital asking if we could talk, and I suggested we do it in a safe, empath-clear zone. It's a bit of a trek, but I like being outside, even when it's cold. It's been pretty mild out for this time of year, but today feels like winter. The exercise makes me feel a little warmer, but there's still a chill that goes down to my bones.

Brody is waiting near the giant oak by the parking lot when I arrive. He's in a huge, puffy navy-blue jacket, but he still looks like he's freezing. He's rubbing his hands together and raising and lowering himself on the balls of his feet.

"Hi," he says.

"Hi."

He looks like he's going to hug me, but then he doesn't, and again, my feelings about it, about him, are jumbled.

There's no one around us, almost no cars in the parking lot due to the weather, and the fact that it's the middle of the afternoon on a weekday. When you have a near-death experience, they let you skip a little school.

"How are you doing?" he asks.

"Oh, you know, as well as can be expected for someone who was almost shot and flung into a waterfall. You?"

"Same." He's watching me so intently, and I find myself fidgeting in front of him.

Neither of us says anything.

He brings his hands up to his mouth and blows into them, trying to warm up.

I run my shoe over a pebble on the ground.

This is awkward.

He must feel it, too. "We got interrupted at the cabin," he finally says, "but I think we should talk about it, about what I said."

"Talk about what?" I cringe at myself. Of course I know. He said Cassie saw him falling in love with me. I wouldn't forget something that big. Why am I being like this?

His mouth breaks into that smile of his, and I can't look away. "About us."

I don't answer.

"Hayden Jefferies at a loss for words?"

"No. Yes." I let out a long breath, and I can see it in the cold air. "I just don't know what *this* is."

"This is me telling you I like you."

I close my eyes. "Because of a vision."

"No," Brody says. "Despite one."

I open my eyes again, and he's looking right into them.

"I want to get to know you better," he says. "Maybe go for dinner or a movie or wherever."

"Like a date?"

He chuckles. "Yeah, like a date."

I suck in my bottom lip. Why am I so scared? I want him, too. Why can't I say it?

"It doesn't have to be anything big. You want to be in a crowd, we can be in a crowd. You want to sit in the park, we can sit in the park. I just want to spend time with you, get to know you, outside of all that we've just been through. See what this is. We can take it however you want, as slow as you want."

"As slow as I want?"

"Yes. You can take the lead."

I study his face. "Okay," I say. "I take the lead."

His smile gets even bigger. "You're not going to regret this."

I don't think I will.

"So, how about maybe leading us to the car, where I can turn on the heat?" he asks. "It is freez—"

I don't give him a chance to finish. I grab his jacket and pull him into a kiss.

His lips, his body, are pressed against mine, and I melt into him. I don't have a vision, no flashes of the past. I'm in the present, in the rush of the moment, lost in Brody.

He pulls me closer, his arms holding me tight. My whole body is buzzing. I don't want it to end. The chill I felt before is gone. All I feel now is the warmth of Brody, the heat of his body, of his kiss.

He stops and looks at me, his eyes going from my eyes to my lips and back again.

"I think I like your lead," he says.

"Yeah? Then you're really going to like this." I wrap my arms around him and pull him in for another kiss.

Epilogue

HaYDen

one month later

"Look at that," Brody says, opening, shutting, and reopening Greta's passenger-side door. "Whoever worked on this is gifted. No stick here whatsoever."

"Just get in," I tell him. Last week he fixed the doors. It took him no time, but I'm pretty sure I'm going to be hearing about it for eternity.

"Give me a minute." He inspects the handle. "I'm enjoying this masterful craftsmanship."

"You know, I could just make you walk."

"But then you'd be so lonely."

"True," I say. "How will I make it the whole minute to Cassie's without you?"

"I really don't know."

"Get in," I tell him again. "I don't want to be late." He takes the pizzas off the roof and maneuvers so he's sitting with them on his lap.

"How many did you buy?" I ask him, even though I can see there are three. He is such an over-orderer.

"Oh, did you want some, too? I can get more."

I give him an eye roll, and he leans over and kisses me. Despite the awkward angle—my seat belt is on and he's hindered by the boxes—it still makes me tingle. It's warm and soft and leaves me wanting more. I press my lips against his one more time, before I force myself to pull away. I don't want to, but I also don't want the pizza to get cold or to keep Cassie waiting.

A few minutes later, we pull up in front of her house. I get out and get Brody's door for him.

"See, it's like magic," he says as he gets out with the pizzas.

"Next time, seriously, you're walking."

He leans down and kisses me again. It's firmer this time, like he's trying to will me strength and support with his lips. "You ready?" he asks.

I've been over to Cassie's a few times since she got out of the hospital, but she was only up for company in small bursts. She's been doing a lot better now, though. Even said she's ready to come back to school, that she wants to get back to normal. To have fun. To put what happened behind her.

"I think so. You sure she's okay seeing us as a couple? Holding hands, all that?"

"I told you, yes—she even encouraged it."

I know he's telling the truth. In one of our visits, she told me the same thing. Still, I want to be sensitive. "Then I'm ready."

We walk up to the door, and I knock.

Audra is the one who answers it. "About time," she says. "We are starving in here."

Brody winks at her. "Well, hello to you, too."

She takes the pizzas from him. "Jackets," she commands. We take them off, and Brody hangs them on the nearby hooks before taking the boxes back. We follow Audra into the living room. Cassie is seated on the couch.

"Hi," I say.

"Hi. Thanks for coming," she says. "I'm glad you guys are here."

Brody puts the pizzas on the coffee table and gives her a hug. "Wouldn't be anywhere else."

"Do you remember what I said about starving?" Audra says, taking the seat next to Cassie.

"Okay, okay." Brody moves to the love seat, so he's no longer blocking the pizzas. I sit next to him, and we all dig in.

"Oh," I say, after I finish my first triple-cheese slice. "I have something for you, Cassie."

"You got me a present?" she asks.

"You could say that."

"You really didn't have to do that."

I wipe my hands on my jeans. "I kind of did." I reach into my bag and pull out a journal.

"You got me a journal," she says.

I hand it over. "Not just any journal."

She flips through it and her mouth opens. "This is mine. The one from when I was taken. How did you get it?"

"Hayden!" Brody says at the same time that Audra screams, "You stole evidence?"

"It's not exactly stealing. I left a notebook in its place." Just adding to my Robin Hood résumé. "Besides, I'm only giving back something that belongs to Cassie."

"That's stealing evidence," Audra says. She doesn't seem mad per se, just a little stunned.

"I was careful. I didn't do anything to jeopardize the case." I turn to Cassie. "I just didn't want you to have to deal with questions about what you can do. I didn't want to give any credence to what Ms. Quill is spouting. No one believes her, and I think we should keep it that way."

Brody laughs. "Yeah, all that ranting about psychic powers isn't doing her any favors."

Quill's already done a slew of interviews from prison. She's telling anyone who will listen that Cassie can "see" things and has been going on and on about how she and Coach Hill only took Cassie because she caught on to their drug dealing. That part keeps eating at me. Despite Cassie's assurances that it's not my fault, I know I'm the reason they thought she was onto them—the reason Cassie, and the rest of us, could've been killed.

Quill insists Cassie wasn't in danger, that they only wanted to see how much she knew, but when they read her journal and found out she was "psychic," they needed more time to figure out what to do next. She says they would have let her go regardless. However, the cement and shovel found in Quill's basement—the stuff bought with Warmack's credit card—tells another story. So does what she tried to do to Audra, Brody, and me.

"My dad is going to kill you," Audra says, snapping me back to attention.

"He won't know," I say.

She gives me a look.

"Okay, fine, but if he didn't want me to take it, he shouldn't have left his keys in the pit, and then had me sweep the evidence room. It was like an invitation, a golden ticket." Part of me thinks that's actually true. The sheriff is a smart man, and he didn't want the info on Cassie out in the world, either. So it may have been a coincidence that he had me sweep up in the evidence room, a room I'd never been allowed in before, *or* he knew exactly what I was going to do and helped me along with no liability to himself.

"The prelim trial starts tomorrow," Cassie says quietly.

"You doing okay?" Brody asks.

"Yeah. Helps knowing Ms. Quill and Coach Hill are going to get what's coming to them."

I may have thought those were just hopeful words from someone else, but from Cassie, I know it's more than that. "You've seen it, haven't you?"

She nods. "I have, and maybe it's wrong of me to relish it, but seeing them pay, it's what's helping me sleep at night."

"It's not wrong. They deserve whatever they get," I tell her.

"Hey, these flowers are gorgeous," Audra says, not so subtly changing the subject away from the kidnapping.

But she's right. This is supposed to be a fun day. We can talk about the trial another time.

"From the Tamisons," Cassie says. "Mrs. Tamison is running for mayor, hoping for an endorsement as the 'keep Lightsend safe' candidate."

I snort, and Cassie raises her eyebrows at me. "That's right, not your favorite family."

"That's putting it mildly," Brody says. "She was convinced Brooke was the one who took you. Confronted her at her house even."

I throw my hands up. "It's not my fault. She's evil."

"She'll get what's coming, too," Cassie says.

"Ooh," Audra says, nudging Cassie with her shoulder. "What did you see?"

Cassie looks at me. "Us. Brooke wasn't at graduation, and I said we made it happen."

I pump my hands in victory. "Yes! I knew I was going to be her undoing. How'd we do it?"

"I don't know," Cassie says, and scrunches her nose.

"What?" Audra asks. "I know that look. You know something."

"I wonder . . . a couple of months ago I had a vision, and in the background your mom was on TV teasing a huge college admissions scandal that brought down celebrities and the mayor of a local town. Mrs. Tamison is running for office here. Maybe it's all connected."

"It's definitely connected," I say.

Brody is staring at me.

"Why are you looking at me like that?"

"I have never seen you giddy. You are practically bouncing right now," he says.

"Well, it's a good day."

"That it is." He takes my hand and locks his fingers in mine.

"We need a toast," Audra says, and pours us all sodas. She holds up her cup. "Here's to a great rest of the year," she says.

"Hear, hear," Brody says.

We all take a sip.

"To Cassie being safe, to friendship, new and old, and to Hayden getting to stay in town," Audra continues.

Brody squeezes my hand, and we all take another sip.

I give a little head bow to Audra. Thanks to her dad, my mom is doing okay. She even promised I can finish out high school here. No moving.

"And now," Audra concludes, "we can sit back and enjoy. The worst is behind us."

"Well . . . ," Cassie says.

When she sees everyone's expressions, she starts laughing. "I'm kidding, I'm kidding. I didn't see anything."

I *think* she's telling the truth.

She winks at me. "It's going to be an eventful year."

That it is. We've been talking. We're going to finish what her mom started. We're going to find answers about our abilities, about others like us out there.

"Hey," Brody says, interrupting my thoughts. "Is anyone going to open the pineapple pizza?"

"I am," Cassie says, reaching in and grabbing an extra-fruity slice.

"Uck." Audra makes a disgusted face. "How can you eat that? You've ruined a perfectly good pizza with that topping. Tell them, Hayden."

"I've never tried it."

"Oh, that is about to change," Brody says. He picks up a slice and holds it out for me to take a bite. The cheese and sauce drip down my mouth. I wipe them away.

"Missed a spot," he says. Brody leans in and brushes his lips against mine. It's just a brief kiss, a peck really. Cassie is here, after all, and this dynamic is new, but my whole body still shivers in excitement.

"That's better," he says.

"Much," I agree.

"Well?" Audra says.

"I think I could get used to it."

She throws herself back on the couch in an overdramatic fashion. "Sacrilegious. All of you."

"Aww, come on," Cassie says, trying to get her to take a bite of her piece. Audra laughs and swats her hand away, sending a slice of pineapple flying onto Brody's lap. He shrugs and eats it.

I could get used to *all* of this.

For the first time in years I feel light. I feel happy.

I have friends. I have a guy I like who likes me back. I have a home. I have a mom who is present again. I have a future I'm looking forward to.

I guess that's the thing with only seeing the past: You never know what amazing things might be coming.

Acknowledgments

So many people helped make this book a reality, and I am so grateful to all of you.

First, my incredible editor, Holly West, for your talent, guidance, friendship and so much more. In my publishing journey, getting to know you has been one of the greatest gifts.

Jean Feiwel, Liz Szabla, Jonathan Yaged, thank you for letting me be a part of this amazing Macmillan family. It really is a dream come true, and I'm so thankful.

Two wonderful interns helped out on this book. Brooke Sokoloski during the early stages and Brittany Groves during the later ones. Thank you both for your help. I know there are big things ahead for both of you, and I'm sure it won't be long before I get to brag that you worked on my book back when you were just getting your start in the industry.

Kathleen "KB" Breitenfeld and Richard Deas, I'm so excited to have your amazing cover on this book. I'm a huge fan of your work.

This book would not have come together if not for production editor Dawn Ryan keeping everything on track through various passes, copyedits and proofreads. It's very appreciated. And of course, Valerie Shea for your copyediting prowess, Emily Heddleson for your proofreading skills, and production manager Celeste Cass for making it into an actual book!

Morgan Rath and Kristin Dulaney, thank you so much for your support of my work!

And to everyone at Macmillan—the editorial, sales, subrights, marketing, publicity, advertising, digital teams, and so on—thank you for all that you do!

The Swoon Squad, you are a wonderful group of authors and people, and I'm happy to be included among such a great crew. Special shout-outs to Sandy Hall for being the first to read my finished draft and making me excited about this book all over again, and to Jenn Nguyen for our check-in chats about writing and everything else! I'm thankful for you both.

Lauren Scobell, thank you for always being there for me. I'm always in awe of your talent, work ethic, and dedication—and am lucky to have you for a friend.

Laura Dail, your help and love of this book means a lot.

The librarians, booksellers, bloggers, social media mavens, readers, and everyone who's helped spread the word about my work—thank you so much! It's very appreciated.

To my family and friends, I could write pages about how special each one of you are, but for now I'll just say you all mean the world to me.

A few special mentions:

Ben Levkov, every day is better with you in it, I'm so happy to have you and your family in my life.

Marilyn, Jordan, and Andrea Petroff, you don't get to choose your family, but I hit the lottery with you guys, and I am beyond grateful for you.

Liam and Alice Petroff, I hope you both know how much you mean to me. You inspire me, make me smile, and fill my heart with love and joy. Always remember you can do whatever you put your minds to—and your Aunt Shani will be cheering you on and supporting you through it all.

And finally my dad, Robert Petroff, who shared with me his love for books. It's just one of the many things you've given me that I'll cherish forever. I miss you so much.

I love you all.